"You look great,"

Kayla mumbled as her sister left the room. "Patrick will be blown away."

Kayla slumped on the sofa and pulled a pillow close to her chest. "It's not fair. Patrick never asked me out to a romantic dinner by the water. He's never asked me out at all. Not that I wanted him to. We're not a couple. But still, he could have...."

Her voice trailed off. Confusing feelings swirled inside her. Why was she jealous? She'd invited her sister specifically to meet Patrick. They obviously got along—he'd asked her out within minutes of meeting her. Kayla's plan had worked. Everything was turning out exactly as it should.

So why did she feel so empty inside—and why was her heart aching?

★ ★ ★ ★ ★ ★ ★ ★ ★ ★ ★ ★

"Susan Mallery dazzles. If you haven't read her yet, you must!"
—Bestselling author Suzanne Forster

Look for
THE SECRET WIFE in September &
THE MYSTERIOUS STRANGER in October

Dear Reader,

What better way to enjoy the last lingering days of summer than to revel in romance? And Special Edition's lineup for August will surely turn your thoughts to love!

This month's THAT'S MY BABY! title will tug your heartstrings. Brought to you by Ginna Gray, *Alissa's Miracle* is about a woman who marries the man of her dreams—even though he doesn't want children. But when she unexpectedly becomes pregnant, their love is put to the ultimate test.

Sometimes love comes when we least expect it—and that's what's in store for the heroines of the next three books. *Mother Nature's Hidden Agenda* by award-winning author Kate Freiman is about a self-assured woman who thinks she has everything...until a sexy horse breeder and his precocious daughter enter the picture! Another heroine rediscovers love the second time around in Gail Link's *Lone Star Lover*. And don't miss *Seven Reasons Why*, Neesa Hart's modern-day fairy tale about a brood of rascals who help their foster mom find happily-ever-after in the arms of a mysterious stranger!

Reader favorite Susan Mallery launches TRIPLE TROUBLE, her miniseries about identical triplets destined for love. In *The Girl of His Dreams*, the heroine will go to unbelievable lengths to avoid her feelings for her very best friend. The second and third titles of the series will be coming your way in September and October.

Finally, we're thrilled to bring you book two in our FROM BUD TO BLOSSOM theme series. Gina Wilkins returns with *It Could Happen To You*, a captivating tale about an overly cautious heroine who learns to take the greatest risk of all—love.

I hope you enjoy each and every story to come!

Sincerely,

Tara Gavin,
Senior Editor

Please address questions and book requests to:
Silhouette Reader Service
U.S.: 3010 Walden Ave., P.O. Box 1325, Buffalo, NY 14269
Canadian: P.O. Box 609, Fort Erie, Ont. L2A 5X3

SUSAN MALLERY

THE GIRL OF HIS DREAMS

Published by Silhouette Books
America's Publisher of Contemporary Romance

SILHOUETTE BOOKS

ISBN 0-373-24118-6

THE GIRL OF HIS DREAMS

Printed in U.S.A.

Books by Susan Mallery

Silhouette Special Edition

Silhouette Intimate Moments

*Hometown Heartbreakers
†Triple Trouble

SUSAN MALLERY

lives in sunny Southern California where the eccentricities of a writer are considered fairly normal. Her books are reader favorites and bestsellers, with recent titles appearing on the Waldenbooks bestseller list and the *USA Today* bestseller list. Her 1995 Special Edition, *Marriage on Demand*, was awarded Best Special Edition by *Romantic Times* magazine.

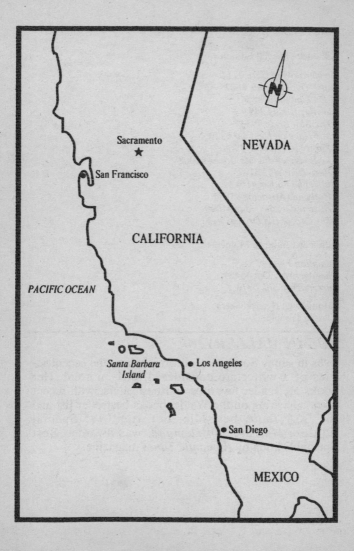

Chapter One

"But Mr. Cookie has never spent the night away from home," the woman in the waiting room wailed.

Kayla Bedford overheard the conversation and rolled her eyes. "Mr. Cookie needs to get out more," she said to herself as she turned on the water and began rinsing the large, soapy sheepdog in front of her.

Duchess endured the bathing stoically, staring mournfully at Kayla, as if silently asking how someone who claimed to love animals could stoop so low as to *bathe* them.

Kayla tilted the dog's nose up so she could rinse her forehead without getting soap in her eyes. "Don't give me that sad little look," she said. "You smell bad. If you'd stop rolling in the mud, your owners would stop bringing you in for a bath. It's your own fault."

Duchess accepted her responsibility in the matter with a sharp bark and a swipe at Kayla's nose. Kayla laughed and ducked back to avoid the pink tongue, not to mention the dog's breath.

"You've got to start flossing, kid," she said.

She finished rinsing Duchess and unhooked the short metal leash that kept her charge in the tub while she worked. She grabbed an oversize towel from a rack on the wall and stepped back. Duchess liked to give herself a good shake before submitting to drying.

"But I haven't seen *all* the facility," the Mr. Cookie's owner said. "What's in there?"

"Our dog-grooming facility. But you shouldn't go in there. Kayla is working with a—"

Kayla heard her boss speak, but it took her a couple of seconds to react. Unfortunately, that was one second too long. The door opened, and a woman stepped into the room. Her clothing obviously cost more than Kayla made in a month. Mr. Cookie's owner had perfectly groomed hair, perfectly done makeup, and enough jewelry to support a family of four about two years.

Mr. Cookie wasn't too bad himself. He was a tiny Yorkshire terrier with a blue bow between his ears.

"Wet dog," Kayla said quickly, positioning herself between the well-to-do customer and Duchess.

She was too late. Mr. Cookie spotted Duchess and barked. The huge sheepdog pricked up her ears. Doggie eyes met. If it wasn't love at first sight, it was something darn close. Mr. Cookie jumped out of his mistress's arms at the same moment Duchess leaped from the tub.

"That hideous creature is going to hurt Mr. Cookie!" the woman shrieked.

Patrick Walcott, Kayla's boss, took the woman's arm. "Mrs. Kane, there's nothing to worry about. Duchess is a well-behaved dog. Mr. Cookie is fine. See?" He pointed at the two dogs, who were sniffing noses. The terrier made low sounds in his throat, as if the moment were too much for him.

"Your dog is going to be fine, Mrs. Kane," Kayla said quickly, "but you're not. Please step back before Duchess decides to—"

Suddenly Duchess braced herself on four stiff legs and shook. Water flew everywhere. It was like getting caught in a rainstorm. Blast that thick coat, Kayla thought as the spray soaked through her smock and T-shirt, down to her skin.

Mrs. Kane yelped and jumped into the foyer. Her high heels narrowly missed Patrick's right foot.

Mr. Cookie endured the downpour, and when Duchess bent her head low to sniff his face, he swiped at her with his tongue. Duchess returned his affection, her long lick nearly knocking him off his feet.

She eyed the smitten couple and shook her head. "Just like Romeo and Juliet. You guys are doomed."

Abruptly Mrs. Kane swept into the room, bent down and picked up her soaked dog.

"Mr. Cookie is a purebred terrier," she announced in the same tone British broadcasters used to point out the queen. "I can't believe you would let a mutt like that roam free in this establishment. This will never do at all. I'm taking Mr. Cookie on vacation with me."

With that, she turned and walked away.

Kayla stared after her and tried to suppress a laugh as Mr. Cookie struggled in his owner's arms. Obviously, a life of luxury was nothing when compared with Duchess's earthier charms. The dog yipped in protest as he was carried from the building.

Kayla cleared her throat and tried to look suitably regretful. "I'm really sorry, Patrick," she said. "If I'd known she was going to open the door, I would have kept Duchess on her leash.''

"It's okay, Kayla. I warned her not to come in. She didn't want to listen.'' He winked. ''Frankly, I wouldn't want to be responsible for Mr. Cookie.''

"Oh, it wouldn't be a problem. We would ask the Andersons if Duchess could spend the weekend, then we'd put them in a cage together. They would have a wonderful time.''

He touched the tip of her nose. ''Wicked child. Don't you know Mr. Cookie is a pure bred?''

Kayla crouched on the floor and wrapped a towel around Duchess. ''So is she. She even has papers. Don't you, sweet girl?''

Duchess licked her cheek.

Kayla grinned at Patrick. ''The dog really needs to start flossing regularly. I've told her, but she doesn't listen. I think you should give her the 'healthy gums and teeth' lecture.''

"It works better if I tell it to the owners.''

A petite blonde walked toward them. ''Dr. Walcott, your next patient is ready.'' She handed him a chart.

He took it and thanked her, then turned back to Kayla. ''What time are you going to Sunshine Village?''

She glanced at the clock on the wall. ''In about forty minutes.''

"I want to come with you. Their resident cat needs to be vaccinated.''

"Of course, you wouldn't think of telling them to bring the animal in here.''

"Of course not.''

"You don't bill them, either, do you?''

He raised his eyebrows. ''Are you angling for an accounting job?''

"Smooth way of telling me to mind my own business, Doc."

Patrick waved and headed for the examining rooms. Kayla stared after him for a minute. She'd known Patrick since she was a freshman in college, seven years ago. He was by far the nicest man she'd ever known. And not bad-looking, she thought, leaning out the door and watching his long-legged stride. His cotton lab coat covered his behind, but she'd seen him in jeans enough to know it was pretty impressive. She'd teased him once that there were probably women who had shrines to his butt hidden away in their closets. He'd brushed her comment off with a self-deprecating wave.

So why wasn't he married? she wondered. In the time she'd known him, he'd dated a lot of women, but no one seriously. What was his problem?

"So what's your problem?" she asked nearly an hour later as they sped down the freeway toward Sunshine Village. The late-afternoon sun drifted toward the horizon, making the ocean glitter as if dusted with golden sparkles.

Patrick drove the van with an easy confidence. He'd abandoned his lab coat and now wore a dark blue T-shirt tucked into jeans. One elbow rested on the open driver's-side window. His skin was tanned.

He glanced at her, his blue eyes nearly as dark as the T-shirt. He had nice eyes, she decided. They were the best part of his face. Well, except maybe for his mouth. He had a good mouth. Firm, well-shaped lips that nearly always curved up into a smile.

"My problem?" he asked.

"How old are you? Thirty-one, right?" She didn't wait for a response. "I've known you seven years. In all that time, you've never dated a woman more than a couple of months. Why is that?''

"Gee, Kayla, stop being subtle and get to the point.''

"So I shouldn't have asked?''

"Why do you want to know?'' *His* question neatly avoided both of hers.

She leaned back in the seat and pointed to their exit, which was coming up. "I'm not going to be here much longer,'' she said. "Two months, sixteen days. Then you'll be on your own. I worry about you. Maybe you should rent my apartment to someone really cute.''

"There's something to think about,'' he said easily. "I've always been partial to redheads.''

Kayla frowned. Although she wanted Patrick to find somebody wonderful and be happy, she wasn't thrilled with the idea of a dazzling redhead taking over her apartment. Kayla rented the one-bedroom unit above Patrick's two-car garage. It was small, but suited her needs. She'd had it since she graduated from college.

"What if I want to keep renting my place?'' she asked. "You know, as a temporary home when I'm between travels.''

"No problem. Just let me know what you decide.''

"I hate it when you're agreeable,'' she muttered.

"Why?''

"Then I come off as the cranky one, and I'm not.''

He gave her a slow, knowing smile.

They pulled into the parking lot at Sunshine Village. The two-story building looked more like a collection of villas than a retirement home. Red tile roofs and gleaming white stucco contrasted with lots of grass and trees. In back was a huge garden tended by several residents. In addition to flowers, they grew vegetables.

Kayla jumped down and went to the rear of the van.

Three large dog cages sat in the back. She opened each cage and clipped a leash on the occupant. Patrick collected his medical bag and joined her.

"I'll get Trudi," he said, taking the dalmatian's leash. Barely two years old, the black-and-white dog still acted like a puppy. After trying to leap up and lick Patrick's face, she danced at the end of her lead, barking with excitement as they moved toward the building.

Elizabeth, a seven-year-old collie, followed more sedately. "Always a lady," Kayla said. She carried Rip, a small black poodle, in her arms.

They walked into the large gathering room downstairs. Several of the residents were already waiting for their arrival. The animals were greeted by name. Patrick handed her Trudi's leash and went in search of the oversize tabby who made her home there.

"You trap that boy yet?" Mrs. Grisham asked as Kayla led Trudi to the large, dark-haired woman sitting on the edge of the sofa.

"Not yet," Kayla said, grinning at the familiar question. "I've tried seducing Patrick, but he's immune to my charms," she teased.

"Then you're not trying hard enough," Mr. Peters said, and wiggled his eyebrows. "A lovely young lady like you? Why, in my day—"

Mrs. Grisham cut him off with a wave of her hand. "We've heard about all your days too many times already. I think Kayla's playing hard-to-get."

"Patrick and I are good friends. I swear. I've known him for years."

"Uh-huh. Who are you trying to convince with that sorry tale?" Mrs. Grisham said.

Kayla laughed. "But it's true."

She moved closer with the dogs. The dalmatian recog-

nized Mrs. Grisham and strained to get closer. Kayla held
her off and commanded her to sit.

"Oh, don't worry. Trudi jumps a little, but I'm used to
it." Mrs. Grisham petted the dog's smooth head. "How's
my pretty girl?" Trudi wriggled with excitement. Mrs.
Grisham took her leash.

Once Trudi was settled, Kayla released Elizabeth. The
collie was well behaved. She circled the room, stopping at
each resident's side. Some were favorites, but she tried
hard to play fair.

Kayla left the two dogs and headed for the stairs. Once
on the second floor, she walked to a suite of rooms at the
back. The door was partially open, and she knocked as she
entered.

Sarah looked up from the book she was reading and
smiled. "Kayla, what a surprise."

Kayla kissed the older woman's wrinkled cheek and set
Rip on the bed next to her. The tiny poodle stepped care-
fully onto Sarah's lap and stared at her happily.

"I've missed you, scamp," Sarah said, petting the small
dog. She held out her free hand to Kayla. "And you." She
squeezed Kayla's fingers. "Pull up a chair. My daughter
sent me the scrapbook."

Kayla dragged over a lightweight metal chair and settled
next to Sarah. "She found it, then?"

"Yes, right where I told her it would be." She pulled
open her nightstand drawer. A faded, dusty book sat on
top. "You get it, dear."

Kayla drew it out of the drawer. The pages were twelve
inches square and bound with ribbon. The cover was plain
except for the word *Memories* scripted in tarnished gold.
She set the book between Sarah's hip and the edge of the
bed.

Sarah turned to the first page. Grainy black-and-white

photos showed a young couple ready to board an old-fashioned plane.

"I wasn't much older than you are now," Sarah said. "Danny, my husband, wanted me to see Paris. It was 1950 and he'd spent some time there during the war."

"Great hat," Kayla said, leaning close to study the picture. Sarah had been wearing a wool dress and a small, stylish hat. Her hair had been dark then, falling to her shoulders in smooth waves. The young man at her side was dapper in a pin-striped suit. His grin embraced the world, and he held his wife as if she were the most precious part of his life.

She sighed. "You look very much in love."

"We were. Oh, there were bad times, of course. But I loved Danny with all my heart. I still do."

Kayla knew Sarah's husband had passed away nearly ten years ago. She touched the older woman's arm. "That's what I want. Love to last a lifetime."

"You'll find it."

"I hope so. I'm nearly twenty-five."

"How long?"

Kayla chuckled. "I'll turn twenty-five in two months and sixteen days. Then the money from the trust fund will be released and I'm off to Paris."

"We stayed at a lovely hotel near the Seine." Sarah flipped through the album. She found a postcard of the building and pointed. "I wonder if it's still there."

Rip flopped over on his back, begging for attention. Sarah gathered him up in her arms and stroked his soft fur. "Aren't you a love?" she said, then nodded at the book. "You look through it, Kayla. Paris has changed in the past forty-something years, but it will give you some ideas about what to expect."

Kayla flipped the pages, stopping at photos of churches

and museums. She studied the streets of the city, wondering what it would look like now.

"I'm very excited," she said. "I've wanted to go to Paris since I was twelve."

"And meet a handsome Frenchman?" Sarah teased.

"Actually, I was thinking of Prince Albert of Monaco. His father married an American."

"Quite right. You're pretty enough to tempt a prince."

Kayla glanced down at her faded T-shirt. There were an assortment of stains from a day spent washing dogs. Her jeans showed white at the seams, and her athletic shoes were so old that if they were tires they would be considered bald.

"Ever glamorous. That's me. Why, just today I was telling Patrick we ought to start serving latte in the waiting room."

"Oh, stop, child." Sarah gave the back of her hand a slight tap. "You *are* a pretty girl. It has nothing to do with what you're wearing. It's in your face and the way you carry yourself. If you don't believe me, ask Patrick."

Kayla closed the photo album and set it back in the drawer. "Patrick sees me as a dependable employee and a good friend. Pretty doesn't enter into it."

"And you've never noticed that he's handsome?"

Kayla glanced toward the door to make sure no one was listening, then leaned toward the other woman and spoke in a whisper. "Not only is he extremely good-looking, but his rear end is perfect. It's all that jogging he does."

"So?" Sarah arched her eyebrows. "Why are you going off to find a prince, when you have one right here at home?"

"Patrick?" She shook her head. "That's silly. He's just...himself."

Patrick? Never, she thought. He was her friend. He'd let

her cry on his shoulder when a young man broke her heart her junior year of college. She talked to him about her plans for the future, helped him write his grant proposals.

"If there was any kind of a spark, it would have already flared by now, Sarah," she continued. "You're going to have to accept the fact that I'm going to marry Prince Albert. But don't worry. I'll invite you to the wedding."

Sarah patted her nearly useless legs. "I'll be there. Even if I have to crawl."

Kayla waved the words away. "Never. We'll send the royal jet for you. Maybe one or two young men to rub your feet on the way, too."

Sarah laughed. "You are a love. I'll miss you when you're gone."

Kayla leaned forward and hugged her. "I'll miss you, too. That's the only bad part about leaving."

"Oh, I almost forgot." Sarah put on her reading glasses and picked up a letter on the nightstand. "I've written to my friend Marie. I told you about her. Danny and I met her when we visited Paris. She's answered me and says she would be delighted to introduce you to her grand-daughter, who is only a couple of years older than you." She smiled. "You'll have friends when you arrive."

"Thank you."

They chatted for a few more minutes, then Kayla collected Rip and promised to return at the end of the week. Downstairs, she found Patrick talking to Mrs. Grisham. Mr. Peters caught her eye and motioned to Patrick, then winked. Patrick turned and caught the gesture. He glanced at Kayla and shrugged, as if to say, "What can we do?"

"Did you vaccinate the cat?" she asked, walking toward Patrick.

"Whiskers is the picture of health, and safe for another year," he said.

She remembered his attempt to vaccinate Whiskers last year. "Did she scratch you?"

He held up his left hand. A long red welt curved across the back, from his little finger to his wrist.

She winced. "At least it's not as bad as last time."

"Small comfort."

"You could have asked me to help."

He looked insulted. "I can handle an eighteen-pound cat on my own."

"It must be tough being so macho."

He reached around her and tugged on the end of her braid. "I'll write you up for insubordination."

"Go ahead. I'm friendly with the boss, and I'll appeal."

Kayla realized all the residents were listening intently. Mrs. Grisham caught her gaze and nodded encouragingly.

Perfect, she thought, then called Elizabeth to her side. "We'd better be going," she said cheerfully, determined to ignore the not-so-subtle matchmaking. "I'll be back on Friday."

Patrick picked up Trudi's leash, and they said their goodbyes as they left the building.

"Are they always that bad?" Patrick asked as he stowed his medical bag behind the driver's seat.

"About getting me in a relationship?" She nodded. "Yeah, they are. It's worse when you're with me. Then they want to turn us into a couple. When you're not around, I'm usually bombarded with pictures of grandsons, nephews, or told to check out the guy cleaning the pool." She secured the latch on Rip's cage.

"Have you told them about your plans to seduce Prince Albert?"

She grinned. "Only Sarah. I don't think the rest of them would approve. I suppose it's sweet of them to care about me."

"Why wouldn't they? You care about them. You started this program two years ago, and they've never had to miss a visit. If you weren't around, you made sure someone else was. They appreciate that." He slammed the rear door of the van. "You're not going to be easy to replace."

She moved toward him and wrapped her arms around his waist. She was five foot seven, but Patrick towered over her by six inches. When he hugged her back, she rested her head on his shoulder and inhaled his familiar scent.

"I'm going to miss you," she said.

"Compared to your rich prince, I'm pretty forgettable."

She smiled up at him. "No way. I bet he can't cook as good as you. And he would probably be very upset to know that I would like to encourage a romance between Duchess and Mr. Cookie."

"*I'm* very upset to hear that. They're both purebred animals. Besides, have you thought about how the pups would look?"

She stepped back. "Not to mention the logistical difficulties of Mr. Cookie trying to—"

"Kayla." He growled her name in mock anger.

She laughed and went around to climb into the passenger's seat.

"What are we doing tonight?" she asked as he pulled out of the driveway.

"We aren't doing anything. I have a date."

Kayla's throat closed unexpectedly, and she found it difficult to ask, "Anyone I know?"

"Maybe."

Usually, his teasing made her laugh. Today she felt a tightness in her chest. She couldn't explain the reaction, and it made her uncomfortable.

"Have a wonderful time," she said, relieved that her

voice sounded completely normal. What on earth was wrong with her? ''Don't forget we have a lot of work to do in the living room before I leave.'' They were stripping off old wallpaper and replacing it with something less floral. ''Of course, if the relationship works out, you can get her to help you,'' she added.

''Gotcha,'' he said.

She turned toward him. ''What? You *don't* have a date?''

He normally wore his hair brushed back off his forehead. By the end of the day, a few strands always tumbled forward. He pushed them away. ''You deserved it, telling me I was getting old and should get married.''

''I never said you were old. I said in the seven years I'd known you, you'd never been involved in a serious relationship.'' She folded her arms over her chest and looked out the window. ''I hate it when you're difficult,'' she muttered.

''I thought you hated it when I was agreeable.''

''That, too.''

''So are you coming over to help me tonight?''

''I shouldn't. I should let you finish on your own.''

''But you won't.''

''Are you cooking?''

''Grilled chicken and a salad. I thought I could cajole you into fixing rice.''

''Did you make your secret barbecue sauce?''

''Does Mr. Cookie want Duchess?''

She laughed, her good humor restored. ''Okay, yes, I'll be there.''

As she watched the familiar scenery slip by, her world righted itself. Next to her two sisters, Patrick was her best friend. She needed things to be okay between them. She couldn't wait to tell him about Sarah's photo album. He would understand what those old pictures meant to her. He always understood.

Chapter Two

Although the sun had long since set, light spilled onto the back patio from the kitchen window and the malibu lights set around the garden. Warmth lingered from the sunny day, although by ten the temperature would drop into the low sixties. Patrick pushed against the concrete deck and sent the swing rocking.

Kayla sighed and rested her head against the soft cushions. "I could spend the rest of the night right here."

She reclined on the swing, her back supported by the swing's right arm and a throw pillow she'd brought out from the living room. She rested her bare feet in Patrick's lap. He rested one hand on her ankles. With his other hand, he stroked the delicate arch pressing against his thigh.

"You're just trying to get out of doing the dishes," he said.

She opened one eye and gazed at him. "But I cooked dinner."

She was the picture of innocence and contentment. All an act, he thought, and grinned. Inside, she had the heart of a pirate. "You cooked the rice and set the table. I did everything else."

"I kept you company by the barbecue. That was work."

He grabbed her feet and tugged, pulling her down so that she lay flat on the swing seat. She tried to giggle and yelp at the same time, the noise she made sounding like a seal.

"Patrick, no," she said breathlessly. "Don't."

"Too late. You're trying to weasel out of the dishes."

"No, no, I'll do them. I'll do all of them. I'll even wash the floor."

"Cheap talk."

He wrapped his arm around her ankles to hold her still. Then, with his free hand, he brought his thumb and forefinger together like a crab's pincer.

"Patrick, don't!" She gasped with laughter as he moved his fingers closer to her feet bottoms. She tried to sit up, but she was laughing too much. "I give. I give!"

He released her. "Let that be a lesson to you."

She collapsed back on the swing. Her jean-clad legs fell across his lap. "I swear I'll do the dishes," she said, and inhaled deeply. "Just give me a minute to catch my breath."

"Lightweight."

She tucked her arm under her head and gazed at him. "We can't all get by on six hours of sleep and running five miles a day. Some of us like to conserve our energy for other things."

"Like what?"

"Like sleep."

He rested one hand on her shin, the other just above her knee. "You need energy to sleep?"

"Sure. If it's done right."

He raised his eyebrows. Kayla had interesting theories on almost everything in life. He wasn't sure he wanted to hear this one.

When he didn't speak, she blinked flirtatiously. "You're not going to bite?"

"Nope."

"It's a great explanation."

"Thank you, no."

"Fine. Be a toad. See if I care." She pouted.

He didn't respond. She was silent for about ten seconds, then poked his thigh. "You always win," she said. "Why is that?"

"I'm a naturally superior being."

That took a heartbeat for her to register. Kayla didn't disappoint him. She sprang up and grabbed his hand, trying to twist it behind his back. He let her tug and grunt, but his arm didn't budge.

"You're not strong enough," he said mildly.

"I hate that." She gave up on his arm and settled for squeezing his fingers together as hard as she could. She generated enough pressure to make him notice, but not enough to really hurt.

A strand of hair drifted onto her face. She released him and brushed it away impatiently. Settling back on her knees, she said, "I've got to start working out. When I'm strong enough, I'm going to kick butt."

He touched her cheek. "I'm a runner, Kayla. You're going to have to catch me first."

"Figures." She smiled. "I swear, you're not winning this one. If I have to, I'll *hire* someone to kick butt."

"Just like I always say. You have the heart of a pirate. When did you get to be so bloodthirsty?"

She twisted around and sat next to him. He dropped his

arm around her shoulders and she rested her head on his chest. "It's part of my charm. You love it." She snuggled closer. "Any news on the grant?"

"Nothing yet. I'm hoping to hear in the next few weeks."

"I know the wait's the worst part, but it's going to work out. They have to give you the money. You're the best candidate. I just know it."

Her faith touched him. "Thanks, Kayla. You were a great help to me. I couldn't have finished the proposals without you."

While Patrick's private veterinary practice was successful, in the past couple of years he'd found himself growing restless. In college, he'd spent as much time as possible working in the research lab studying disease in house pets. His goal had always been to return there.

"Is the lot you were looking at still for sale?" she asked.

"It was the last time I drove by." He squeezed her shoulders. "Don't get your hopes up too much. This is a very ambitious project. Not only does it require building an entire six-story building, but then it has to be staffed. We're talking about millions of dollars."

"What about the clinic?" she asked. "Will you still work there?"

"I'm not sure. I think I'd prefer to focus on the research for the first couple of years. Of course, it's going to take some time to get the building constructed. I'll hire a couple of vets and ease them into the practice."

"A couple? You think you work that hard?" Her voice teased.

As she stared up at him, he saw the light from the window reflected in her green eyes. Cat eyes, he thought. All-knowing and beautiful. She'd showered before she came over. She rarely bothered with perfume, so her sweet scent came from soap, shampoo and her smooth skin. Her hair hung loose down her back, the natural curls teasing his forearms.

He remembered her as a slightly awkward, shy eighteen-year-old. Over the past few years, she'd become an attractive woman. While they'd never been a couple, they were good friends. He was going to miss her when she was gone.

"You're going to need two replacements, as well," he said.

Her mouth straightened. "You think so?"

He nodded. "I'll get a part-timer in to take care of the grooming. The more difficult problem is finding someone to take over the visitations to Sunshine Village."

She ducked her head and leaned against his chest again. "I know. I've been worrying about that, too. We're going to have to find someone who really cares about the people there. I think I'll start asking around. Maybe someone at one of the colleges, or a stay-at-home mom looking for something different to do while her kids are in school. I'll make sure it's right before I leave."

"Are you going to find me a new best friend, too?" he asked, only partly kidding.

She wrapped her arm around his waist and squeezed. "Oh, Patrick, it's not like we'll never see each other again. I'll be back, and we'll stay in touch."

"I know, kid. It'll be fine."

He heard the smile in her voice as she said, "I'm not a kid anymore."

"I know."

He could feel her breast pressing into his midsection. Reminding himself that Kayla was just a friend didn't stop a sliver of interest from sparking to life. He ignored the sensation. He'd felt the occasional spark before and done nothing about it. He preferred Kayla in his life as his friend. That way, there were never any scenes, angry words or false expectations, and there was no risk of breaking up.

If he was going to be completely honest with himself, he didn't want her to go. But not wanting her to leave him wasn't enough to convince him to ask her to stay. Kayla had spent years planning this trip. Her whole dream in life was to travel. She wanted to see the world. He'd grown up moving from one military base to another. What was the old cliché? She wanted wings, and he wanted roots.

He cared enough about her to wish her well on her journey. When she was gone, maybe he would take her up on her suggestion that he start dating. That would distract him from the hole her absence would create in his life.

He pulled his arm free of her and stood up. "You're trying to make me forget that there are dishes to be done. Don't think I'm going to let you get out of your duty."

She grumbled under her breath, then held out her hands. He pulled her to her feet. "All right, Mr. Tyrant. I'm coming. Maybe you should chain me to the sink so I can't escape."

He lightly kissed the top of her head. "Whine, whine, whine. And here I was going to be nice and let you dry."

She darted in front of him and spun until they were facing each other. Her eyes crinkled at the corners as she laughed. "Yes, Patrick. Please let me dry. You know I hate washing."

Ten minutes later, he was up to his elbows in soapy water. Kayla sat on the counter next to him, holding a dish towel and waiting for the next glass.

"I'm sorry I got so weird when you said you had a date tonight," she told him. "It just sort of caught me off guard.

With so little time before I leave, I guess I selfishly want you to spend your free time with me.''

He smiled, remembering her cranky expression. ''No problem.''

She took the glass he offered and began to dry it. The overhead light reflected off Kayla's hair, turning blonde into spun gold. She wore a plain white T-shirt tucked into clean, worn jeans. Her feet were still bare. Loafers rested by the front door. The first thing she did upon entering her home or his was to kick off her shoes.

''Do you ever think about getting married?'' she asked.

He rinsed a plate, then handed it to her. ''Sometimes. I don't think I'm ready yet.''

''You're thirty-one.''

''So you reminded me earlier today.''

''What aren't you ready for?''

He shrugged. Marriage was a big step. ''I've avoided long-term entanglements,'' he said. ''Much as you have.''

She tossed her head and flipped her hair over her shoulder. ''I'm saving myself for Prince Albert. What's your excuse?''

He reached for the pot she'd used to cook rice and pushed it under the water. The bay window in front of him wasn't curtained, so the glass acted as a mirror, reflecting his image and the room behind him. He stared at the reflection for a couple of seconds.

''I don't have one,'' he admitted at last.

Kayla leaned toward him and touched his shoulder. ''It's your dad, isn't it?''

''Yeah. I guess. According to what everyone told me, my folks were really in love.''

''But that's a *good* thing. You should want that, too.''

He shrugged. ''I don't have a memory of it. She died when I was two. What I do remember is my dad mourning her. It was as if he'd lost a leg and was forever cursed to walk with a limp. Except the missing part of him was his heart. He lived another twenty years, and there wasn't a day that he didn't pray for her to return.''

Patrick remembered coming home from school early once. He must have been nine or ten. He hadn't known his dad was in the house, so he'd let himself in the front door, using the key he wore around his neck. He'd found his father in the dining room. The older man had sat at the table, the wedding album open in front of him. Silent tears had poured down his face. He hadn't made a sound as he turned pages and wept.

The memory was as clear today as it had been then. He'd felt his father's pain. The depth of the wound had terrified him. As a child, he'd feared being abandoned by his only living parent. He'd crept out of the room without letting his father know he'd seen him.

"I don't want to love like he did," Patrick said softly. He picked up the pot and began scrubbing it. "It was tragic."

"It's wonderful and romantic. That's what I want."

Patrick shook his head. "Too much pain. I respect and admire my dad, but I think he was weak. He could have recovered. He chose not to. I don't want any emotion controlling me that much."

Kayla looked at him. "You might not get a choice in the matter."

"There's always a choice."

She eyed him speculatively. "You need a good woman to snap you out of this funk."

"I'm not in a funk."

She ignored him. "A woman. But what kind?" Her brow furrowed. "Someone who likes animals and is patient. Someone you can really talk to." She tilted her head toward the living room. "Someone who won't mind the fact that half your walls are being stripped of wallpaper and the other half need to be."

"A redhead," he put in.

Her sniff was the only reply. "Pretty, smart, funny," she went on. "In short, me!"

Patrick was pleased he was only washing a pot, because her words caused him to let go and the metal container clattered into the sink.

He stared at her. She met his gaze and grinned.

"Well?" she asked. "Are you speechless?"

"Yes."

"Good. I adore being in control." She batted her lashes.

"Kayla, I—" He paused, not sure what to say.

"We'd be perfect together. We get along, we like each other. I'm charming, you're sensible."

He sensed she was teasing him, but he couldn't respond. It was as if he couldn't catch his breath. He looked at her, trying to figure out her game. There had to be one. Him and Kayla? After all this time? No way.

But once the seed was planted, he realized it wasn't as shocking as he'd first thought. Kayla and him? Was it possible she'd been harboring some romantic feelings for him? He didn't think so. Surely he would have sensed something.

"We're friends," he said at last.

"Agreed. But we do have enough in common to be a great couple."

Her expression was happy, her eyes were bright with humor. She didn't look lovesick. There was a piece missing. There had to be.

"We want different things in life," he said, deciding to play along and see where she was going. "You want to travel, I want to settle in one place."

"We share the same values," she said. "We care about each other. We have mutual respect. Isn't that important?"

It was, but he didn't want to answer her. "What are you getting at?" he asked.

She gave an exaggerated sigh. "Okay, here's the deal. I think you really do need to be with a woman, and I have one in mind."

"You want to set me up?"

"Don't sound like you're getting vaccinated against some tropical disease. You'll adore her. I promise."

"I've heard that before."

He reached for the pot and rinsed it off. She wasn't declaring undying love, she just wanted to set him up. Good, he told himself, and ignored the tiniest flicker of disappointment. Better for both of them. They *were* great friends, but they would never make it as a couple. He couldn't imagine caring for her that way.

Kayla jumped off the counter and touched his arm. "I'm not kidding. You'll adore her. And here's the best part. She looks just like me."

He opened his mouth, but she gave him a warning look. "Don't even think about saying anything tacky, Patrick. I'm holding a wet towel, and I'll make you pay."

He winked. "Whip me, beat me, tie me up—"

"Patrick!" She cut him off with a shriek. "Be serious. I'm going to call my sister Elissa and invite her out for a weekend. You guys can meet. She might be the woman of your dreams."

He sobered quickly. He didn't want to meet the woman of his dreams. He'd given up on dreams of love a long time ago. The price was too high.

Kayla waited, shifting her weight from foot to foot. She was obviously impatient to have him approve of her plan. He had no interest in meeting her sister, but he wouldn't hurt her feelings by telling her that. She would enjoy having one of her sisters spend the weekend with her. He could meet the lady, talk politely, then be on his way. Elissa's visit wouldn't change anything.

"Do your worst, kid," he said.

She gave him a quick hug. "You're going to love her," she said. "I promise."

"That's what you told me about sushi."

"Elissa is much nicer than sushi."

"She'd better be."

"Have I ever been wrong?" she asked, then wrinkled her nose. "Okay, don't answer that. But I'm not wrong this time. You'll see."

Chapter Three

"*Quelle heure est-il?*" the voice on the tape intoned.

"Kell err a teal," Kayla repeated dutifully over the yapping of dogs in the kennels. Her alcove of an office was right off the boarding area, which normally didn't bother her, but today she was trying to learn French.

"You guys aren't helping me," she called over her shoulder. "I'm trying to ask the time." The volume of the barking increased. She leaned closer to her small tape recorder. "Apple what? Oh, forget it." She pushed the Off button. "I'll listen to it tonight."

She rose to her feet and headed into the kennels. At the sight of her, most of the dogs quieted, with whimpers of pleasure replacing the barking. Kayla paused and greeted them all. She took a few extra minutes with the dogs being boarded. Although pets had a good time going on walks and playing with other residents, they missed their families. Kayla stepped into a kennel and knelt in front of a large, gentle golden Labrador. Big brown eyes met hers but the dog didn't raise his head from where it rested on his paws.

"Come on, Sammy. Don't be sad. They're coming back today."

Sammy's expression didn't change. Kayla glanced over her shoulder to make sure no one was around. The staff would tease her unmercifully if they knew what she was about to do.

Easing against the concrete wall of the kennel, she sat on the floor. To her left was a doggie door that lead to a twenty-by-eight foot outdoor area. Each dog had its own run. On her right was a raised, padded platform that served as a bed. Sammy's toys were scattered around, although he hadn't played with them much.

She stretched her legs out in front of her and patted her lap. The large dog slowly lumbered to his feet. He moved closer, then cautiously stepped onto her thighs. Kayla tried not to wince as the sixty-five-pound animal sat on her lap and leaned heavily against her chest. She wrapped her arms around Sammy and began to softly sing about the purchase price of a dog in a store display.

She continued the song, rocking Sammy, rubbing his back and head. He sighed heavily. After a few minutes, his tail started thumping against the ground. By the time she'd completed the song for the fourth time, he'd shifted off her and picked up one of his chew toys.

They wrestled with the toys for a while. A dog in the next kennel barked, challenging Sammy to a race. The Labrador took off out the doggie door, racing to the back fence. Kayla smiled as she let herself out.

"Mission accomplished," she said as she walked toward the exit. She checked bowls as she went, making sure they all had water. Although the kennel wasn't her responsibility, she didn't mind looking things over when she was back here.

At the door, she paused and counted empty kennels. Just three. Only about half the residents were paying boarders. The rest of the dogs either came with her to Sunshine Village or were strays.

A familiar feeling of guilt tightened in her chest. Word had gotten out that Kayla took in strays, so there was a steady stream of them. Placement wasn't too difficult, although sometimes it took a while. Unwanted dogs were treated, fed, housed, all for free. Patrick never complained, never hinted that the strays cost him a lot of money, not just for their food and medicine, but in what he could be making if he was able to take in more paying boarders.

Patrick understood why she cared about the strays. He understood everything. There was a strength about Patrick. Solid—that was how she would describe him.

She pulled the door open and found the object of her thoughts standing in her alcove.

She laughed. "Patrick. I was just standing in the kennel thinking about how wonderful you are. And here I could have told you to your face."

He didn't return her smile. His expression was grim.

"What's wrong?" she asked. "Is there an emergency?"

"A lady has brought in a stray," he said curtly. "Is there room in the kennel?"

She nodded. Patrick only got angry about strays if they'd been mistreated. "How bad?"

He shrugged. "I haven't examined her yet. Skinny, scared. About what you'd expect. Everyone else is tied up. Can you help me with the examination?"

"Sure."

She followed him to the waiting room.

A small woman with pale skin and short, graying hair

sat on the bench against the wall. Her face was drawn, and dark shadows had taken up permanent residence under her eyes. Next to her was a little mixed-breed dog. Shaggy hair, big eyes. A shudder rippled through the dog every few seconds. Kayla had a bad feeling that when she picked the animal up she would be able to feel all its ribs.

"Mrs. Francis?" Patrick asked.

The woman nodded.

"I'm Dr. Patrick Walcott. This is Kayla." He settled next to the woman and gestured for Kayla to sit by the dog. Patrick pulled a pen out of his lab coat and adjusted his clipboard. "Tell me about the dog."

"Don't know much," Mrs. Francis said, and shrugged. "Been around the neighborhood a year, maybe two. Sweet dog. Gentle, loves kids. Never bitten anyone, not that some of the boys in the neighborhood haven't tried her patience. I've rescued her a time or two myself." Mrs. Francis twisted her hands together.

Patrick's voice was low and soothing. "That's very good of you. Most people don't bother."

The older woman smiled. "I like animals."

"When was she abandoned?"

"I can't rightly say. Been close to a month, I think. Her owners, I never knew them well, just moved. Left her behind."

"You don't think she got left behind by accident?"

Mrs. Francis's mouth twisted down. "I heard things about her family, and they weren't nice. They didn't forget her." She placed her hand on the dog's back, stroking it. "I wanted to keep her myself, but it didn't work out." Color crept onto her cheeks. "Sometimes there's barely enough food for my children, but I've been making it work. Then I got a promotion. I work full-time now. There's going to be more money for all of us, but I won't be home during the day. I can't leave her out in the yard. Not with those boys around. It's not safe. So I hoped if I brought her here you could find a place for her with some nice people.''

Patrick asked a few more questions and made notes. Kayla had to swallow the lump in her throat. She reached out her hand and let the little dog sniff her fingers. A fuzzy tail thumped against the plastic cushions on the bench.

''Pretty girl,'' Kayla said quietly, and received a pleading look from big, sad eyes.

''Does she have a name?'' Patrick asked.

''Not that I know of. My middle girl says she looks like that dog that used to be on TV. You know the one.''

''Benji,'' Kayla filled in.

''That's it.'' Mrs. Francis offered a wan smile. ''I was afraid I couldn't keep her, so I didn't let my kids name her. I figured naming her would make it too hard to let her go.''

Patrick rose to his feet. ''Mrs. Francis, I appreciate all you've been through. You've obviously grown attached to the dog, and I suspect it's going to be hard for you to give her up, too.''

The older woman stood up. ''Maybe,'' she said, casting a glance at the little dog. ''But I want to do what's right.''

Patrick placed his hand on her shoulder. ''We'll take care of her. Kayla is in charge of finding homes for our dogs, and she'll make sure this dog gets a good one. I promise.''

Mrs. Francis blinked several times. ''Maybe one with children.''

''Of course,'' Kayla said. ''A loving family with a big fenced yard. She'll be very happy.''

Patrick walked to the desk and said something to the

receptionist. She reached into a drawer and handed him a slip of paper. He returned to Mrs. Francis's side.

"One of the grocery store chains in the area has been very supportive of our attempts to place strays. They've offered to offset the cost of feeding and caring for an animal when good people like you take the time and trouble to rescue them." He handed her a gift certificate. "You can use this at any of their stores."

Mrs. Francis stared at the certificate. "A hundred dollars?" she breathed, then glanced at him. "I didn't spend anywhere near that much. She doesn't eat but a little."

He smiled. "I know, but you had to get here, didn't you? And you've rescued her more than once. You deserve it, Mrs. Francis. Please accept it, and tell your children thank-you."

Kayla picked up the little dog. As she'd feared, she could easily count the ribs. She held her close and felt her shiver.

The woman touched his arm. "Thank you, Dr. Walcott. You're a good man." She kissed the dog on the top of her head, then walked out into the parking lot.

Kayla blinked several times.

Patrick glanced at her. "You gonna cry, kid?"

"I hope not. This kind of stuff always gets to me."

"Yeah. Me, too." He took the dog from her arms and held it expertly. "Come on, little girl. Let's see how you're doing."

Fifteen minutes later, Patrick had completed the exam. Kayla assisted. The little dog didn't squirm or try to get away. She lay still, completely docile.

"I can't decide if she knows we're trying to help her or if she's given up," Kayla said, knowing he would hear the worry in her voice.

"I see some life in her. I think she's going to be fine.

Aren't you, sweetie?'' He stroked the dog's head.
''There's obvious malnutrition, and fleas. We'll have to
test her for worms. She's probably never had any shots,
but I want to wait a couple of days to start her on that.''
He glanced at the clock. ''Jo should be here.''

He walked to the phone attached to the wall just outside
the examining room. After picking up the receiver, he
punched a couple of buttons, and then his voice came over
the loudspeakers. ''Jo, please come up to examining room
three.''

Less than a minute later a black-haired nineteen-year-
old burst into the room. ''Yes, Dr. Walcott?'' she asked.

''We've got a new resident.'' He gestured to the dog.
''She's in pretty good shape, except for a few fixable
things. Get her a basket and some soft blankets.'' He
frowned. ''Are you on tonight?''

Jo nodded. ''Until 6:00 a.m.'' The teenager hurried to
the little dog and gathered her up. ''Oh, what a pretty little
girl.'' She cuddled the dog close. ''Does she have a
name?''

''Not that we know of,'' Patrick said.

''I suppose Muffin is out of the question.''

''Absolutely.''

Kayla smiled. Jo had been trying to name strays Muffin
ever since she started working here, nearly a year before.
Patrick had never agreed.

''Mix up some of that special feed,'' Patrick continued.
''Small servings. No more than half a cup. But feed her
every couple of hours, all night. Lots of water. See if she'll
go for a walk with you. You know where the extra leashes
are. Use flea powder for now. I don't want to shock her
by giving her a bath. That can wait. Oh, and I'll need a
sample to test for worms.''

''Done,'' Jo said, and carried the dog from the room.

Kayla stared after them. "Gee, and I was going to offer to take her home with me."

Patrick walked to the sink and washed his hands. "I know," he said over the sound of the water. "I could see it in your eyes. If Jo hadn't been on duty tonight, I would have encouraged you. But she's the best."

Someone was on duty at the clinic every night. There was a small room in the back with a comfy cot, a desk with an office chair and good light. When Kayla first worked for Patrick, she'd spent her share of nights at the clinic. Some of the ill animals required medication or post-operative treatments every couple of hours, but apart from that it was easy duty. She remembered getting a lot of studying done. Of course, more than once she'd brought one of her favorite dogs into the room with her. She'd often awakened to find a bemused Patrick shaking his head in disgust while a large canine took up more than half the cot and used her legs for a pillow.

"Next Thursday I'm scheduled to speak at a children's center downtown," Patrick said. "If our new guest turns out to be as calm and good-natured as she seems, then I'd like you to come along and bathe her. I want the kids to see how to do it right. Maybe they can even give her a name."

"Not Muffin," she teased.

He grabbed a paper towel and dried his hands. "No Muffins, no Buffys."

"What about Mr. Cookie?"

"I refuse to even comment on that one."

"I happen to like pet names. You want all of them to have people names."

"Of course."

She laughed. "Why?"

He put his arm around her shoulders. "I don't have to answer to you."

They headed for her alcove. "I know why," she said. "You think dogs are people, too."

He ignored her and moved to her littered desk. After pushing aside a couple of folders, he found her desk calendar and wrote down the appointment for the children's center.

"You don't trust me to remember?" she asked, trying to work up some irritation.

"I know you."

Her emotions weren't in the mood to bubble and boil. Probably because Patrick was right. She did sometimes forget appointments.

She crossed to the calendar on the wall. The picture on top showed the Seine and the Left Bank of Paris after a storm. Everything was wet, all grays and dark browns, except for a spray of bright yellow and pink flowers resting on a table by the river. A black marking pen hung from a string next to the calendar. Kayla glanced at the clock and saw it was after five.

"Another day closer," she said, and made a big *X* in the box with today's date.

Patrick looked at the calendar, but didn't say anything. What did he think about her leaving? she wondered. She knew he would miss her. But how much?

"Any news on the grant?" she asked.

"Nothing." He shoved his hands in his lab-coat pockets. "It'll be a while, so stop asking."

"I want them to hurry. I want to know what's going to happen, and I don't want to find out after I leave."

He smiled and lines fanned out from the corners of his blue eyes. "I'll call them up and tell them they have to let me know by July first."

Several months ago, Kayla had thought her birthday would never arrive. Now it was just around the corner. "I'm not leaving that day. How long will it take to start construction?"

He leaned against the edge of her desk. The overhead light made his short light brown hair gleam. "I've already picked the construction company. I suppose they can break ground as soon as the check clears."

She sat in her chair. "This is going to be an exciting project. I'm thrilled for you."

"I hope it all works out. I haven't done any serious research since college. I've been keeping current on what's going on, but that's not the same as being in the middle of it. People lose pets to diseases that should already have a cure. And we never know what part of our animal research is going to spill over and help humans."

She tilted her head and studied him. "You're a good man, Patrick Walcott. One of the last nice guys."

He frowned. "Gee, thanks. All men want to be told they're nice."

"Okay, you're nice, good-looking and sexy. Is that better?"

"Nice try, but I don't believe you."

She stiffened in her chair. "But I'm telling the truth."

"If I was so good-looking and sexy, how come you didn't have a crush on me when you first came to work for me? Jo does."

Kayla tried to keep calm. She didn't want to start blushing. She'd had a crush on Patrick when she started at the clinic. Thinking about him had kept her up more than one night. But she'd been terrified to let him know. She'd been just a kid, and he an older, mature man. Now the age difference was no big deal, but at eighteen, seven and a half years had felt like a lifetime.

The phone on her desk rang. Kayla picked it up. The voice at the other end asked for Patrick, and she gladly handed over the receiver.

While he was busy talking, she made her escape. How odd of him to bring up the subject of crushes. Thank goodness he didn't know about hers; he would tease her unmercifully. Although it had been a long time ago. Why should she be so sensitive about it now?

She didn't have an answer. All she knew for sure was that she would do almost anything to keep Patrick from knowing how she'd once felt about him.

"Remember," Patrick said. "You know your pet best. If you think something is wrong, then bring the animal in."

He glanced around the crowded room. The Children's Community Center had been built almost entirely with donations. It sat in a poor section of the city, nearly dwarfed by large office buildings. Traffic sounds spilled in from outside, but in here was a haven for children.

The center served as an after-school day-care facility for children ages six to thirteen. It stayed open through the summer, offering different programs for kids whose parents had to work. Patrick had been coming here since he first opened his practice.

"Anybody here ever get vaccinated?" he asked.

A little girl in blond pigtails pulled her fingers out of her mouth long enough to ask, "What's that?"

"Shots," an older boy announced. "You got 'em when you were a baby. They're so you don't get sick."

"That's right," Patrick said. "What's your name, son?"

The boy, maybe eleven or twelve, sat a little straighter. "Jackson."

"Jackson, should pets get vaccinated, too?"

The boy thought for a second. "Sure. They get sick, just like us. And if you don't, they're gonna get rabies, then everybody dies."

Several children gasped.

Patrick held up his hands. "Wait a minute. Jackson's half-right. Your dogs and cats need vaccinations to keep them from getting sick. One of the vaccines is against rabies. But very few domestic animals get rabies these days, and even if a rabid animal bites you, you're not going to die."

Kayla stood next to him. "They're not going to like the cure much, though," she said in a soft voice.

He smiled at her. "I wasn't planning to tell them what it was."

"Good thinking."

He returned his attention to the children. "My clinic is open on the second and fourth Saturday of the month. You can bring your dogs and cats to me, and I'll vaccinate them for you. You don't have to remember my name or the days I'm there. I put up a flier on the bulletin board." He pointed to the bright yellow sheet of paper.

Jackson eyed him cautiously. "Shots cost money. Sometimes there's not even enough for dog food."

"I know," Patrick said. He'd dealt with this question several times before. "If your pet needs shots, bring it in. We'll worry about paying for it later. Also—" he addressed the whole room "—if your pet is sick, don't wait for those two Saturdays. Call the office and tell them you need to come. Any other questions?"

Kayla leaned close. "You're going to be swamped with work from this."

He shook his head. "I've made the offer before. Only a couple take me up on it. Most of these kids can't afford to have a dog or cat. I wish it was different. I would rather worry about my bottom line and have their lives enriched by a pet.''

''Just like I said. One of the good guys.''

''As long as you don't call me nice.''

''Yes, boss.''

When he answered the children's questions, he'd moved aside to let Kayla take his place. She set their latest stray on the portable table he'd brought with them. He spoke to Mrs. James, one of the volunteers who worked at the center. She showed him where to fill the tub with warm water, then offered several pitchers so they could rinse the dog.

''Someone brought her into the office,'' Kayla was saying when he returned. The children had left their seats and gathered around the table. ''A family moved away and left her behind.''

A beautiful girl with expressive brown eyes and coffee-colored skin petted the dog. ''On purpose?'' she asked.

''I'm afraid so. Sometimes people do that.''

He set the tub in front of Kayla. She smiled her thanks, then returned her attention to the children. She handled their new charge gently, soothing the animal with continuous touches.

They'd only had the dog six days, but already she'd started to gain weight. Her eyes were clear, her expression was interested. She'd stopped shaking a couple of days ago.

Kayla worked quickly and efficiently. She told the children that the dog didn't have a name. Would they like to pick one?

''Benji!'' someone called.

''Benji's a good name,'' Kayla agreed, ''but this little dog's a girl.''

They argued over names for a couple of minutes, and then Jackson stepped forward. ''How about Rhonda?''

The girl in pigtails nodded. "Rhonda was nice. She used to work here, then she moved away."

Kayla glanced at their faces. "Everyone agree?"

The kids nodded.

"Rhonda it is." She looked over her shoulder at him. "That okay?"

"Anything but Muffin."

She grinned.

Kayla finished rinsing the dog, then wrapped her in a fluffy towel. Patrick watched the proceedings. Kayla talked to the children as if they were intelligent adults. They responded to her attention and practically glowed when she favored them with a smile. He knew what that felt like. Sometimes when she turned her smile on him he felt—

He frowned. He wasn't sure what he felt. He shouldn't feel anything. They were friends.

She finished towel-drying Rhonda and released the little dog. The animal approached the children slowly, interested but cautious. Kayla urged them to sit on the floor and be very still. They did as she asked. In a matter of minutes, Rhonda was racing from kid to kid, yapping happily, her whole body vibrating from the vigorous sweep of her tail.

Kayla looked on, obviously pleased. Her full lips turned up at the corner. Odd that he'd never noticed how smooth her skin appeared, or the slender line of her neck. She wore a baggy T-shirt tucked into worn jeans. A uniform he'd seen her in a hundred times before. Yet today he admired the curve of her hips and the tempting roundness of her behind.

It didn't matter that she'd only been teasing him, trying to set him up with her sister. One sentence had changed everything.

We'd be perfect together.

He couldn't forget or let it go, and he didn't know why.

Was he attracted to her, specifically, or to the idea of having a relationship with someone? If it was the latter, then he was fine. It meant he was ready to look around and maybe take a chance on caring. Not love—that was way too risky for him—but affection. Respect. Mutual understanding. If it was the former, if he was attracted to Kayla, then he was in trouble.

Kayla stood up and walked toward him. When she reached his side, she wrapped her arms around his waist and sighed. "You're doing a good thing here." She nodded toward the kids, who were playing tag with Rhonda. The little dog raced around small feet, ducked under chairs, and had them all laughing.

"But I'm not nice, right?"

She laughed. "You were nice to me. You took in a lonely, homesick eighteen-year-old and gave her something that mattered. I wouldn't have made it through college if it hadn't been for my job at your clinic."

He remembered that time. She'd missed her sisters desperately. "I never understood why the three of you didn't go to the same college. You'd been together all your lives. It must have been hard for all of you."

"It was," she agreed. "But we wanted to do it. We'd always been the Bedford triplets. It was time to learn how to be ourselves." She looked up at him. "So, nearly seven years after the fact, thank you."

Her earnest expression made him uncomfortable. "I didn't hire you as a charity case."

"Why did you?"

He smiled. "Do you remember our interview?"

"Not really."

"I was examining a particularly uncooperative hundred-and-ten-pound Doberman named Thor. You were earnestly trying to sell me on your meager qualifications. The more nervous you got, the more you patted the dog. By the time the interview was over, he was licking your hand and didn't even flinch when I gave him his shots. I knew then you were a natural.''

"So it worked out," she said.

"Agreed." But why hadn't it worked out romantically?

The question came from inside his head, and he didn't know how to answer it. Before he could try to figure out what that meant, Mrs. James approached them.

The woman was about his age, pretty, with soft brown hair. She smiled at him, then turned her attention to Kayla. "I know you take dogs to visit senior citizens. Do you work much with children?"

"I can," Kayla said, and stepped away from Patrick. "What did you have in mind?"

"I heard about a girl through a friend of mine. Her name is Allison, and she's about nine, I think. She was in a horrible accident. She's in a body cast at a rehab center. She's not supposed to move at all. Of course, she's very upset, and not responding to anyone. I thought if you had time, you might visit her."

Kayla didn't hesitate. "I'd love to."

Mrs. James smiled. "Let me get the address and phone number. I don't think she can have visitors other than family until next week, but I'd like to be able to call her mother and tell her you're coming."

"Please do."

While the woman went off to get the information, Kayla sighed. "I know exactly how that girl feels," Kayla said.

Patrick remembered Kayla talking about a similar situation when she was twelve. A car accident had put her in the hospital for close to a year.

He leaned close and kissed the top of her head.

"What's that for?" she asked.

"Because you're one of the nice guys, too."

She smiled. "And I'm more understanding. Being called nice doesn't offend me."

He studied her familiar face.

"Why are you suddenly looking so serious?" she asked.

"I hope Prince Albert appreciates what he's getting when he falls for you."

Chapter Four

Kayla poured herself a cup of coffee and glanced at the clock. Two minutes until nine. She still had time. She added milk and sugar, picked up her plate of toast and moved to the sofa in the living area.

Saturday morning had dawned bright and clear. The temperature would warm into the high seventies. She'd heard a lot of other places described as paradise, but as far as she was concerned, San Diego had the best weather in the world. She couldn't imagine living anywhere else.

She stared out her large window. Her second-story west-facing view provided her with just a hint of the ocean. If she stood on tiptoe, she could see a sliver of blue. This morning she didn't bother checking. It was enough to know the water was there.

Promptly at nine, her phone rang. Kayla picked it up and heard two other voices already chatting. The operator announced that their third party was on the line, then clicked off. Her sisters paused long enough to welcome her to the conversation.

"How are you, baby sister?" Fallon asked.

Kayla grinned at the familiar greeting. Fallon was the oldest. Elissa had been born exactly six minutes later, with Kayla a full twelve minutes after Elissa. "I'm fine. What about you guys?"

"We're switching computer systems," Elissa said, then groaned. "I can't tell you how many hours I've been working. They swear it will be done on Monday, but I know they're lying. I figure Wednesday, maybe Thursday. At least it will be over this week."

"Tell me about it," Fallon said. "The school is putting on a summer festival just before school gets out. Ten-year-old boys do *not* want to dress up as any kind of plant, especially not flowers."

"Gee, my job is going great," Kayla said. "I have no horror stories to share."

The three women continued to chat. Kayla listened as her sisters brought her up to date, and then she told them what was going on with her. There were people who said that in addition to looking exactly alike, the triplets sounded the same, especially on the phone. Kayla didn't agree. She could always tell who was talking, although she was willing to admit that much of that came from context, as well as sound.

Elissa changed the subject. "Has anyone been out on a date recently?"

Silence filled the line.

Kayla laughed. "I guess that's a no, huh?"

"I don't get a lot of single guys coming through my classroom door," Fallon stated. "What's your excuse, Elissa? Don't tell me there aren't some gorgeous doctors at the hospital."

"You've been watching too many television dramas. Of course there are single doctors. At least I assume there are. But I work in administration. I don't get to spend a lot of time hovering around the surgery unit."

"I, of course, have an excuse," Kayla reminded them.

"That's right. The ever-single, ever-rich, ever-royal Prince Albert." Fallon hummed a couple of bars of the "Wedding March." "Have you written him yet to warn him of your intentions?"

"Of course not. I don't want him to think I'm crazy."

"The implication being you're completely sane?" Elissa teased.

"Mock me all you want, ladies. You're just jealous because I have a plan. When our trust-fund money is released, I'm going to make changes in my life, and neither of you can say the same."

"I have plans." Fallon sounded superior. "Sensible plans."

"What? Buy a couple of savings bonds and put a fresh coat of wax on your car?" Kayla sipped her coffee. "Fallon, you've got to get over being so darn sensible. Live a little."

"I do live. Just because I don't want to run off to Europe and fall in love with a stranger doesn't make me a stick-in-the-mud."

Kayla retreated. She didn't want to argue with her sister. Especially not on such a perfect day. "What about you, Elissa? Any plans?"

The line was silent so long, Kayla asked, "Elissa? Are you still there?"

"Of course." Her sister's voice sounded strained. "I've been thinking about a few things I'd like to do. Nothing is settled yet. Are you leaving on our birthday?"

"No. I thought we'd spend it together," Kayla said. "Isn't that what we've planned?"

Fallon cut in. "Of course it is."

"I think it will take me a week or so after that to get ready," Kayla continued. "I haven't bought my tickets yet."

"Don't forget our Christmas plans," Fallon said. "You'll be back for that, won't you?"

"Are you kidding? Christmas in the Caribbean... I wouldn't miss it for anything." Kayla smiled at the thought. She and her sisters had been planning a holiday in the tropics for years.

"Fallon, I think you should go ahead and pick out a hotel," Elissa said. "I don't mind where we stay."

"As long as it's nice," Kayla put in. "Five stars for sure."

"I'm happy to. My class is studying the history of the area, so I have a lot of research material. Something quiet and secluded."

"With warm sand and blue ocean," Elissa said dreamily.

"And cute pool boys," Kayla added, chuckling.

"What about Prince Albert?" Fallon asked.

"Oh, royal weddings take a long time to put together."

"How convenient. Okay, I'll take care of it." Fallon paused. "This is going to be different from our camp outs."

"I know," Kayla told her. "I can't wait. You remember the one we took during our junior year of college? Boy, the tents were getting ratty."

"Hey, we were traveling on a budget."

"I remember." Kayla frowned. She also remembered how their mother hadn't been interested in the triplets anymore. Once they stopped cooperating with her plans to have a show-business career, she'd emotionally abandoned them. So the three girls had clung to each other. They'd worked part-time jobs in high school, saving enough money to buy some camping gear. After that, they'd spent as much time as possible away from home. Even though they went to different colleges, they'd managed to spend long weekends together.

"Didn't we invite some guys to that camp out?" Fallon asked.

This memory was more pleasant than thinking about their mother. Kayla grinned. "Yes, we did. I distinctly recall having a serious talk with them, explaining that there absolutely would be separate tents."

"Why didn't they believe us?" Fallon sighed. "Never mind. I know the answer. They're guys."

"One of them—gosh, I can't even remember his name—got so bad, I had to push him in the lake."

Fallon chuckled. "Didn't he leave after that?"

"Can you blame him?" Kayla shook her head. "What fun we had." She had the fleeting thought that it would have been nice to invite Patrick along. But back then she'd been all of twenty, and he'd been her boss. They had always gotten along, but they hadn't been friends like they were now. She would have been too intimidated to ask him to join them.

"What do you remember, Elissa?" Fallon asked.

Their middle triplet cleared her throat. "I didn't go. I'd already left college."

Her voice sounded sad. Kayla wondered if Elissa was ever going to let her past go.

"Oh, that's right." Fallon quickly changed the subject. "I'll let you two know what I find out about the hotel. Are we still talking about staying from the twenty-second of December through the twenty-ninth?"

"Sounds good to me," Kayla said.

"Fine," Elissa answered.

"Okay, great. Look, I've got to run. I've got tons of errands, and it looks like it might rain. Talk to you guys next week. I love you."

"Love you, too," Kayla called, and Elissa joined in.

There was a click on the line as Fallon hung up. Kayla stared out the window and tried to decide if it was appropriate to talk about Elissa's past.

"Are you all right?" she asked.

"Of course," Elissa answered quickly. "Why?"

"You sounded sad for a minute."

"I'm not sad. It's just with our birthday coming up so quickly, and the trust money being released, I have a lot to think about. Some of it is serious."

Kayla understood completely. Elissa had gone down a different road from either of her sisters. "I'm here for you," she said. "If you want to talk or anything."

"I appreciate that."

Kayla drummed her fingers on the arm of the sofa. "I've been thinking. Why don't you come down here for a long weekend? We haven't seen each other in a while, and it would be fun."

She didn't bother mentioning her plans to fix up Elissa with Patrick. Maybe some quality time with one of the good guys would cheer up her sister.

"Are you sure?" Elissa asked. "You're going to be busy getting ready for your trip. I wouldn't want to intrude."

"Come on. You're never in the way. We always have a good time. I think it's what we both need."

Elissa laughed. "You're right. I've got plenty of vacation days. I've already carried over a week from last year.

I'll do it. The computer program will keep me busy for about three weeks. When's convenient after that?''

They quickly settled on a date. "Bring something sexy to wear," Kayla said. "We're going out on the town."

"Kayla, what are you planning?"

"You'll just have to wait and see. But I promise, you'll love it."

Kayla had nearly finished washing her kitchen floor when someone started pounding on her front door. She straightened and leaned the mop against the wall.

"I'm coming," she called as she stripped off her yellow rubber gloves and dropped them on the floor.

As she headed for the door, she crossed her fingers, hoping her visitor was Patrick. After the phone call with her sisters, she'd decided her apartment needed a thorough cleaning. She'd been at it for a couple of hours. She was sweaty, not wearing a speck of makeup, her ponytail was coming undone, and she wore cut off shorts and a shirt that should have been tossed six months ago. Patrick was used to seeing her looking scruffy; any other neighbor would be shocked.

The pounding continued. She pulled open the door. Patrick stood beaming on her front porch. "Where's the fire?" she asked.

His grin broadened. "I got it!"

She stared at him, not sure she understood. "Got what?"

He waved a multicolored overnight-mail envelope. "The grant." He stepped into the apartment and tossed the package in the air. "I got it!"

She screamed his name, then opened her arms wide. "You did it! I knew you would!"

He swept her close and swung her around the room. She

held on tight, laughing with him. Joy filled her. "This is so perfect," she said.

"Tell me about it." He lowered her to the ground and took her hands in his. "They gave me all the money I'd asked for. Enough for the building, the equipment, everything. I can hire the scientists and the staff."

"I'm so happy for you."

She couldn't stop smiling. She figured she was probably glowing as much as Patrick. His irises glittered with excitement. A lock of light brown hair tumbled onto his forehead, and she brushed it back.

He hugged her again. She squeezed his muscled body. "You've worked so hard," she said. "This is great. I'm thrilled and proud."

"Hey, I couldn't have done it without you. We both spent a lot of hours on those grants. I owe you."

She chuckled into his chest. "No, now we're even. You've done a lot for me, Patrick. I helped because of that, and because I wanted to."

She pulled back slightly. He looked down at her. "Okay, we're even. That means the glory belongs to both of us."

Her hands rested on his sides. She could feel his strength. "I'm always willing to accept the glory."

"This time, you earned it. Thank you."

He raised a hand to her cheek. He cupped her face gently, then bent down and kissed her.

Kayla raised herself up on tiptoe to meet him halfway. For that split second before their lips touched, she didn't think anything of it. She and Patrick had kissed lots of times. Pecks on the cheek, brief brotherly-sisterly kinds of greetings. They'd tickled each other, given back rubs, cuddled when it was cold, clung together during scary movies.

She didn't notice anything different when his lips first

brushed against hers. Without thinking, she slid her hands up his chest to his shoulders. His fingers touched her waist.

She started to smile in anticipation of what she would say next. But the words disappeared as Patrick's mouth lingered against hers.

Confusion blossomed first, then a faint tingling that started at the tips of her fingers before skittering down her arms. Heat came next. Surprising heat that stole her breath and made her want to cling to him.

His lips moved gently, softly, sweetly. Her world spun suddenly, nearly knocking her off balance. His grip on her waist tightened, and she found herself leaning into him, wanting her aching breasts to press against his chest.

She'd been kissed before. Short kisses, long kisses, kisses that felt as if the guy were trying to perform a medical procedure. But she'd never been kissed by Patrick. Not a real kiss.

Her breath caught in her throat as she waited for him to deepen the pressure, to touch his tongue to her lips and let her invite him in. He did neither. Just when she was ready to surrender, he pulled back and released her.

"This is going to be great," he announced, ruffling her bangs as if she were a ten-year-old. "We're both going to get what we want."

"Huh?" The tingling lingered, and her mouth ached so much, she couldn't form words.

"You're going off to Paris, and I'm going to build a research center."

"Oh. That. Um, sure. It's going to be wonderful."

Kayla stared at him, searching his face for some proof that he had also been affected by the kiss. But Patrick looked the same as ever. No fire darkened his eyes, no passion tightened his body. His lips barely looked damp.

Was *she* crazy? Hadn't he felt the fire between them? Or hadn't it happened at all? Had it just been her imagination?

She stepped back and moved to the window. For once, the familiar view didn't comfort her.

The measles, she thought quickly. A relapse, like with malaria. Or she was getting that flu everyone had been talking about.

There had to be a perfectly logical explanation for her reaction to his kiss. She wasn't attracted to Patrick; she couldn't be. He was her friend, and it would be wrong to feel that way about him. Besides, she was leaving. She had places to go, people to meet, including Prince Albert.

Fortunately, Patrick didn't seem to notice her preoccupation. He moved next to her and touched her arm. "I've got to get to the office," he said. "Someone is bringing in a pregnant cocker spaniel and wants me to supervise the birth." He ran his hand through his hair. "There's so much work to do. I've got to start interviewing replacements."

He bent down and kissed her on the cheek. Much to her amazement, the tingling started up again.

Before she could protest or examine what was happening to her, he'd stepped back and headed for the door. "We're celebrating tonight," he announced. "Steaks and champagne. I won't even make you cook anything. Say seven?"

"Ah, fine," she murmured, unable to do anything but stare at him. As the door closed behind him, she continued to look at the place where he'd stood and wonder what was wrong with her.

When she heard his car backing down the driveway, she shook her head and tried to break the spell. She glanced at the clock. She had nearly six hours to figure out her strange reaction and what had caused it. Then came the tricky part. She needed either an antidote or a way to make sure it didn't happen again.

Chapter Five

Patrick flipped channels and listened to the splashing sounds coming from the kitchen.

"I hope you appreciate this," Kayla called. "You know how I hate to do the dishes."

"I wish I could get grant funding every day."

She laughed. "Then it wouldn't be special, so we wouldn't have to celebrate. Therefore *I* wouldn't have to do the dishes."

"I knew you'd try to weasel out of it."

"I'm here, aren't I?"

That she was. She'd arrived on time, bringing him a huge plant and a bottle of his favorite Scotch. She'd even dressed for the occasion, replacing worn jeans with newer ones, and her ancient T-shirt with a long-sleeved white blouse that buttoned down the front.

He returned his attention to the television, but nothing looked interesting. He glanced at the clock. It was nearly nine. Maybe there was something good coming on. He clicked the channel for the cable listings and read through the offerings. One of the all-family networks had a special Saturday-night feature. He chuckled, then turned to that channel.

"Kayla, come out here."

"Just a sec. I'm nearly finished." Several cupboards banged shut as she put the pots and pans away. There was a moment of silence, and then the refrigerator door opened. "You want more champagne?"

"Sure."

She came out of the kitchen carrying her glass and the half-full bottle. As she walked toward the sofa, he increased the volume on the television. The sound of children singing filled the room.

Kayla stopped in her tracks, stared at the TV, then at him. "Turn that off this instant."

He grinned. "No way, kid. Come on." He patted the sofa cushion next to his. "You can take it."

She shuddered visibly. "I haven't seen one of these for years. And I would prefer to keep it that way. Tell me it's just one episode."

"Sorry. A four-hour marathon, until well after midnight." He patted the sofa again. "You're here for the duration, so make yourself comfy."

She plopped down with a groan and handed him the champagne bottle. After setting her glass on the light oak coffee table in front of her, she pulled her knees up to her chest and buried her face. "I can't stand it."

Patrick glanced at the television. The credits finished, and the first scene opened. Several children played in a courtyard. Girls jumped rope, while the boys were involved in a game of baseball. A pretty eight- or-nine-year-old skipped onto the screen. Her hair was a mass of gold ringlets, her eyes were bright green. A yellow-and-white gingham dress flared out to her knees, and she wore black and white oxfords.

She walked up to the pitcher and smiled prettily. "Let me play, Billy," she said.

The older boy dismissed her with a wave. "Get out of here Sally. Baseball is just for guys. Girls aren't smart enough or good enough to play."

"Boys against the girls," Patrick said. "Let me guess. Sally rallies the girls to form their own team, there's a play-off game and the girls kick butt."

Kayla rocked slightly and moaned. "I can't believe you're making me watch this."

"Is it really that awful?"

She raised her head and glanced at the TV. "I guess not." She studied the screen for a minute. "At least that's not me. I think it's Elissa."

She relaxed a little, letting her feet slide to the floor. Patrick leaned back against the sofa and shifted his weight. Then he cursed silently. For the first time since buying the couch four years ago, he noticed the damn thing had a high back. Too high for his purposes. The top of his head barely cleared the top. There was no way he could casually rest his arm along the back.

He tried to picture another way of making it work, then had to hold in a laugh when he realized he was acting as desperate as he had on his first date in high school. Back then, getting his arm around Christina's shoulders had been paramount. He vaguely recalled succeeding, because he could remember her gazing up at him, as if inviting him to kiss her. Of course, he'd been too scared to try. He'd left that for their second date.

This isn't high school, he reminded himself. He wasn't a nervous sixteen-year-old. He was a grown man, and he'd known Kayla for years. If he wanted to put his arm around her, he could. He'd done it countless times.

But tonight was different, and he had no one to blame but himself. It was that kiss. He hadn't been able to forget it all day.

Had it really happened the way he remembered it? Had that incredible passion been real? All through the afternoon, when he should have been thinking about his grant and the new research facility, not to mention a pregnant cocker spaniel, he'd thought about Kayla. She'd haunted him. He'd heard her laugh, seen her smile, imagined the shape of her body. He'd relived the kiss until his body heated with desire.

He didn't have any answers. He just knew that if he didn't touch her soon, he would go mad.

Casually, he let the remote control slip from his hand. Instead of just bending over to pick it up, he rose and poured them both more champagne. Then he picked up the remote. But when he sat back down, he moved closer to her. Close enough that their arms were almost touching.

Kayla winced at the show. "Some of this dialogue is really bad. Or maybe it was just the delivery."

A commercial came on, and Patrick muted the volume. "How long did you and your sisters appear on 'The Sally McGuire Show'?"

"We started just after our eighth birthday and completed four seasons. At first it was fun, but after a year or so, we were ready to get out." She brushed her hair off her shoulder. "None of us wanted to be Hollywood kids. It was unfortunate, because that's all our parents wanted from us."

The show came back on. He increased the volume. Sure enough, Sally had organized the girls into a rival baseball team. They had cute pink-and-white uniforms. Even their mascot, a little white poodle, wore a matching coat and cap.

Kayla pointed to the girl on the pitcher's mound. "That's Fallon. She was the best pitcher of the three of us."

"How can you tell?" In his eyes, all the Sallys on the show looked exactly the same.

"I don't know. I just can. I recognize her, of course, but I also remember shooting most of the episodes."

When Sally came up to bat, Kayla laughed. "That's me. I even run the bases. Elissa had started out with this scene, but she fell and skinned her knee. They didn't want that showing, so she isn't in much of the baseball-game show."

"I've never met your sisters."

"Really? I guess not. The few times they've visited me here, you've been gone. But Elissa is coming out for a weekend, and you'll meet her."

He turned to Kayla and frowned. "You're *not* going to set us up. Understand?"

"Why not?"

Because right now he couldn't think of anything but how to get his arm around her. "I can find my own women."

"I haven't seen any hiding out here. Apparently you're not doing a great job."

"Kayla." His voice was a low growl.

"All right. I won't fix you up. I'll just introduce you. If you like her, ask her out yourself. If you don't, no harm done. I didn't tell her about you. Don't get all in a snit."

"I don't do snits."

She rolled her eyes. "Of course you don't, Patrick. You are the most even-tempered, perfect—" She glanced at the screen. "Oh, look."

A commercial came on for a popular children's shampoo. A beautiful young mother sat with her daughter, and they were watching "The Sally McGuire Show." The show went into a commercial, and it showed the triplets talking about how much better their hair was since they'd started using the new brand.

"Commercials, too?"

She nodded glumly. "I'd wondered why we were getting residual checks. Now I know. They're using part of an old commercial in the new one."

"Did you three work all the time?"

She shifted toward him, resting one knee on the sofa and sitting on her foot. "Sometimes it felt like that. Mom put us in commercials when we were babies. Because we were perfectly identical, we could be interchanged at will, thereby allowing the commercials to be shot faster. There are restrictions when working with children. We had a few parts in some forgettable movies, then the series started when we were eight." Her green eyes darkened with emotion.

"You don't like that part of your life, do you?" he asked.

She shook her head. "We just wanted to be normal kids. When we weren't working, we went to this upscale private school. But we weren't ever there long enough to make friends. So it was just the three of us. At least we had each other. I feel sorry for the kids who have to go through that alone."

He tried to imagine her childhood, but it was completely foreign to him. Over the years she'd told him bits and pieces, but this was the first time he'd heard the whole story. "Did you explain to your parents that you were unhappy?"

She shrugged. "We were too scared. We knew what would happen. Then I was in that bad car accident just before our twelfth birthday. I was in the hospital for weeks, then in rehab for almost a year. Fallon and Elissa refused to continue the show without me. No triplets, no Sally McGuire. They talked about bringing another character in, but some viewer polls showed that the audience wouldn't accept that. There was a movie of the week in the fall after my accident. Elissa and Fallon handled the part alone. Sally and her friends were all adopted, and the orphanage closed down. Everybody was happy.''

He knew her well enough to figure out there was more to the story. ''Including your parents?''

She wrinkled her nose. ''Oh, let's say they would have preferred a different ending. They were furious at my sisters, but there was nothing they could do.'' She leaned her shoulder against the back of the sofa. ''My parents ended up fighting so much, they got a divorce. Then it really got ugly.''

He touched the back of her hand. ''You don't have to tell me any more of this.''

''I don't mind.'' She squeezed his fingers, but didn't meet his gaze. ''I know we've talked about this before, but I guess I never told you details because I was embarrassed.''

''About what?''

''I don't know. I was never a big star or anything, but people get weird when they find out about the show.''

''Why would that matter?''

She glanced at him. ''I know it wouldn't *now*, but when I first met you, well, I was afraid you would think I didn't really need the job. Then, after I'd kept the secret for a while, there didn't seem to be a good time to tell you. Are you mad?''

Their fingers entwined. ''No, Kayla, I'm not mad. I understand it must have been difficult for you. What happened after the divorce?''

"My parents were very bitter about the money,'' she said. "The judge was afraid they would spend it all, so she set up a trust for us. We were allowed to withdraw funds for college tuition and board. Nothing else until we turned twenty-five. Then it's released to us. In college, we all had to work part-time to pay for books, gas for the car, spending money, that sort of thing. So I did need my job with you.''

Her eyes were huge pools, nearly as clear as emeralds, with a faintly haunted expression tugging at the corners. Lamplight reflected the gold in her hair and made her skin look pale and smooth. Why had he never noticed that she was so much more than pretty?

"At least now your trust fund makes sense,'' he said. "I'd always wondered where it came from.''

"Now you know.''

"You did the right thing,'' he continued. "Look at where you are now. You're all grown, with a terrific future planned.''

"Thanks,'' she said, smiling shyly before turning her attention back to the screen. The first show had ended, and another one had started. "Oh, my.'' She pointed. "This one is awful. Just as filming started, we all came down with chicken pox. And do I mean all of us—every kid on the set. Worse, I recovered first, and I had to do most of the acting.''

"Why is that so bad?''

She shuddered. "Because I have so little talent. There's a very heartfelt speech in this show. I practiced and practiced. It still came out horrible.''

"I can't tell the difference when you're on the screen.''

"You're being very kind.''

She faced front and started to watch the show. Patrick kept his attention on her. They weren't holding hands anymore, and he missed the connection. The sofa back continued to defeat him.

Just put your arm around her, a voice in his head ordered. *She won't mind.*

Okay, he knew that was true. She wouldn't mind. But he wanted more than that. He wanted her to want him. Or at least be thinking about him the same way he was thinking about her. The fact that he didn't know exactly what he was thinking about her didn't matter.

He shifted a couple of times, but couldn't seem to get in a good position to casually hold her. He swore silently and leaned against the sofa. Enough, he told himself. This was crazy. If he and Kayla were attracted to each other, something would have happened a long time ago. Attraction and passion didn't suddenly explode in an already established relationship. Obviously, he had to get out more.

Kayla placed her elbows on her knees and hung her head. "Here it comes. Oh, I don't think I can watch."

The little girl on the screen stood on a narrow bunk in a long dormitory. She clutched a pillow to her midsection. Around her, children sat listening intently.

"We all want a family," Sally said earnestly. "And I know in my heart, someday we're going to find one. I pray for it every night. There's a mommy and daddy for each of us. Until they come to get us, we still have each other."

One of the little girls started to sniff. Kayla moaned. "It gets worse," she muttered.

"I'm enjoying it."

"Then you're a sick man."

He smiled.

"We are our own family. We love each other and take care of each other. That's what families do."

Kayla shrieked. "I can't stand this." She threw herself against Patrick and buried her face in his chest. "Turn it off, please. I beg you. I'll do anything."

He stared at her in amazement. Mission accomplished, he thought as he wrapped his arms around her. She snuggled close.

"If you won't turn it down," she said, "I'm going to hum loud enough so I can't hear it."

He didn't want to let go of her long enough to grab the remote, but he figured he would like the humming even less. He touched the volume control twice, and the sound quieted.

"Better," she murmured.

He agreed silently.

She had her arms around his waist, her head against his shoulder. With one hand he stroked her back, with the other he played with her silky hair. The curly strands slipped through his fingers, cool and soft. Tempting.

They were close enough that he could smell her scent and feel the heat of her body.

As they watched the rest of the show together, he felt a certain "rightness" in their being in each other's arms. He also wrestled with concern. He knew better than most the cost of loving and losing. He'd watched his father slowly die for twenty years after his wife died. Patrick didn't want to have to suffer that much for anyone. He wanted to belong, but not get hurt.

At least he was safe with Kayla. While he couldn't explain what was going on between them, he knew it wasn't love. They were just friends dealing with wayward hormones. In a few days, everything would return to normal. He would have bet on it.

Kayla laughed and reached for the remote control. She increased the volume, then pointed at the screen. "I remember her," she said as a woman in her late forties or early fifties chased three children out of the orphanage's kitchen. The woman raised her fist menacingly, but the children just grinned and held out the cookies they'd stolen.

"Her name is Mrs. Beecham, and she was always so sweet to my sisters and me. She made cookies every Friday on the set, remembered our birthdays." She sighed. "She used to talk to us about all the places she'd traveled and the men she'd met. Of course, with the hindsight of an adult, I've figured out that most of what she told us was probably made up, but that doesn't make it any less wonderful."

"I'm glad you had her in your life."

"Me, too. She used to say that love was like a tornado. It would sweep into our lives and carry us away."

"Interesting analogy, when you consider tornadoes tend to destroy everything in their path."

Kayla looked up at him and frowned. "That's not how she meant it."

"But it's true."

"Maybe, but I don't believe it." Her expression softened, and her eyes focused on something far in the future. "When Prince Albert dances with me, I'm going to feel that tornado."

Patrick tried not to stiffen, but it was damned hard not to react. Here he'd been holding her in his arms, thinking romantic thoughts, and she'd been dreaming of Prince Albert.

"I hope the two of you are very happy," he said, and released her. Before she could protest, he moved to the far end of the sofa.

Kayla stared at him, bewildered. "What's wrong?"

"Nothing."

"Then why are you acting weird?"

"I'm not. I just find it interesting that an independent woman such as yourself is dreaming about being rescued by Prince Charming."

"I don't want to be rescued," she said. "I want to be swept away. There's a difference."

"And only a prince can accomplish that?"

"It is a nice touch." Her voice sounded teasing.

He wasn't amused. "He's got to be close to forty, and a little jaded with life."

"I don't care. It's not even him, it's what he represents." She leaned back against the sofa and sighed. "I'm going to Paris. I'm going to buy wonderful clothes and get my hair cut and speak French. I'm going to sit in sidewalk cafés and be sophisticated."

"You can't buy sophistication."

She waved him off. "Don't interrupt my fantasy. Men are going to find me irresistible. I'm going to write witty letters to all my friends and be perfectly happy."

Something dark and unexplained turned over in Patrick's chest. It wasn't that he objected to Kayla's dreams, or even her travel. What he didn't like was the fact that she planned to leave him behind without a second thought.

"With Prince Albert—" she glanced at him "—or a Prince Albert–like person, I'm going to see the world. He'll take me riding and on his yacht. We'll drink champagne."

"I thought that's what we had been doing," he growled, nudging the nearly empty bottle with his foot.

"Patrick, if you're not going to participate, then at least don't make fun of me."

Confusion filled him. Confusion and annoyance. He

couldn't compete against a prince, or any other perfect man she imagined. He was just the local vet, with dreams of his own, none of which could hold a candle to a castle or a yacht.

Without stopping to consider the consequences, he turned toward her. Rational thought fled. He reacted to what she'd said, to what he was feeling, and to what he really wanted.

He grabbed her shoulders and pulled her against him. Kayla didn't resist; she simply stared up at him, her eyes wide, her mouth parted.

"See if Prince Albert makes you feel like this," he said. Then he kissed her. Really kissed her.

Kayla was too stunned to react. Patrick hauled her closer, held her in his arms and settled his mouth against hers. She sensed his anger, which she didn't understand, his confusion, which she shared, and his passion, which tempted her as she'd never been tempted before.

Of their own accord, her hands rose to his shoulders and rested there. He was solid strength, the only stable part of a world that had started spinning.

His mouth clung to hers, touching, taunting. She felt the firm pressure and wanted more.

He read her mind. Even as she thought of him deepening the kiss, he did so. He parted his mouth and brushed her lips with his tongue. She parted for him, anticipation stirring her body into passionate restlessness.

He invaded slowly, as if he were a petitioner and she sacred ground. He paused to whisper her name, as though it were a prayer.

From the sleek softness of her inner lip, to her teeth and at last to her tongue. He moved slowly, discovering pleasure points dormant since her birth. He stroked these small sparks into roaring flame that threatened to consume her.

She slid her hands up his neck to his short hair. Individual strands tickled her palms. She learned the shape of his head, his ears, then cupped his jaw, caressing smooth skin with just the faintest hint of stubble.

His head tilted, allowing him to move deeper inside her. She met him, alternately blocking progress and leading the way. When she hesitated, he paused, as well, touching her gently, showing her how much better it would be if she allowed him to pleasure her.

He moved his hands against her. First they traced the length of her back, then her hips. He placed his palm on her knee, warming her, then urged her to move toward him.

She resisted, not sure what he wanted.

He broke the kiss and stared at her. Desire darkened his irises to dark blue velvet. His mouth was damp, his skin flushed. She'd forgotten why he'd kissed her in the first place. She had the vague recollection of him trying to prove a point. If he was to ask her at this moment, she would swear that he had won and not care what or how. She only wanted him to kiss her again.

He brought one of her hands around to his mouth and pressed his tongue against her palm. Heat flared up her arms and settled in her breasts. Hot, bright need filled her with sensations she neither understood nor controlled, yet she wasn't afraid. Not of Patrick.

"Come closer," he whispered against her now damp skin.

She shifted toward him.

"Closer."

He put his hand on her hip and urged her to straddle him. She hesitated, unsure of herself, if not of him.

"Please."

The single word was more air than sound, yet it touched

her soul. She did as he requested, sliding one thigh over his, settling herself on him, their most intimate places only inches apart.

Her hands once again rested on his shoulders. Because of her position, she sat slightly higher than he. She could see all of him—his face, the breadth of his shoulders, his powerful arms, the way her knees cradled his hips.

He threaded his fingers through her hair and drew the long strands away from her face. ''Cat eyes,'' he said. ''So beautiful.''

She ducked her head and flushed, not sure if the blush came from pleasure or from confusion. Questions filled her head. In the name of sanity, she needed to answer them. She needed to stop and think about what they were doing. But she didn't want to. She wanted this moment to go on forever.

He raised his head slightly. She met him more than halfway, lowering her mouth to his. This time, he parted, and she was allowed to enter the sacred place. She discovered the texture of his mouth, tasted him, felt the heat, the need that drove them both forward.

The uncharted course should have frightened her. Perhaps, if she'd allowed herself to think, it would have. But she refused to consider, or weigh what was happening. She only wanted to feel.

His hands moved slowly from her thighs to her hips to her waist. Fire coiled low, liquid flames stretching toward her breasts, making them swell and tighten. His fingers reached up and stroked the underside of her breasts.

She froze in place. Even her breath caught in her throat. Waves of pleasure filled her. They were like nothing she'd ever experienced before. A small whimper escaped when she tried to breathe.

Strong, capable hands slipped higher, taking her curves

in their palms, cupping her gently, reverently. She broke the kiss, unable to concentrate on anything but his touch and the feelings he invoked. His fingers swept around, discovering her, moving closer to the taut centers, nearing but not reaching. Ache and fulfillment combined into the sweetest sensation.

When he moved his hands higher still, she nearly wept in frustration. Then she felt him unfastening the top button of her shirt. Too shy to look or help, she arched her head back and closed her eyes.

Whispers of cool air licked against her skin. The shirt parted easily, and he pulled it off her shoulders. Without thinking, she relaxed her arms and let the garment slip to the floor.

He placed his hands on her back and drew her closer. She went to him, her thighs sliding along his until they touched intimately. Her fingers laced behind his head. She knew what he would do next. Knew and eagerly anticipated. Every part of her tensed, until at last she felt his warm breath, moments before his mouth claimed the valley between her breasts.

Moist, hot, firm. There weren't enough words to describe the sensation of his mouth on her skin. He moved a little, licking the full curve, then moved again and settled over her left nipple.

Through the thin layer of her bra, he teased her. Teeth barely brushed against the tight peak. She sucked in her breath. Not able to control herself, she pressed her fingers into his scalp and urged him closer.

He obliged her silent request, opened his mouth and drew her inside.

Relief was instant. His mouth closed around her as his tongue sweetly tormented the sensitized peak. What she had felt before faded in the light of this new pleasure.

Want and need melded until her very life depended on this exact moment. Sharp cries gathered in her throat until she couldn't control them. When one escaped, she stiffened slightly.

"Don't stop," he whispered against her, then transferred his attention to her other breast.

He moved back and forth, creating such fire inside her that she thought she must glow from the flames. Involuntarily her hips arched against him.

This time, he was the one to suck in his breath. His hands moved to her hips and encouraged her to repeat the action. She did, moving as he guided her. In her aroused state, it took her a minute to realize the significance of the hard ridge pressing between her thighs, brushing erotically against her jeans and creating friction in that most private place.

She pulled back and looked at him.

Patrick's face was alive with passion. She'd always thought him attractive, but now the tight lines of his jaw and around his mouth made him more than just someone she'd known. Need transformed him into a tempting stranger...someone dangerous.

Someone she wanted more than she wanted her next breath.

They stared at each other. As the passion faded, sanity returned. What were they doing? she asked herself. This wasn't right. They weren't lovers.

He touched her bottom lip and smiled faintly. "Do you want me to apologize?"

His voice was low and husky. She knew if she glanced down she would see the proof of his arousal straining against his jeans. A shiver rippled through her. Not one of fear or cold, but, instead, of anticipation. The innate understanding of how wonderful it would have been.

She shook her head. "Of course not. I'm just a little confused. What happened?"

"I don't know. I—" He dropped his hands to the sofa. "I guess we're lucky we never tried that before."

"I guess."

She slid back until her feet touched the floor, then she straightened. Although her bra covered her adequately, she felt self-conscious about being shirtless and quickly retrieved the garment.

Her insides were shaking. Not so much from passion anymore, but in reaction to what had happened…and almost happened.

Patrick stood up and approached her. She finished buttoning her blouse, then risked glancing at him. The fire was gone, and he'd returned to being the man she'd known for years.

"Hey." He touched her face. "Don't be scared, okay?"

"I'm not." She wasn't frightened, exactly. She wasn't sure what she felt. "But I'd better get home."

He walked her to the door. When she stepped onto the porch, he called her name. "Do you want to pretend this never happened?"

As if she had a choice. She had a bad feeling that she would remember this night—in sensual detail—for the rest of her life.

"I need you to be my friend, Patrick. I depend on you."

"I understand," he told her. "We'll both forget."

As she walked back to her apartment, she wondered if he was going to have to work as hard as she would to act normal.

She told herself it hadn't meant anything, that it *wouldn't* mean anything. They could both go on as they had before. Nothing had changed.

When she unlocked her door, she glanced over her

shoulder. Patrick stood watching, as he did every night when she walked home. He wanted to make sure she was safe.

She waved, then ducked inside.

Once she was alone, she sank down on the floor and tried to make sense of it all. She and Patrick were friends, and friends were different from lovers. Everyone knew that. Not that she had a whole lot of experience. She'd never had a lover.

A shiver rippled through her, this one leftover sensation from their time in each other's arms. The intimacy should have frightened her. For years she hadn't been able to imagine doing that with a stranger. She still couldn't. Yet with Patrick, everything had felt right. Maybe because she trusted him.

She didn't trust many people. Not since she'd watched her parents fight over everything when they were divorcing. Their raw anger had terrified her. Surely they had been in love once. What had gone wrong?

She didn't want that for herself. That was why the dream was so much safer than reality. But Patrick was real, and he didn't scare her.

She pressed her hands to her face and sighed. Was there an answer? Should she bother looking for one? Or should she just wait? When she got to Paris, life would be so much simpler.

Everything would be perfect—just as she'd always planned.

Chapter Six

Mrs. Carter, the director of the rehabilitation facility, smiled. "We don't usually allow dogs on the premises, but in this case, we'll make an exception."

Rhonda sat on Kayla's lap. At the woman's words, her tail wagged, as if she were pleased at being allowed inside. Patrick knew dogs didn't understand what was being said, but sometimes he believed they had more powers of interpretation than they were given credit for.

Kayla stroked the dog's head. "I hope we can help, Mrs. Carter. I've taken the dogs to a retirement home for a couple of years, and they have really made a difference. Sometimes I think it's easier to relate to animals than to people, especially when the person involved is sick or injured. Dogs don't demand witty conversation and are grateful for a quick pat or cuddle."

"We have to do something." The director drew her eyebrows together. She was in her early thirties, well dressed, in a red suit. Dark eyes spoke of her concern and compassion. "Allison has been here nearly a week, and she hasn't said a word to anyone. Apparently it was the same at the hospital. It's not that she can't talk, she simply chooses not to. She's smart and verbal...at least she was until the accident. Her family is concerned, as is her doctor. At this point, we're considering psychiatric intervention."

Patrick leaned forward. He hadn't met the child, but already he felt his heart go out to her. "She was injured in a car accident?"

"She was on a bike," Mrs. Carter said. "A car hit her. There were almost no head injuries, so in that respect, she was lucky. We're hoping for a full recovery, but one can never be sure. She's in a body cast. She's only nine. This is difficult for her."

"Let's see what we can do," Kayla said. She picked up Rhonda, then rose to her feet.

"Would you like me to come with you?" Mrs. Carter asked.

Kayla shook her head. "Just tell us where the room is. I think we'll do better if we slip inside casually. It will look less like a setup. Not that she isn't going to figure out why we're here."

Mrs. Carter gave them the room number and directions. They said their goodbyes and promised to stop on their way out. Once they were in the hall, Kayla released the breath she'd been holding.

"Poor kid," she said quietly.

"Yeah. I can't imagine what it must be like."

Kayla glanced at him. "I can, and it's pretty tough." She hugged Rhonda. "You're going to work magic, aren't you?" The dog swiped at her nose with her pink tongue. Kayla giggled.

Patrick followed her down the cool, silent corridors. If Rhonda didn't work magic, then Kayla would. He remembered her talking about her own accident. He didn't know the details; Kayla didn't talk about them. Over the years, he'd put together enough of the story to know that she'd been badly injured and spent a year in recovery. For a while, the doctors had thought she wouldn't be able to walk, but she'd proved them wrong. Looking at her today, it was difficult to believe she'd ever been that seriously injured. The only lingering physical evidence was the faint network of scars on her thighs and torso.

They paused in front of the last door at the end of the hall. Windows at the end of the corridor showed a beautiful rose garden. He figured the rooms on either side would have the same view. So far, the rehab center had been impressive. Little Allison was in good hands.

"Do you want me to wait out here, or do you want me to come inside?" he asked.

Kayla touched his arm. "I think I might need the moral support."

"That's why I'm here."

They went inside together.

The room was large and bright, with white walls and colorful posters on the walls and ceiling. The latter was explained by the position of the occupant on the hospital bed in the center of the floor. A sheet covered her from her feet to her chest, but the thin layer of cotton didn't disguise the large cast over her body. The thick material covered her from her ankles to her neck and trapped her arms to just above the elbow.

Music drifted through the room, its source a stereo system in the corner. There was a television mounted up high, the screen dark. On various tables and chairs scattered around were dolls, stuffed animals and books. Yet the child lay in solitary stillness.

Around her, on the floor, were a few more stuffed animals. From their awkward positions, he assumed they'd been placed on the bed and she'd thrown them off. A chair, tall enough to allow the visitor to be at equal level with the girl, sat next to the nightstand.

Kayla moved to the bed. "Hi, Allison. My name is Kayla. My friend Patrick and I thought you might like a visitor today." She set the small dog on the bed and smiled. "Her name is Rhonda. She's very friendly and very sweet. Do you like dogs?"

Silence.

Patrick stepped closer and looked at Allison. Shiny raven hair framed a pale face. Large blue eyes stared blankly at the ceiling. She had the innocent beauty of an angel, but the dark shadows under her lower lids and the tight set of her mouth told him that she'd spent more time in hell than in heaven.

It was all he could do not to hold the girl tight and promise to make it all right. He held back. No doubt her father had already tried that, and it hadn't helped. He could only hope Rhonda would succeed where the rest of them had failed.

"Rhonda's a special dog," Kayla said, stepping around to the far side of the bed. She sat in the chair and looked at the child. "She was left in our care so she could visit people and make them feel better. Dogs are wonderful friends. They love you no matter what. They want to be with you, even when you don't feel good. They don't even mind if you don't want to talk."

Rhonda sniffed at the sheets, then at the girl's hand. Her tail swept back and forth as she licked the slender, pale fingers.

Nothing. Not a flicker of response.

Kayla looked at him, and he shrugged. He felt helpless in the presence of this child's pain. What did he know about healing her?

"When Rhonda first came to us, she didn't have a name," Kayla said. "She was skinny and dirty, but when we fed her and cleaned her up, she turned out to be a very pretty dog, with a sweet, loving nature. It's amazing what you can find when you take the time to look on the inside. That's what's happened with you, isn't it? You've got a different outside. I'm sure you hate the cast, but when it's gone, there will be a whole new you on the inside."

This time, the silence wasn't as unexpected. Allison blinked every few seconds, but aside from that, there was no sign of life. The cast prevented him seeing the rise and fall of her chest.

Kayla glanced around the room. The sunlight caught her gold-blond hair and made it glow. She was in her usual attire of jeans and a T-shirt. No makeup, no jewelry save an inexpensive watch. Yet, to Patrick, she was as beautiful as she'd ever been.

She picked up a photograph on the nightstand. "This is your family. You guys look great together. Your mom's real pretty. You look a lot like her. I see you have a younger brother. I never had a brother. Just two sisters. It was fun. We shared clothes and played together."

Rhonda nudged at Allison's fingers, but they didn't move. The dog snorted in frustration, sank onto the mattress and tried to squeeze her head under the girl's hand. When that proved unsuccessful, she rested her muzzle on Allison's wrist and closed her eyes.

"I don't see a dog in the picture. Do you have any pets at home?"

There wasn't an answer.

Kayla set the photo back on the nightstand. Patrick wondered if she would give up. She didn't. She stared at Allison for a long time, then reached over and brushed the girl's dark bangs off her forehead.

"I know," she said quietly. "Everyone is telling you how sorry they are and pretending they know exactly how you feel. They don't, though. They don't know what it's like to be trapped in a room day after day. They don't know how scared you are. They don't know that you lie awake at night, that you don't want to go to sleep, because when you do, you dream about the accident. They don't know that you're afraid you're going to spend the rest of your life in a cast, that sometimes you just want to scream so loud the world splits in two. They don't know how much you hate everyone who can walk and play and run and jump. They don't know that you hate your family most of all—your brother because he can do all the things you can't, and your parents because if they really loved you, they would be able to fix it."

Patrick sank into a chair by the door. He tore his gaze away from Kayla long enough to glance at Allison. So far, there was no reaction, but she seemed to be blinking a little faster.

"I know," Kayla said. "I know everything. You see, it happened to me, too. I was twelve. You were riding your bike when you were hit by a car. I was in a car when another car hit us. The man driving me was killed, and I almost died. I was in a hospital for weeks. They told me I wouldn't walk, that I would live in a wheelchair for the rest of my life."

She touched Allison's cheek with her fingers and smiled slightly. "I didn't believe them. I thought it was a dream. I kept trying to wake up, but I couldn't. My arms were in casts and I was in traction. I couldn't even pinch myself so I could wake up. I kept thinking if I could just pinch myself, everything would be okay.''

While continuing to stroke the girl's cheek, she used her free hand to wipe her own face. Her tears made Patrick ache. But he didn't go to her. Instead, he remained in his seat, sensing that the telling of this story was as important for Kayla as it was for Allison.

"It's been over twelve years, and I still cry when I think about that time,'' she continued. "I was in hospitals and places like this for almost a whole year. My sisters, the ones I told you about, came to see me. They really cared and tried to make it better, but they only made it worse. You see, my sisters look just like me. We're identical triplets. So every time I looked at them, it was like looking at myself, only I couldn't do all the things I used to do. I felt as if I were looking in a mirror, the kind they have at carnivals. Instead of seeing myself, I saw an ugly joke. Someone else walking and playing. Someone who used to be me, but wasn't anymore.''

Sometime while she was talking, the music had stopped. Patrick glanced at the stereo and saw that the CD had ended. Kayla hadn't noticed. She sucked in a deep breath, as if the rest of the story would require even more emotional energy.

"I hated being in bed, and I hated being in pain,'' she said. Her voice was thick from tears. They fell freely now. One touched Allison's cheek. The child turned her head toward Kayla, who, with her head slightly bowed, didn't notice.

"After a while I started wishing I'd died in that accident,'' she whispered. "I prayed every night that God would let me die. Then one day I really did start to get better. It was slow at first, and it took a long time. There was a lot of work and a lot of frustration. But I made it.

And then I was glad I hadn't died." She looked up and smiled at Allison. "I even got to be a regular girl again, and you're going to get that chance, too. I promise."

Tears trickled out of the corners of Allison's eyes. Kayla gently wiped them away. "It's good to cry," she said. "It helps wash away the sadness."

Patrick concentrated on staying in his chair. Every instinct screamed at him to go to Kayla and hold her tight, yet he knew there was nothing he could give her, no comfort he could offer. He'd heard her talk about her accident many times before. She often joked about it, made fun of her scars, or dismissed that year out of her life as unimportant. He realized now that there were scars he'd never known about—scars crisscrossing on the inside, scars that touched her heart.

She had a depth, a sense of self, he'd never fully understood. The circumstances of her past explained her interest and compassion with the elderly and the animals. She always looked out for those in need. She was a hell of a woman.

Rhonda stood up and stepped cautiously around Allison's shoulder encased in the cast. She bent over and began to lick away the child's tears. Allison sniffed, and then a smile tugged at her lips.

"She's very pretty," Allison said, speaking for the first time.

"I think so, too." Kayla stood up and walked around the bed. When she was by Rhonda, she moved the dog back so that Allison could pet her. "She has a soft coat. Would you like to touch her?"

Allison nodded and stroked Rhonda's head. The small dog's body shook with pleasure, and she gave a little yip of excitement. Allison laughed.

"Hi, Rhonda. You're a nice doggie, aren't you?"

Rhonda snuggled close in agreement.

"What do you feed her?" Allison asked.

As Kayla started to explain the intricacies of pet care, the door next to Patrick's chair opened. A nurse stepped into the room.

"I just came to check on—" The young woman paused in midsentence. She stared at the smiling child, then looked at Patrick. "What happened? Was it the dog that finally got through to her?"

"Rhonda helped, but mostly it was Kayla. She's been through a similar situation, and I think Allison is pleased to finally find someone who understands what's happening to her."

"I've got to tell Mrs. Carter," the nurse said. "I'll be right back." She closed the door, and Patrick heard her soft footsteps hurrying away.

A few minutes later, Mrs. Carter stepped into the room. "Amazing," she breathed.

Patrick rose to his feet. "I think so, too."

"Her parents are going to be thrilled. The doctor, too. Do you think Kayla will be willing to come back and bring the dog with her?"

Patrick stared at the woman he'd thought he knew so well. After seven years, he was just beginning to see the real Kayla Bedford.

"I know she'll come back," he said. "That's the kind of person she is."

Mrs. Carter excused herself and went to call Allison's parents. Patrick waited patiently while Kayla and Allison talked about Rhonda and what Allison missed most. He heard Kayla promise to sneak in some french fries the next time she visited.

The ache in his chest intensified. Every fiber of his being longed for her. Not just sexually, although he desperately needed her in his bed, but also in other ways. He wanted her in his life.

He'd spent the past four days trying to forget what had happened between them last Saturday. Nothing he did or thought had been able to erase those memories. They had embedded themselves in his person, much as the scars from her accident had left her physically changed.

For now, his scars didn't cause any pain, because she was still with him. But in time, he was going to have to let her go. No matter what he thought about her, no matter what he felt, he had no right to keep her beside him. She'd lived through too much, waited too long. She deserved to have every one of her dreams come true. Even if those dreams didn't include him.

Kayla squinted at the magazine, but that didn't help her understand the words. She laughed. "I keep feeling that if I stare at this long enough, it will make sense. But it's not working."

Sarah glanced up, looking over the half glasses resting on her nose. "I thought you were listening to your French tapes and doing the lessons in the workbook."

Kayla cleared her throat. "Yes, well, I've been trying, but with the dogs and all my additional responsibilities, I don't really have time."

"You need to make time, dear. This is important."

"I know."

She felt guilty, but that didn't give her any more hours in her day. The past four weeks had just flown by. Between her duties at the clinic, visiting Sarah and her friends and spending three afternoons a week with Allison, there wasn't a spare minute.

"If I'm not at work, I'm here, or at the rehab center. In

the evenings I've been helping Patrick replace his wall-paper. I barely know what day it is.''

"I didn't know that you were seeing Patrick." Sarah raised pale eyebrows.

"Oh, don't start on me, Sarah. There's absolutely nothing going on. I swear.''

But as she spoke the words, she felt a faint heat climb up her cheeks.

There was no reason to blush, she told herself. She hadn't lied. There was *nothing* going on. Since that night…since he'd kissed her in a way she'd never been kissed before…he had done as he promised. He'd forgotten the incident. Not by a look or a word had he hinted they'd ever spent passionate moments in each other's arms.

Frankly, she preferred it that way. Better for both of them if they remained just friends.

But sometime over the past few weeks, those logical words had ceased providing comfort. At times she wondered how he'd been able to forget so easily. Hadn't he felt the same incredible heat? The same need?

Unless she was willing to risk humiliation, she was never going to find out the answer to those questions. And she would rather be covered with honey and staked out naked on an anthill than ask him anything.

Eventually she would forget. At least that was what she told herself a hundred and fourteen times a day.

She tossed aside the French magazine and stood up. As she walked to the window, she tried to shake the restlessness that gripped her. She'd noticed that tingling jump-out-of-her-skin feeling more and more in the past week or so.

"We've put together a list of places you should go while you're in France," Sarah said. "I've put a little mark by Mr. Peter's suggestions. He's not as reliable as one would like. I have a feeling he might be sending you to a brothel.''

Kayla laughed. ''That would be interesting for everyone.''

The vegetable garden was visible from Sarah's room. Young, tender plants sprouted in the rich soil. This year, she wouldn't be around to take home fresh green beans and carrots. In the fall, the pomegranates she loved so much would dry up on the tree. No one else ate them.

''What's wrong, dear?'' Sarah asked. ''You look out of sorts.''

Kayla turned and smiled at her friend. ''That's what I forgot when I was getting dressed this morning. My sorts.''

Sarah didn't return the smile. She patted the side of the bed. ''Tell me.''

Kayla settled next to her and touched the older woman's hand. Sarah's skin was still soft, but it was tissue-thin. The network of veins was easily visible.

''I don't know what's wrong,'' Kayla said. ''Sometimes I just want to run and run until—'' She broke off and shrugged.

''Until what?''

''I'm not sure. Maybe if I had the answer to that, I'd feel better.''

''Are you having second thoughts about your trip?''

''No,'' Kayla said quickly. ''I want to go. I've wanted to go since I was little. I've been waiting for years.''

Sarah pulled her hand free and touched Kayla's chin. ''We grow, dreams change.''

''Not mine.''

Sarah nodded. ''Then your problem is solved. When you leave, you're doing the right thing.'' The older woman rubbed Rip's ears. The black poodle, stretched across the bed and using her stomach for a pillow, groaned in contentment.

"I hope so." Kayla grimaced. "I worry about Allison. She's making great progress. In my head, I know she'll be fine, but in my heart, I want to be here to see it. Which is silly. She has a lot of friends and family. She's able to enjoy their visits more. She doesn't really need me."

"Maybe you need her."

Kayla wanted to dismiss Sarah's remark, but she knew better. "Maybe. I suppose watching her reminds me of myself. It's bringing back a lot of memories I thought had been long buried."

"You have many friends. Unfortunately, you're going to have to leave them behind when you fly to Paris. But our memories and our love will go with you."

Kayla leaned close and rested her head on Sarah's shoulder. The older woman wrapped her arm around her.

"I tell myself that's enough," Kayla said. "Then I worry that it isn't. I think my adventure would be a lot better if everyone I cared about came along with me."

"Sorry, but I've made plans for that day."

Sarah's tone was light and playful, but Kayla knew her friend would love to see Paris again. Kayla would have invited her in a heartbeat, but Sarah's infirmity prevented her traveling.

For a moment, she allowed herself the fantasy of having Patrick at her side as she explored Paris. But he had the new research facility to worry about, people to hire, changes to make. He didn't have time for anything else. Besides, having a man along would interfere with her plans to meet and get swept off her feet by a prince.

"I think I'm going to talk to Allison's mother and see if the family wants to adopt Rhonda," Kayla said.

"That's nice. I'm sure the child would adore to have Rhonda around."

"I agree. I'm going to make sure Patrick gets someone fun to bring the dogs here."

"He'll do a fine job, but your replacement will never be you, Kayla. We'll miss you."

"I wish—" Kayla broke off. What was there to wish for? She was getting everything she'd ever wanted. She should be the happiest person in the world.

Patrick stared at the university transcripts in front of him, then shifted his attention to the résumé on his desk. Melissa Taylor had recently graduated from the University of California at Davis. Her degree was with honors, and her work experience included hands-on practice in a clinic about the same size as his own. She had letters of recommendation from professors he remembered from his time spent at the same university. She was perfect for the job.

"I'm impressed," he said, stacking the papers into a neat pile and closing the folder. "I'm surprised you don't want to go to work for a larger practice, or at one in an affluent neighborhood."

Melissa smiled. She had auburn hair that tumbled down her back, a lithesome figure, and legs that seemed endless. If she didn't want to be a vet, she could probably make a great living as a cover model.

"I've had other offers," she said, her voice low and husky. "I suppose I could go into a different kind of practice, but this is what I prefer. I like dealing with family pets and regular people." She glanced away, as if suddenly shy. "I'm willing to admit that once I found out about your research project, I was intrigued. If you hire me, I hope you'll consider me for that, as well. I understand my primary duties would be to the clinic, but in my free time…'' Her words trailed off.

"I appreciate the honesty," he told her. "It would be an advantage to have you help out."

He rose to his feet, and she followed suit. They shook hands.

"I'll be in touch," he told her. "I'll be making my decision in the next two weeks. Please let me know if you accept another position in the meantime."

She paused by the door and gave him a smile that could have sold gas heating to nuclear-power executives. "I probably shouldn't tell you this, Dr. Walcott, but I have no intention of accepting any other offers until I hear from you. You're my first choice." She smiled, then left.

He slumped back in his chair and waited. Unfortunately, his hormones did not come to life. In fact, no part of his body had been particularly moved by Melissa Taylor's charms. He wanted to think it was because he was more tired than usual. But he knew the truth was more devastating than that.

He could tell himself that Melissa wasn't funny enough, or experienced enough, or any number of other lies. The truth was, he would hire her and be grateful to have someone of her caliber to work at the clinic. Then, when she worked out perfectly—and he knew she would—he would do his best to ignore her only flaw.

After all, it wasn't her fault she wasn't Kayla.

Chapter Seven

Kayla shifted her weight from foot to foot as she hovered by the front door of the clinic.

"You're going to wear out the tile," Cheryl, the petite, dark-haired receptionist said. "I'll tell you when your sister arrives."

Kayla shook her head and glanced at her watch for the fourteenth time in five minutes. "I'm too excited. She'll be here any minute. It's the middle of the day. She shouldn't have hit much traffic driving down."

Sure enough, before she could check her watch again, a familiar white Honda pulled into the parking lot. Kayla was out the door and down the walkway in a flash.

Elissa stepped out of her car and laughed. "I guess I don't have to ask if you're happy to see me."

"Of course not. And I happen to know you're just as thrilled to be here."

They embraced and grinned at each other. Elissa

touched her sister's hair, then stepped back and looked her over. "You're just as beautiful as ever."

Kayla grinned at the familiar compliment. "As are you." Keeping her arm linked with Elissa's, she led her toward the clinic's front door. "I still find it amazing we've gotten away with telling each other that for years and no one has figured out how conceited we're being."

"It's not conceited," Elissa said. "It's—" She paused, her green eyes dancing. "It's a kindness to make others feel good about their physical appearance."

"Oh, right. But when most people compliment each other, they aren't talking to someone who looks exactly like them."

Kayla pulled open the glass door, and they stepped into the facility. She turned toward the counter. "Cheryl, this is my sister, Elissa."

The receptionist stared blankly. "Oh, my goodness."

"Didn't you warn her?" Elissa asked.

"Of course. Does it ever help?"

Cheryl walked around the counter and stopped in front of them. She glanced from one sister to the other. A large mirror hung on the far wall. Kayla could see what Cheryl saw—two women who looked exactly alike. Oh, the clothes were different. She wore her usual jeans and T-shirt, while Elissa dressed like a Laura Ashley model. Today she'd tucked a pale pink long-sleeved blouse, complete with a bit of ruffle around the collar, into a soft, flowing calf-length gray skirt. She wore gray flats and pearl earrings.

But the clothing and accessories were the only differences. They had the same gold-blond hair, the same green eyes, the same faces, hands, smiles, the same everything else.

Cheryl shook her head in amazement. "There's a third sister?"

"Yes," Elissa said. "Fallon. She's also identical."

"You girls must get a lot of attention when you're out together."

Kayla rolled her eyes. "Constantly. It was worse when we were younger. At least now we can choose not to dress alike."

"Oh, remember those velvet dresses every Christmas?"

"I bet you three were darling," Cheryl said.

"Maybe," Kayla told her, "but we were also really uncomfortable. Those big collars itch."

They continued chatting for a few more minutes, then Kayla took Elissa back to show her the rest of the clinic. She'd planned their route so they would end up in Patrick's office last.

"You didn't dress to meet dogs," Kayla said as she pushed open the door to the kennel.

"I didn't think it would matter what I wore," Elissa told her. "I assumed all your dogs were well-behaved."

"They should be." Kayla glanced at the pale, expensive-looking skirt. "I think I'll keep Trudi safely behind bars. She likes to jump on people."

They slowly walked down the center corridor. Kayla pointed out different boarders. Duchess was back for her monthly grooming. Kayla had already bathed and dried her, so she was fluffy and sweet-smelling.

"Duchess had a gentleman admirer a few weeks back," she said as she stuck her fingers through the gate. Duchess gave her a friendly lick. "Mr. Cookie, an eight-pound Yorkie, fell madly in love. Unfortunately, his owners objected, and the young lovers were torn apart, never to see each other again."

Elissa eyed the very large, very hairy Duchess. "An

eight-pound Yorkie? Maybe it was for the best. I don't think they could have overcome their rather obvious physical differences.''

Kayla grinned. ''Love can be spiritual, as well as physical.''

''I'm not sure dogs see it that way.''

''Maybe you're right.'' She motioned to the last cage. ''This is our newest addition. Her name is Rhonda.''

When Kayla opened the gate, Rhonda walked out. Elissa crouched down and patted the friendly dog. ''This is the one you were telling me about, isn't she? The one helping you with that little girl?''

''Yes. Rhonda and I visit Allison three times a week. She's made great progress. The doctors are impressed with how quickly she's healing. The initial reports are good. There shouldn't be any permanent damage.''

''She was lucky,'' Elissa said.

''I know. If that car had been going a little faster, or had hit her differently, she could have been paralyzed or killed.''

''That's not what I meant.'' Elissa picked up Rhonda, then rose to her feet. She cuddled the dog in her arms. ''Allison is lucky to have you to help her. You understand what she's going through. I wish you'd had someone like that when you were in the hospital.''

Kayla shrugged, the praise leaving her feeling uncomfortable. ''Anyone would have done the same thing.''

''Most people would have wanted to, but you're one of a very few who could actually help. I'm trying to pay you a compliment. Accept it politely and say thank-you.''

''Thank you. Let's get out of here.''

Kayla lead the way to her alcove. Elissa spotted the calendar right away. She set Rhonda down and pointed to the crossed-out days.

"Doesn't this bother people?" she asked.

Kayla frowned. "Why would it?"

"You're leaving a week after your birthday, our birthday, which is right around the corner. You've made friends here. I'm sure they're going to miss you."

"Sure, but what does that have to do with the calendar?"

Elissa stared at her as if she'd grown a second head. "You're rubbing their nose in the fact that you can't wait to get away. Wouldn't you be offended if one of your friends did that to you?"

Kayla opened her mouth, then closed it. She didn't know what to say. Everyone had seemed happy for her, vicariously excited about her adventure. "I didn't mean it like that," she managed at last.

"I know. I'm sure they know, too. I'm being silly. Just forget it. What else is there to see around here?"

Kayla continued the tour. Rhonda trotted along beside them. Kayla pointed out examining rooms, the storage area, the small room where the employee on duty spent the night. But all the while she made conversation with her sister, a small part of her brain turned over Elissa's words. She remembered the strange look on Patrick's face when he'd seen her crossing off the day on the calendar before she went home. Did he think she was an insensitive clod?

They turned into the corridor. "That's the grand tour," Kayla said, forcing herself to concentrate on the moment. She could deal with the rest of it when she was alone. "There's only Patrick's office."

Elissa frowned. "I'm not sure this is such a good idea."

"It's perfect. You two belong together. You're going to have to trust me on this."

"The last time you said that to me was when I didn't

want to jump my bike over the ravine behind the house. You said to trust you, and I ended up with a broken arm.''

Kayla laughed and gave her a hug. "Hey, at least the attending physician was cute. That sort of made up for it, don't you think?''

"As I was the one stuck in a cast over Christmas, no, it doesn't make up for it. But I forgive you anyway.''

"Thanks. Besides, Patrick is a lot less scary than that ravine. He's funny, intelligent, and very good-looking. You two went to the same college.''

Elissa's smile faded. "I only lasted two years. I never graduated.''

"That's not the point. You were there, weren't you?''

"I suppose.'' Elissa crossed to the window overlooking the parking lot.

"Do you have regrets?'' Kayla asked.

"About leaving college?''

"About all of it.''

"I haven't decided. I made the best decision I could under the circumstances. I was only twenty. That's awfully young to make those kinds of choices.''

Kayla remembered that time. "I always admired you for what you did.''

Elissa turned toward her and raised her eyebrows in surprise. "Why?''

"Because you followed your heart. I remember Mrs. Beecham on the show talking about love being a tornado. That's what happened to you.''

"Exactly. That *is* what happened to me. Look where I ended up. Love might be a tornado, but storms with that kind of power tend to destroy everything in their paths.''

Kayla gave a start as she realized Patrick had said the same thing. "I don't care,'' she told both her sister and the memory. "I want to be swept away.''

Elissa managed a shaky smile. "Then I'm sure you will be."

"What about you? It's not too late. When the trust money is released, you could go back to college."

"Maybe. I've thought about it. I have a lot of decisions I need to make."

Kayla didn't want to upset her sister, so she changed the subject. "I appreciate you helping me out with Patrick. One of the doctors he's hired is this evil woman. We have to protect him from her."

"Evil?"

Kayla sighed. "Well, maybe not evil, but I don't like her. She's beautiful, really tall, really smart. Oh, and she has red hair, which is, unfortunately, Patrick's favorite. I know she wants him." She shuddered. "I can't let that happen. You're my only hope."

Elissa laughed. "How can I refuse such an impassioned plea? Lead on, Kayla. Introduce me to this poor man in desperate need of rescuing."

They were still laughing when Kayla knocked on the door, then pushed it open.

Patrick stood up as they entered. He glanced from one sister to the other. "I know you warned me, but it's an amazing resemblance. However, I think I can tell you apart by your clothes, if nothing else." He came around the desk and held out his hand to Elissa. "I'm very pleased to meet you. Kayla has been singing your praises for weeks."

Elissa smiled. "So you only have the bad things left to discover."

"I doubt there are any bad things."

Elissa glanced at her. "Is he always this charming?"

Kayla nodded, even as she remembered all the times Patrick had taken great pleasure in pointing out *her* faults. They were, she noticed, still holding each other's hands.

As if sensing her attention, they reluctantly released the contact.

"Please have a seat," Patrick said, pulling out a chair for Elissa. He left Kayla to find her own seat.

She picked up several charts resting on a chair and set them on the corner of his desk, then slumped down next to her sister.

"Kayla tells me you live in Los Angeles," Patrick said.

"That's right. Santa Monica."

"By the beach. It's pretty there."

"You know the area?"

"I've been there a few times. Actually, I've spent more time in Marina del Rey. I sailed out of there."

Elissa leaned forward in her chair. "Really? I didn't know you sailed."

"Nothing very big. Most twenty-five- or thirty-footers. Day trips, mostly. I've gone over to Catalina a couple of times."

Elissa shot her a glance. "You didn't tell me Patrick sails."

Kayla stared at her employer. "That's because I didn't know. You don't sail around here."

He barely spared her a smile. "I have. You must have been gone when I went out."

Or he hadn't bothered to invite her along. Maybe he used a day at sea to seduce his women. Her gaze narrowed. What other secrets did Patrick keep?

"How long are you going to be in town?" he asked. "Maybe you can make time for a sail."

"That would be lovely. Kayla and I haven't really discussed our plans for the weekend yet. Can I get back to you?"

"Sure."

The conversation continued to flow easily between

them. Kayla folded her arms tightly across her chest and told herself she was really happy. Thrilled. She couldn't have been more excited. Elissa and Patrick chatted as if they'd known each other for years. They were perfect together.

It couldn't have worked out better.

So why did she want to throw up her hands and scream?

Take deep breaths, she told herself. Slow, calming breaths. She tried to force the tension from her body. Unfortunately, once it started to fade, she was able to feel something hot and painful in the pit of her stomach. It sat there heavily, like a ball of poison.

Patrick focused all his attention on Elissa. She might as well not have been in the room. Had he been like this when he interviewed Melissa Taylor? The thought stabbed her like a scalpel. How dare he—

She pressed her lips together. How dare *she?* She had no rights where Patrick was concerned. They were friends. She'd often encouraged him to find someone and start a relationship. She'd introduced him to Elissa with the hopes the two of them would hit it off. Why was she suddenly having second thoughts? And why was Patrick so damned interested in Elissa?

She looked at her sister. Except for the different clothing, they were exactly alike. So it wasn't Elissa's looks. Was it her personality? Elissa was the middle of the triplets and acted like a middle child. She was calm and caring, settling fights between Fallon and Kayla. Maybe he was drawn to Elissa's gentle, restful spirit. Kayla knew she had many good qualities, but a restful spirit wasn't one of them.

In seven years, Patrick had never once looked at her the way he was looking at Elissa. It was all she could do not to grab her sister and hustle her from the room.

Before she could act on her impulse, the phone buzzed. Patrick excused himself and hit the speaker button.

Cheryl's voice came over the intercom.

"Is Kayla in with you? There's a package up front for her. It's from her travel agent."

"She's right here," Patrick said, at last sparing her a second's worth of attention. "She'll be right up." He hit the speaker button again to disconnect the call. "I'm sure it's tickets, or something equally wonderful. Don't worry. I can keep Elissa company."

"Yes, I know," she said before she could stop herself, then quickly left the room.

All the way to the front desk she told herself she was acting like a fool. This was what she wanted, and she would learn to be happy about it. Even if she had to fake it for the rest of her life.

As she stopped in front of the reception desk, Cheryl waved a box in the air. It was about as long and wide as a shoe box, but about a third as tall.

"Something exciting," Cheryl said.

"I hope so." Right now, she needed a distraction.

She grabbed a pair of scissors and slit the tape sealing the box. The top slipped off easily. Cheryl stared over her shoulder and gave a gasp of surprise. "Africa?"

"I'm not sure," Kayla told her. "I'm going to be in Paris for a while, then I'll come back to spend the holidays with my sisters. I thought I might try a photo safari in the spring."

Cheryl picked up one of the brochures. "It's beautiful."

Kayla nodded as she read over the letter from her travel agent. There were several documents attached. Visas were required for some countries, and there was a vaccination list. If Kayla was going to seriously consider the trip, she would need to start some of her series of shots now.

"Series of shots?" Kayla echoed out loud, then swallowed hard. She flipped to the next page, then the next, until she found the sheet she wanted.

She stared at the list of required shots and felt her stomach fall to her toes. She'd wanted a distraction, and she'd sure gotten one.

Series of shots? The last time she gave blood, she'd fainted. She sank into the nearest chair and lowered her head between her legs. Maybe Africa wasn't such a good idea.

After Kayla left, Elissa rose and closed the door. When she resumed her seat, she stared at Patrick.

He returned her gaze. At first the similarities between the women had been startling. Now he was starting to see that there were tiny differences in their features. While they both used their hands when they talked, Kayla had a body language that was unique. Her smile was broader, her gaze more intense. Irrationally, he thought she was prettier. Which told him he was in more trouble than he'd first realized.

Elissa leaned back in her chair and rested her hands on her lap. "That was a very impressive performance, Patrick. If I didn't know better, I would be flattered by the attention."

He swore under his breath. "Was it that obvious?"

"Yes." She smiled. "You said all the right words, but your heart wasn't in it. Were you trying to make Kayla jealous?"

He wasn't sure. When Kayla walked in and introduced her sister, something inside him had snapped. He'd been furious that she'd gone ahead with her plan to get him involved with another woman. Not only was he insulted by her assumption that he couldn't get a date on his own, he resented her not figuring out that she was the one he wanted to be with.

"It's a little more complicated than that," he said.

"Too bad, because the plan worked."

"You think so?" he asked, not wanting to sound too eager.

"I was afraid she was going to drag me out of here by my hair." Elissa leaned forward. "To give her credit, I think she genuinely wanted us to like each other. But then something happened. I don't suppose you'd be willing to fill in the details."

"There aren't any. Kayla and I are good friends."

"If I could have hooked up a battery to the sparks flying between the two of you, I could have run an electric car for a month. If nothing's going on, why the act?"

She had him there.

"I want to help," Elissa said. "Kayla's my sister, and I love her. I want her to be happy. I've known there was something wrong for a while, but I didn't know what. Now that I've met you, it all makes sense."

"Then maybe you could explain it to me."

"Are you attracted to my sister?"

"I don't know." He held up a hand before Elissa could interrupt. "I mean that sincerely. If you'd asked me the same question six months ago, or even three months ago, I would have said no. I've known Kayla for years, and in all that time we've only ever been friends. Lately, though, something is different."

"Go on."

He fought a smile. "It's almost eerie talking to you, Elissa. You look so much like Kayla."

"Could you tell us apart?"

"Sure. Why?"

The corners of her mouth turned up. "No particular reason. I was curious. Some people can't. What's changed between you and my sister?''

"A while back, out of the blue, she announced that she and I would be a great couple. She listed all the reasons we belonged together. To tell you the truth, I was stunned. Then she laughed and said it was joke. That she was leaving and wasn't really the perfect woman for me—you were.''

Elissa shook her head. "Sometimes Kayla can be stubborn. She gets an idea in her head and nothing can budge it. So that comment started you thinking?''

"In a way.'' He shifted in his chair. "Then there was this kiss.''

Elissa raised her eyebrows.

"It's not what you think,'' he said, telling himself it wasn't a lie. He *had* been talking about that first kiss, the one at her place when he found out about the grant. The second kiss, the one that had set him on fire and left him sleepless with longing, was too private to share with anyone.

"Kayla and I have always kissed,'' he continued. "You know, as friends. Brother and sister, even. But it changed. I don't know why or how.''

"Do you love her?''

He thought for a moment. "I care about her, but she's leaving in a few weeks. I don't want her to go, yet I'm not about to ask her to stay. She's been planning this trip for as long as I've known her, probably longer. She deserves a chance to make her dreams come true.''

"I agree,'' Elissa said. "But is this her real dream, or something left over from when she was a child? Kayla has an unusual past. She learned how to put her life on hold.''

"If you're talking about the accident, I know about it.''

"I'm surprised she told you. She usually doesn't talk about it."

"I'd heard bits and pieces. She pretends that it wasn't anything. I didn't get the details until recently."

Elissa nodded. "Then you can understand why dreams are so important to her. For nearly a year, dreams were all she had. Lying in that hospital bed, she decided something wonderful was going to happen when she grew up. After the trust fund was established, she made the decision to see the world and marry a handsome prince."

If she was trying to make him feel better, she was doing a lousy job. Patrick pushed his chair back a couple of feet and rested his ankle on his opposite knee. "I can't compete with that."

"Oh, I'm not so sure. You've got the handsome part taken care of."

"Thanks. I'm not sure Kayla shares your opinion."

"Oh, but she does. She told me herself."

He refused to let himself hope. His feelings for Kayla were new and unexpected, and he had a bad feeling he'd already left himself open to heartbreak.

Elissa glanced over her shoulder, as if making sure the door was still closed. "I have a plan," she said quietly, leaning toward him. "It's a great way to test the waters without anyone getting hurt."

"I'm listening."

"I want you to invite me out to dinner tonight. Somewhere romantic, with dancing."

"Not that you wouldn't be a delightful companion, but how does this help me with Kayla?"

Elissa grinned. At that moment, she looked so much like her sister that he couldn't help grinning back.

"I won't be going," she said. "At the last minute, I'll tell Kayla I can't go through with it." She waved her hand.

"There are some things in my life that will make her believe me. I'll insist that she go in my place so you won't feel stood up. Your job is to pretend not to know. If I'm right, and I'm sure that I am, she's going to be very upset that you've asked me out. She'll jump at the chance to spend the evening with you. Then the fun starts. She'll be with you, but as me. That will give her something to think about."

The plan had merit. If Kayla was pretending to be her sister, she might slip up and say something she wouldn't normally. Maybe he could get an idea of her feelings for him. Even if he didn't learn a thing, at least he would get to spend the evening with her.

"Are you sure this is all right with you?" he asked. "After all, you're being abandoned on your first night here."

"I don't mind." She looked pensive for a moment. "Kayla is trying to do a nice thing. While I appreciate that, it wouldn't have worked out between you and I. Not that you're not everything she promised," she added quickly.

"Thanks."

"There are a few other things I have to take care of before I can start dating. Besides all that, I don't think Kayla has really thought this through. Her feelings for you seem a little confused to me. Maybe a date will clear up everything. I'd like you to give it a try."

"I'm willing," he said.

"I'm glad you agree. I know that traveling and fulfilling her dreams are important to Kayla. She deserves to do both. But I'm afraid she's spent so long living in her dreams, she's forgotten that the life she already has is pretty wonderful."

Chapter Eight

"He really asked you out for dinner?" Kayla asked, trying to keep the disbelief out of her voice.

Elissa stuck her head out of the bathroom and smiled. "I've told you fifteen times, yes, Patrick invited me out for dinner." Her gaze narrowed. "What's wrong, Kayla? Don't you want me to go?"

"Of course I want you to go," she answered quickly. "I'm thrilled. This is what I hoped would happen. It's terrific. Really."

She forced herself to hold perfectly still and look pleasant, when all she wanted to do was scream.

Apparently Elissa bought the act. She nodded and stepped back into the bathroom. "If you're sure."

"Oh, I am."

Kayla leaned against the door jamb and watched her sister put on makeup. Elissa wore her hair in a loose ponytail on the top of her head. Electric curlers sprouted from the rubber band like metallic flowers. She wore a towel wrapped around her, with the end tucked in by her left arm. The white terry cloth covered her from breasts to midthigh. She'd finished most of her makeup, and she reached for a tube of mascara to apply the final coat.

When she was done, she shooed Kayla out of the way. "You haven't seen this dress, and I want it to be a surprise. Go wait in the living room until I'm ready," she said.

Kayla stepped back and shuffled into the main room. "You'll look great," she mumbled under her breath. "Patrick will be blown away."

She slumped on the sofa and pulled one of the throw pillows close to her chest. "It's not fair. Patrick never asked me out to a romantic dinner by the water. He's never asked me out at all. Not that I wanted him to. We're not a couple. But still, he could have…"

Her voice trailed off. She wasn't sure what Patrick could have done, but there had to be something. Confusing feelings swirled inside her. Questions and thoughts mingled and separated.

Why was she jealous? She'd invited Elissa down specifically so her sister could meet Patrick. They obviously got along—Patrick had asked her out within minutes of meeting her, and Elissa was nearly dressed and ready, a good half hour before their date. Kayla's plan had worked. Everything was turning out exactly as it should.

So why did she feel so empty inside? Why was her heart aching and her body heavy with dread?

She wanted to believe it was because she sensed something wrong with the relationship, that she had a premonition that Elissa and Patrick shouldn't be together. Unfortunately, the reason wasn't that noble. She had an ugly suspicion that she was playing dog in the manger with

Patrick. She didn't want him for herself, but she didn't want anyone else to have him, either.

But why? She'd never been like that before. It wasn't in her nature. She wasn't a mean-spirited person, and certainly not about her sister and her best friend. She cared about them both.

The bathroom door opened, interrupting her thoughts. Elissa stepped into the tiny hall, then forward into the living room.

The last rays of sunlight flowed through the window and caught the gold in Elissa's hair. The shimmering curls tumbled over her shoulders in casual, sexy disarray. Makeup highlighted large green eyes, brightening them to the color of summer grass. The short black dress ended several inches above her knees. Twin pairs of skinny straps secured the fitted bodice and waist, while the fuller skirt swayed with each step. Dark stockings and black pumps completed the outfit.

Kayla's breath caught in her throat. "You're beautiful," she said. This time there was no mistaking the bitter stab of jealousy, but she put her feelings aside. Tonight was for her sister. Elissa deserved some fun in her life. If that meant Patrick fell for her, then Kayla would learn to be happy with that.

Elissa twirled in a circle. The skirt fluttered with the movement. "You really think so?"

"I'm positive. Patrick isn't going to know what hit him."

Elissa's smile faltered. She bit her lower lip and sank into the love seat next to the sofa. "I can't," she whispered, and covered her face with her hands.

"You can't what?"

"I can't go through with this." She motioned to the dress, then touched her hair. "It's not right."

Kayla firmly squashed the first hint of elation. She was determined not to be selfish. "Why? Patrick asked you out, and you want to go. What's the problem?"

Elissa straightened. "Cole." She spoke the single word with two parts pain, one part resignation.

"You haven't spoken to him?" Kayla asked cautiously.

"Not since—" Her voice broke, and she waved her hand, as if that were enough to complete the thought.

It was. Kayla was at her side in an instant. She took Elissa's hand and squeezed it. "I'm sorry," she said. "It's been so long that I thought you were ready. I thought it would help you to meet someone else."

"I thought so, too, but it's not time. I just can't do this."

In an odd way, Kayla didn't feel relieved. She loved her sister and hated to see her unhappy. If Patrick could have helped Elissa recover from her past, then Kayla would have lived with the consequences.

Elissa drew in a deep breath. "I'll call Patrick and tell him I can't make it. I hope he doesn't get angry. I don't want to go into the reasons why I'm canceling our date."

"He won't be mad," Kayla said, as a flicker of expectation fluttered through her. If Patrick didn't go out with Elissa, he wouldn't have a chance to fall for her. She hated herself for thinking that, but she couldn't seem to make the thought disappear.

"I'm going to sound like a flake," Elissa said. "It's really too bad. He seems so nice, and I know he's a close friend of yours. But he dates a lot, right? It's not as if I'm the first woman he's asked out in months. This isn't going to upset him."

"Ah, right," Kayla said, and swallowed. Just as Elissa didn't want to discuss her past with Patrick, she knew Patrick wouldn't want her telling Elissa about his lack of a social life over the past couple of years. Elissa *was* the first woman he'd asked out in months. He very well might think he'd been blown off.

"What?" Elissa asked. "Why do you have that funny look on your face?"

"I don't. It's just—"

"He's going to be hurt."

"No, it's just—"

Elissa sprang to her feet. "I knew it. This is crazy. I should never have accepted. I wouldn't have, but you seemed so eager for us to go out. I didn't want to let you down."

Kayla felt as if she were having tea with the Mad Hatter. "This is *my* fault?"

"If not yours, then whose? Patrick is going to be crushed, I'm upset, all because we were trying to make you happy."

"But I— You—" She leaned back on the love seat and closed her eyes. "Fine. Everything is my fault. I'll call Patrick and explain that." She held up her hand to stop Elissa's interruption. "Don't worry, I won't say a thing about you and Cole. Patrick is polite. He won't ask questions."

She walked over to the phone hanging on the kitchen wall. When had everything gotten so out of control? Two months ago she and Patrick had been good friends and she hadn't cared about who he dated. Two weeks ago she'd been sure Elissa was the perfect woman for him. Ten minutes ago she'd been eating herself alive with jealousy because her sister was going out with Patrick. Now she was the bad guy for setting them up together. Maybe that African safari wasn't such a bad idea. At least there she wouldn't be able to mess up anyone's life, including her own.

She started dialing the familiar number. Before the call

went through, Elissa grabbed the receiver and broke the connection. "Wait a minute. I have a plan," she said.

Fifteen minutes later, Kayla dropped the blush brush on the bathroom counter. "This is never going to work."

"Sure it is. Patrick doesn't know me at all."

"But he knows *me*."

"Exactly. So don't be yourself. Be me. We used to trade places all the time."

Kayla wrinkled her nose. "That was in junior high school. We haven't done it in years. Besides, I was never good at that game."

Elissa waved away her concerns. "He won't be expecting this at all. It's just dinner. The alternative is one of us calls him up and tells him I can't go. Frankly, I think he deserves better than that."

Kayla stared at her reflection in the mirror and had an eerie sensation of déjà vu. Her hair had been pulled to the top of her head in a ponytail. Electric curlers pressed against her scalp. Instead of a towel, she wore a short white robe, but otherwise, she could have been Elissa getting ready for her date.

Elissa handed her the mascara. She took it, but didn't put it on. As much as she wanted to go and spend a romantic evening with Patrick, there was one ugly truth she had to face. "He asked you out, not me."

"That's hardly important."

Kayla turned to face her. "It's very important. He's never asked me out. If he was interested in me that way, he would have."

"Are you sure about that? Have you ever given him a hint that *you* were interested in him in that way? Aren't you the one always talking about what good friends you are?"

"Yes."

"Then why would he ask you out? It's not as if you're secretly longing for him. Right?"

Longing for him. She liked the sound of that. It fit her feelings perfectly. Longing wasn't as big as love, but it seemed larger than friendship. She thought about him all the time, and didn't understand why. She longed to be with him, near him, maybe even held by him. She longed to repeat those amazing kisses.

"It's all very confusing," Kayla said, avoiding her sister's question. If Elissa noticed, she didn't let on.

"The bottom line is, he's your friend and you don't want to hurt him. Isn't that all that matters?"

"I guess."

Kayla finished applying her makeup, then pulled the curlers and rubber band out of her hair. By the time she'd slipped on the dress, applied a final layer of hair spray and hunted down her dressy black pumps, Patrick was due to arrive.

Tiny shudders rippled through her. She knew they were just a combination of nerves, excitement and a bit of dread. Would she be able to pull this off?

Elissa handed her a small black handbag. "He should be here any minute," she said. "I'll go wait in the bedroom. Our plan has a better chance of working if he doesn't see us together. After all, he knows you well enough that if we're next to each other, he might be able to tell us apart. And we don't want that."

"Okay."

Elissa kissed her cheek. "Have a great time. I won't wait up."

"We're not going to be out that late."

"You never know."

There was a knock on the front door.

"Don't forget you're supposed to be me," Elissa murmured, then waggled her fingers and disappeared into the bedroom.

Kayla walked to the front door, took a deep breath and pulled it open. Here goes nothing, she thought.

Until he saw her standing in front of him, Patrick wasn't sure Elissa would actually be able to pull off the switch. But the moment the door opened, he recognized the woman in front of him. The relief was instant, as was the anticipation.

"Hi," he said, as Kayla stared at him. "You look amazing."

"Ah, thanks. So do you. I've never seen you—" She stopped suddenly. "That is, you look great in a suit."

"Thanks."

He stepped toward her and glanced over her shoulder. "Where's Kayla?"

"What? Oh, she's in her bedroom. Um, lying down. She has a headache."

"I'm sorry to hear that. I should probably pop my head in and say hi."

Kayla grabbed his arm, then, just as quickly, let go. "I don't think she wants to be disturbed."

"All right. Be sure to tell her I hope she feels better."

"I'm sure she'll appreciate your concern."

He held out his arm. "Shall we go?"

Kayla stared blankly for a moment, then slipped her hand into the crook of his elbow. As they walked down the steps to the driveway, he felt the faint tremors in her fingers. Turning his head so she wouldn't see him smile, he sent a silent "Thank you" back to Elissa.

At first he'd had his doubts about her plan. Would it make a difference if he was out with Kayla pretending to be Elissa? But now he saw the possibilities. For the first time, they were on a date.

He'd had his car washed. It gleamed in the porch light. When he held open the passenger's door, she glanced at him before slipping in. Confusion darkened her eyes. He understood her apprehension. Nerves had a grip on him, too. But this was a time for them to get to know each other in a whole new way.

He waited until she'd secured her seat belt, then walked around the back of the car and got in beside her. Before starting the engine, he glanced at her.

He'd seen her in makeup before, and he was reasonably sure he'd seen her dressed up. Yet in some ways it was if she were a stranger. A beautiful, mysterious stranger he'd just discovered.

"Is something wrong?" she asked, her voice low and husky.

"No. I was just thinking how beautiful you are." He touched her bare shoulder. "The dress isn't bad, either."

Color flared on her cheeks. Her gaze lowered as she murmured, "Thank you."

He hoped for that one moment she'd forgotten she was supposed to be her sister. He wanted her to know the compliment was meant for her, and no one else.

Perhaps the reason they had never clicked as a couple was that they had never allowed themselves to see each other that way. Tonight was their chance. They could show that side of themselves. The night, he thought with a smile, had many possibilities.

The small, dimly lit waterfront restaurant was as romantic and seductive as satin sheets and chilled champagne. Their table sat in front of the window. Lights from the building and a nearby dock reflected on the inky ocean, providing just enough illumination for Kayla to see the pale foam of waves breaking against the pilings.

The place settings had been arranged close together, allowing them to talk intimately and stare out at the view. The last fingers of sunlight had disappeared as they were seated, and the darkness outside gave Kayla the impression that she and Patrick were alone.

It wasn't true. Bits of quiet conversation drifted to them from other tables. A four-piece band played in the far corner, and several couples moved together on the dance floor. The night, the place, the music and the man were all perfect. Except he thought he was with someone else.

The waiter returned with a bottle of white wine and a free-standing ice bucket. He presented the selection, holding the foil-wrapped top with one hand while resting the bottle against his opposite forearm.

Patrick glanced at the label. "That's the one," he said.

The waiter opened the bottle and poured a small amount into Patrick's glass. He sipped, then nodded. After the wine had been poured, Patrick raised his drink.

"To a wonderful evening."

"My thoughts exactly," she said, and tasted the wine. "It's very nice."

"An old favorite," he said. "I like it on special occasions. But don't expect me to be an expert. I know a little about wine, but I'm more a beer or soda kind of guy."

Kayla remembered their celebration when he'd received his grant. They'd opened a bottle of champagne. "How do you feel about champagne?" she asked, trying to act innocent.

"I like it. In fact, I had some recently. When I—" He broke off and shook his head. "I don't want to talk about me. I want to hear about your life. You work in a hospital? What do you do there?"

Kayla gave him a brief description of Elissa's job, leaving out technical details because she didn't know them. It would be easier, she decided, if they talked about things she knew about.

"I toured the clinic today," she said. "I was impressed. You're doing good work there."

"Thank you. It's not just me. I have a great staff. Did Kayla take you back into the kennels?"

"Yes. I met several of your permanent residents."

Her forearm rested on the padded arm of the captain's chair. He shifted in his seat, moving closer. As his body angled toward hers, he stroked his fingers against the back of her fingers. The sensation was so unexpected, so electrifying, she lost her train of thought and couldn't pay attention to what Patrick was saying.

Not that she cared. No words could be as life-changing as the feel of his hand touching hers. He moved slowly, gently, teasing her. Nerves ignited. Untouched, undiscovered parts of her body began to make their presence known.

She stared into his blue eyes and knew that if she found a way to crawl inside Patrick's heart, he would hold her close and keep her safe forever. The thought should have terrified her. Perhaps, when she thought about it later, it would. Except this *was* Patrick, and she trusted him with her life.

"...so there stood Kayla, facing down this guy," he said, as if he'd been talking for several minutes.

She realized he probably had. With an effort, she wrenched her attention away from the delicious sensations he produced with his touch and tried to focus on his words.

"He was huge," Patrick continued. "Six-four, maybe six-five. A former linebacker with a pro football team. At least two hundred and fifty pounds of solid muscle. He'd bought a house in the area, had a successful business, and wanted to adopt a cat."

Kayla's mind cleared long enough for her to remember the incident. Working with a couple of local shelters, the clinic had sponsored an Adopt-a-Pet afternoon one Sunday last year. Kayla had put together the event by herself, and she'd been very picky about who took home the animals. She didn't remember anything extraordinary about that day, and wasn't sure why he was telling the story.

"It was late in the afternoon," he said. "We were down to a couple of dogs and one kitten." He grinned at the memory. "It was a tiny thing. All black, with big yellow eyes. A female, barely seven weeks. You know, when they still look like fur balls rather than small cats."

Kayla nodded.

"This one was a tiger at heart. She spit at everyone. Families with children had been afraid to take her home."

"She was too young to be with a household of children," Kayla said without thinking.

At Patrick's inquisitive look, she sank back in her chair. "I've, ah, been around small kittens. It's easy for them to get hurt."

"Oh. You're right."

She exhaled slowly and reminded herself she was Elissa. Elissa didn't work at the clinic. Pretending to be her sister was harder than she'd thought.

"So in walks this guy. I can't remember his name. Peter, I think."

His name had been Paul, but Kayla didn't dare correct him.

"He took one look at the kitten and fell in love. Of course, when he tried to pick her up, she spit and scratched until the poor man was bleeding."

Kayla smiled, remembering the crushed look on Paul's face. It was as if he'd been kicked by his own mother.

"What happened?" she asked, still not sure what intrigued Patrick about that afternoon.

"Kayla told Peter that the kitten had been handled all day and was scared. He had to show her he was safe. She made him lie on the floor on his back. Then she put tuna in his palm, his forearm, and a tiny dab of it on the front of his shirt." Patrick grinned. "No napkin, no plate, just tuna on the man's shirt."

Kayla felt herself flush. She hadn't thought about using a napkin until later, when Paul tried to rub away the smell.

"I was in the corner, trying not to laugh. This little tiny kitten, maybe three whole pounds of fur and not much else, came sneaking up to this big guy. She ate the tuna on his hand and arm, then climbed up to his chest. Now, kittens have needle-sharp claws. They really hurt. Peter flinched with each step, but he didn't budge. The kitten ate the tuna on his chest, stared into his face for a minute, then curled up and went to sleep."

Kayla smiled at the memory.

"Peter didn't want to get up and disturb her, so he stayed on the floor for about a half hour, until we were ready to leave."

"Did things work out with the kitten?" she asked, already knowing the answer.

"Absolutely. That cat runs his life. He brings her in every six months for a checkup. I keep telling him he only needs to come in once a year if she's not sick, but he won't listen." He shook his head. "Kayla is the only person in the world who would have dared to tell this rich, successful, famous guy to lay on the floor and then smear him with tuna, all because of a damn cat." Amusement crinkled the lines fanning out from the corners of his eyes. "She's one unique woman, and she's going to be impossible to replace."

Pleasure filled her. She wanted to thank him for the compliment and for thinking so highly of her. She held the words back, knowing that he wouldn't like her nearly as much if he knew she was here masquerading as her sister.

He squeezed her hand. "Sorry, Elissa. This night is so you and I can get to know each other, and here I am talking about your sister. You must think I'm a jerk."

"Not at all," she said quickly. "I like Kayla, too. Besides, she is the one person we have in common."

He stared at her. "You're right about that."

She wanted to ask what he meant, but the waiter appeared with their menus.

She glanced over the selections. Everything looked delicious, but she knew she was too nervous and excited to eat much. Patrick commented on several items, and they discussed the fresh fish of the day, then placed their orders.

"Aren't you hungry?" he asked when the waiter had moved off, leaving them in relative privacy.

"First dates make me nervous," she said, knowing she spoke the absolute truth. She and Patrick might have been friends for years, but this was their first official date. Except for the fact that she was lying about her identity, she thought it was going pretty well.

"Are you going to be leaving your job at the hospital?" he asked.

She stared at him. "No. Why do you ask?"

"I wondered if all three of the Bedford triplets would be taking off for parts unknown once the trust money was released."

Privately Kayla thought her two siblings were unadventurous and missing a great opportunity—but both had chosen not to come with her to Paris. Still, she couldn't say that.

"We all have plans," she said cautiously as she realized she wasn't sure what Elissa wanted to do with her money. Her sister had always been frightened of wealth. "But Kayla is definitely the traveler. In some ways, I envy her the trip she'll be taking in a few weeks." She took a sip of wine. "We plan to spend the holidays together in the Caribbean. That will be fun."

Patrick's mouth straightened. "You'll have to forgive me for not sharing your enthusiasm. Kayla's been a part of my life for a long time. I can't remember what the clinic was like without her, and I'm not looking forward to having to rediscover it. She's going to be impossible to replace. I'll miss her."

Kayla met his gaze. She read the sorrow in his eyes, the promise of pain he would suffer on her behalf. Her chest tightened. The knowledge that Patrick cared about her wasn't new; they'd always cared about each other. Maybe it was the depth of his feelings that surprised her...or the fact that he was telling a stranger things he'd never said to her face.

"I'm—" She cleared her throat. "She's really going to miss you, too."

"I doubt that. She'll be too busy chasing after European aristocracy. She wants to marry a prince."

"No, really. She is going to miss you. You mean a lot to her. She talks about you all the time. You're an important part of her life."

His mouth turned up in a faint smile. "You're being kind."

"I'm telling the truth. I swear." She made an X over her left breast. "Kayla thinks you're wonderful."

"I think she's great, too. I've always wondered one thing."

Her breath caught. What had he wondered? Why they'd

never gotten together? She was starting to seriously ask that question herself. Being with Patrick felt so right. She could talk to him about nearly anything. It might have been difficult to admit her feelings to him as herself, but as Elissa it was amazingly easy to confess everything. That she liked him more than he knew. That she replayed his kisses over and over in her mind. She smiled. Okay, maybe it would be nearly impossible to work the comment about the kissing into a casual conversation, but she really wished there was a way to let him know.

"Kayla is so bright and funny. Nearly as good-looking as her sister."

He flashed her a grin designed to add to the compliment. Kayla wasn't sure if she was flattered or insulted.

"And?" she asked, hoping he would lay it all out on the table, confess everything. Then she could tell him the truth, and they would—

"Why hasn't some guy swept her off her feet? She never goes out. I keep hoping for someone special to come into her life, but it doesn't happen."

Kayla sagged back in her chair. Great. Patrick thought she was a lonely old maid in need of a social life. Not exactly the romantic declaration she'd anticipated.

Before she could formulate an answer, he touched her hand again.

"Elissa, you must think I'm the biggest jerk around. I keep talking about your sister, when you're the one I'm interested in. Can you forgive me?"

"Sure," Kayla mumbled, even though it wasn't true. Forgive him? For being interested in Elissa? Not likely. Didn't he get it? Didn't he sense the connection between them? Oh, yeah, of course he did; he thought the chemistry was between him and Elissa, not between him and her.

"Let's dance," he said, standing up and holding out his hand.

She let him lead her to the small floor in the far corner, all the while not sure what to make of her feelings. In a way, she should be happy that he couldn't stop talking about her. But it annoyed her that he kept apologizing for it. Nothing made sense.

Then he took her into his arms, and she didn't care about making sense or her sister or anything but being with him.

Her heels put her at exactly the right height to rest her chin on his shoulder. He pulled her close right away, and she didn't think to protest until it was too late. Frankly, she didn't care. This was Patrick, and if he thought she was acting brazen, what did it matter? He was with Elissa.

They touched from shoulder to thigh. One of his hands settled on the small of her back, the other held her fingers tucked in against his chest. She could feel the steady pounding of his heart—the strong and solid beat so much like the man himself.

They swayed together with a familiarity that belied the truth that this was their first dance. The music surrounded them like a sensual fog, leaving her dizzy and disoriented. Yet safe. Nothing bad would ever happen while she was in Patrick's arms.

The hard, muscled planes of his body provided the perfect counterpoint to her yielding curves.

"We do this well," he said lightly as the combo switched to another slow dance.

"I agree. I was going to tell you I'm not much of a dancer, but I guess that's not true with you."

His cheek rested against her forehead, and she felt him smile. "It must be my close contact with Kayla. You two are so much alike."

Kayla didn't want him to think about Elissa right now. "Have you danced much with Kayla?" she asked.

He chuckled. "No. We've never been romantically involved."

She had to struggle to keep her tone light, but she was determined to ask the question. "Why not?"

"She was never interested in me that way."

His statement hung in the air, floating on the music. A half-finished thought that begged for completion.

Were you ever interested in her...that way?

She didn't ask, and he didn't offer.

The right answer would fill her with elation and make her face her own questions. The wrong answer would leave her devastated. Rather than risk it, she contented herself with silence and the stirring pleasure of being in his arms.

By the time the dessert dishes had been cleared away, Kayla had given up worrying about the fact that all Patrick's attentiveness, all his gentle touches to her hand, arm and back, were actually meant for Elissa. Her sister wasn't here, she wasn't the one making Patrick laugh, so Kayla refused to worry about giving her the credit.

"You must have been very proud when you opened the clinic," she said.

Patrick nodded. "I'd wanted to be a vet since I was a kid. It was a dream come true. The first year was tough, but the community supported me in a big way."

"Now you're famous and you have a big staff."

He laughed. "I'm certainly not famous, but the staff is a decent size. They work hard, and I appreciate that. Especially you-know-who."

The not-so-subtle reference to her made her smile. The wine had relaxed her, as had the passion flaring in his eyes. She decided to up the stakes of the game.

"I have a confession," she said softly, leaning close.

He mirrored her posture, placing one hand on her back and tilting his head toward hers. "Which is?"

"You have to promise not to tell anyone. Especially Kayla."

For a moment, Patrick looked puzzled. Then his expression cleared. "You have my word. What's the confession?"

"Kayla had a huge crush on you when she first started working at the clinic."

Instead of laughing, Patrick turned serious. "She hid it well. I never had any idea. When did she get over it?"

Now it was Kayla's turn to be uncomfortable. It wasn't that she didn't want to speak the truth; instead, she wasn't sure what the truth *was*. When had she gotten over the crush? Or had she at all?

He settled the problem by taking her hand in his and squeezing gently. "You're trying to spare my feelings. She was over me in a week."

"You're not even close."

He shrugged. "Kayla and I take great pleasure in tormenting each other. I have a confession of my own. She thinks I have a thing for redheads. I talk about it all the time."

Her heart pounded a little faster. "You don't favor them?"

"No. I like—" he reached up and touched one of her curls. "—blondes." His hand dropped to her bare shoulder. "You're so lovely."

"Thank you."

She became lost in his steady gaze. She had no recollection of gathering her purse and leaving the restaurant, but suddenly they were standing on the dock overlooking the dark ocean. The restaurant was behind them. They could see other couples dining, but no one saw them. The side of the building and a wooden gate created an alcove of shadow that sheltered them in privacy.

The moment was so perfect, no words were necessary. And when he pulled her into his arms, she knew this dance had nothing to do with music, and everything to do with the rhythmic heat swelling between them.

His mouth came down on hers, a tender, welcome assault. Lips pressed to lips. She inhaled his scent, absorbed his taste, clung to him, to his broad shoulders. He wrapped his arms around her, pulling her close, so close she felt the edges of their beings start to meld together.

His fingers teased at her nape, seeking sensitive hollows under the protective layer of her curly hair. At his touch, electric shivers raced through her, making her rise up on her toes and kiss him more firmly.

His mouth parted, as did hers. They both waited a breath, then their tongues met, pressing tip-to-tip at the place where their lips clung.

As her body awakened to passion, her heart also embraced new and exciting sensations. They had no name. Some part of them, almost the echo of their presence, was familiar. As if a shadow of them had been present before.

She wasn't ready to identify them. It was enough to be with Patrick, to know those feelings existed in her world.

She slipped her arms around his waist and felt the strength of his back. Tracing the length of his spine, she moved her hands up to his shoulder blades, then slipped down to the waistband of his trousers. Her fingers itched to cup the tight, muscled shape of his rear. The itch went unsatisfied. Neither Kayla nor the pretend-Elissa had the courage to do that.

As if he'd read her mind, he broke the kiss and exhaled

sharply. "You have no idea what you do to me," he said, his voice husky with passion.

"If it's what I'm experiencing, I have a good idea."

His gaze met hers. In the darkness, his irises looked like bottomless pools. She wondered how it would feel to disappear inside him.

"I knew tonight would be special," he said.

"Me, too. I've never felt like this before."

He hugged her tight. "Thank you for saying that." His mouth touched her cheek, her jaw, then moved lower, to her neck. She arched back her head, sinking into mindlessness as he forged a damp trail to her collarbone.

Intense pleasure made her toes curl. She needed this moment to last forever.

He licked the hollow of her throat. "I want you," he murmured. "Sweet Elissa, I want you."

Chapter Nine

Now what? Kayla asked herself as they drove through the dark streets. She focused her attention on the lit signs they passed, on the clear night sky, on her hands, clenched tightly in her lap. Anything to keep her from glancing at the man calmly sitting next to her.

Soft music drifted out from hidden speakers. Mood music—slow and romantic. Was that part of his plan? To relax her with the right combination of nighttime and sax solo?

Now what?

He wanted her. He'd kissed and held her and told her he wanted her. She'd felt the heat from his body, felt his passion, shared the moment.

But he thought he was with Elissa.

Her heart ached, with a dull, twisting kind of pain that made her want to get out of the car and start walking. Maybe if she went long enough and far enough, she could leave the misery behind. Maybe she would eventually forget.

How could he want her sister after just one evening, when he'd never once wanted her, Kayla? And he'd been with *her.* She pressed her lips tightly together to keep from swearing. It wasn't fair. She'd been his friend, she'd worked for him. How many nights had they sat up together, tending sick animals, or even each other? When he caught that bad flu three years ago, she'd been the one to make him soup and spoon-feed it to him. She'd been the one calling the doctor at three in the morning, then running out to get the prescription filled.

When a nasty bout of food poisoning laid her low for several days, Patrick had been there for her, too. He'd held her as she huddled in a ball and moaned in pain. He'd forced her to drink water so she wouldn't get dehydrated, and he'd cheered when she was able to keep down a piece of dry toast.

What about helping him with his grant and wallpapering his living room? What about the shared time on his porch, what about the sunsets and the laughter? Didn't they mean anything to him? How dare he think he wanted Elissa and not her!

That was the worst of it, she admitted to herself. Patrick's reaction was to her. She'd been the woman at the restaurant. His lips had touched *hers,* not Elissa's. She'd been the one to turn him on. But he didn't know that, and she didn't know how to tell him.

As they neared the house, she risked glancing at him. His expression gave little away. He looked relaxed, which wasn't fair at all.

What was she going to say? Should she confess all? If she didn't, she was going to have to explain to Elissa what had happened. After all, Patrick would expect to see Elissa again, and after tonight he would think they were more than friends.

She squeezed her eyes shut and whimpered softly. What a mess. She didn't want to tell him the truth; it was too humiliating. However, there didn't seem to be another choice. Elissa hadn't been able to go on a friendly date with Patrick. There was no way she could deal with the relationship as it had evolved.

Unless Kayla kept pretending to be her sister.

A recipe for disaster, or a shortcut to happiness?

Before she could decide, the car slowed. She opened her eyes and saw that they'd pulled into Patrick's driveway. Instead of stopping by the detached garage and walking her up the stairs to her—make that Kayla's—apartment, he continued to the main house and parked the car near the front door.

After turning off the engine, he angled toward her. The porch light illuminated the left half of his face, highlighting strong planes and penetrating eyes.

"Despite what I said at the restaurant, I don't have plans to ravish you," he said lightly. "At least, not without your permission. With those ground rules established, would you like to come in?"

"Yes," Kayla said, without thinking. A small piece of sanity screamed out that it was a really bad idea. The rest of her didn't listen. It was tough to hear the voice of reason, when every cell of her body yearned to be in Patrick's arms again. Maybe a good ravishing would clear her mind.

He walked around the car and opened the door for her. As she stepped out, he took her hand and brought her fingers to his mouth. He touched the tips to his lips, dampening each sensitive pad with his tongue. The combination of the romantic and the erotic made her thighs tremble. She felt as if she'd just run five miles.

He pulled her close and kissed the top of her head. "I promise to act like a gentleman, no matter how tough that's going to be," he said, his voice thick. He slid his hands through her hair, cupped her scalp and raised her chin. "I want to kiss you. Is that all right?"

He hadn't closed the passenger's door, and the dome light allowed her to see his expression. Passion flared in his eyes. She could both feel and see the heat. The fire touched her skin, but instead of burning her, it caressed her, dancing against her in pirouettes of pleasure.

The problem of her identity disappeared in the need of the moment. Did it matter who she was, when she was the woman he wanted? If this was just a game, then she'd waited far too long to play. The rules weren't clear, nor was she completely familiar with the ultimate goal, but she was willing to risk losing, if that meant she would have the pleasure of watching Patrick win.

His question still hung between them. He waited patiently for her reply. Words formed in her throat, but a flood of emotion prevented her from speaking. Instead, she raised on tiptoe and pressed her mouth to his.

It was a chaste kiss. Closed lips clung, captivated by unleashed need. Kayla ached for more. She wanted his tongue in her mouth, his hands on her body, bare skin next to bare skin. And yet, this was right. Pure. As if it were important for their souls to join first.

First? Were they going to make love? Was that what she wanted? Patrick as her lover...her first lover?

He pulled back and stared at her. "You take my breath away."

"I know what that feels like," she said, and was pleased when her voice didn't shake. She was still wrestling with the idea of them becoming lovers. Was that what she wanted?

"Do you want me to take you home?" he asked.

Unexpectedly, tears sprang to her eyes. The gentle question made her want to throw herself at him. Even now, even with the desire raging between them, he was giving her a choice. That was the kind of man he was. Thoughtful, understanding, caring, considerate.

He would make love the same way he kissed—with quiet force and unbelievable passion. She'd never felt comfortable enough to give herself completely to the other men she'd dated. Maybe it had been a matter of not trusting them enough. She trusted Patrick.

She blinked away the tears. She wasn't ready to leave him, not tonight. "I'd like to come in," she said.

He closed the car door, then put his arm around her. They walked to the front door, which he unlocked, and then she led the way into his house.

The living room looked exactly as it had a hundred times before. Wallpaper was missing from two walls and partially peeled off a third.

"Redecorating, I see," she teased.

He shook his head. "It looks awful, I know. But it's not my fault. Your sister is supposed to be helping me. She's great with the animals, but not exactly committed when it comes to helping me around here."

"You look smart enough to take care of it yourself. After all, this is *your* house."

"Yeah, but the new wallpaper was her idea." He took off his suit jacket and tossed it over the sofa. "Do you really want to talk about decorating?" he asked, loosening his tie and moving close to her.

She tilted her head so she could meet his gaze. "Not really."

"Me either."

He placed his hands on her shoulders. Strong fingers

kneaded her bare skin, and then he plucked at the skinny straps holding up her dress.

"These have been driving me crazy all evening," he said. "Just these little scraps of cloth. Weren't you worried they'd break?"

Her breathing increased. She placed her evening bag on the back of the sofa and wondered if he would think he was brazen if she stepped out of her shoes.

"They're sewn on well," she told him. "They don't break."

"But they do slide down."

The image his words painted filled her mind. In reality, the dress was snug enough that even if the straps were cut off, nothing would fall. Releasing the zipper in the back was another story. Would he want to do that, too?

Unable to speak, she nodded.

He bent and touched his mouth to her neck. Instinctively, she tilted her head to give him more room. He rewarded her with an openmouthed kiss against her already heated skin.

She couldn't think, she couldn't move, she could only stand there absorbing the wondrous sensation of erotic dampness, of his tongue licking her, tasting her. Her body grew heavy. An ache began in her chest and between her legs. She pressed her thighs tightly together, but that didn't help. She needed more; she needed him.

He slipped the straps off her shoulders, following his fingers with his mouth. First on her left side, nibbling at the curve of her shoulder, moving his mouth lower, to the top of her chest, pausing to trace the line of her collarbone before repeating the actions on her right side.

Her hands fluttered in the air. As he dipped toward her breasts and touched the exposed, shadowed valley between, she swayed and caught herself by placing her hands on his waist.

"Touch me," he said, the words muffled against her skin.

Touch me. A man's plea for a woman's gentle embrace. Raw need exposing vulnerability. Did he fear her reaction—and the potential for rejection—or did he trust her?

Touch me.

"I want to touch you," she said, and slipped her hands up his chest.

Tense muscles quivered with her every move. The defined ridges and valleys of his stomach rippled as she passed over them. His body broadened, and she had to spread her fingers to caress all of him. When she reached his shoulders, she glanced up and found him watching her.

In her head, she knew Patrick was a man, with the wants and needs men experienced. But until that second, until their gazes locked and she felt the impact of his arousal, she hadn't thought of him as a sexual being. Hunger tightened his mouth, his nostrils flared with each breath, a muscle twitched in his right cheek.

His power overwhelmed her. For the first time, she felt small and fragile next to him—female to his male, her curves and softness designed to receive that which he gave.

He took one of her hands in his and brought it to his mouth. He kissed her palm, then gently bit the fleshy place below her thumb. Never breaking eye contact, he pressed her hand against the center of his chest. Slowly, but with a determination that left her no doubt about his final destination, he moved her hand lower. Past the smooth cotton of his shirt, past the cool metal of his belt buckle. Lower, until she felt the placket covering his zipper, lower, until she cradled the hard ridge.

While she was still a virgin, she wasn't completely inexperienced. Some of her dating relationships had lasted several months, and in that time, she'd felt comfortable enough to fool around. It wasn't as if she didn't know what an aroused man looked like. She'd seen and touched and even tasted, but she'd never gone all the way.

But touching Patrick was different. It was as if she'd never been with anyone before, yet she wasn't afraid. Perhaps it was because, for the first time, the situation felt right.

She traced the length of him, feeling him flex against her hand, even as his eyes half closed and the hand touching hers tensed.

He leaned forward and kissed her. Her lips parted, and he slipped inside. His tongue circled hers, setting up a rhythm that called her with an ancient and irresistible beat. She could imagine them together, locked in each other's arms, bodies slick and ready, joining, sharing, reaching, becoming one. The image was so clear, she had the oddest feeling they'd made love before, if not in this lifetime, then in another.

He nudged her hand away and pulled her up against him. His hardness pressed into her belly. His hands touched her shoulders, her back, her hips, before dropping lower and cupping her rear. Her hips flexed, bringing her closer to him. She arched into the contact, released, then repeated the thrusting motion. He buried his face in the crook of her neck and groaned. She fought back a sigh of her own as that place between her legs grew damp, and need pumped through her like liquid fire.

He straightened, then took a single step toward the hallway, and the bedrooms beyond. A single step, and he paused.

"Do you want me to stop?" he asked, once again giving

her complete control over what happened—or didn't happen—between them.

No, of course not. She wanted them to make love. She wanted to know what it was like to be in Patrick's arms, to feel safe and cared for. She wanted him to be the first man to touch her in that unique way that would bond them as one.

But a lie stood between them.

She didn't know what to say. He took her silence as affirmation. "I'll walk you home." Nothing in his body language or tone hinted that he was disappointed. His graciousness only made her feel worse.

"I don't want to go home," she said quickly, and turned away from him. "I just—" She shook her head. "It's not what you think."

The carpet was amazingly interesting, she thought as she stared at it, unblinking. The color, the weave. If she concentrated very hard, maybe she could pretend she didn't have to tell him the truth.

"It's exactly what I think, Kayla."

"No. I've been pretending."

"You don't want me?"

She spun toward him. "Of course I do. You're—" Her hands fluttered in front of her waist as she searched for words. How could she tell him how much this night had meant to her? Even though he thought she was Elissa, his physical response had been to *her*. She was the one he'd talked to and laughed with. He'd kissed *her* lips, touched *her* body, been held captive by *her* hand on that most male part of him.

"It's just..." Her voice trailed off. Her brain cleared slowly, as if waking from a vivid dream. Words filtered through. Words he had said. Words—a word—that just now made sense.

She straightened her arms and stared at him. "What did you say?"

One corner of his mouth turned up. "I said it's exactly what I think."

"After that."

"I asked if you had been pretending about wanting me."

Her body tensed as the truth sank in. "In between those two statements."

"I said your name. Kayla."

She nearly sank to the floor. As it was, she had to consciously tighten her leg muscles to keep standing. "You knew?"

"The moment you opened the door." He had the audacity to smile. "We've been friends a long time, kid. Did you really think you could fool me?"

"Me, fool you? If anyone's been fooled, it's me. You let me go on pretending? You let me talk, say those things?" Her face burned as she recalled admitting her crush and who knew what else. "You could have told me."

The humor fled his face. "I could say the same thing."

"But I—" Her confusion disappeared, leaving behind embarrassment and shame. "Elissa couldn't go through with the date. I can't go into the reasons, because they're personal, but they have nothing to do with you. She was afraid you would think she was blowing you off. Neither of us wanted to hurt your feelings. She suggested we trade places. I'm not sure why I agreed. I suppose I thought it was a good idea at the time."

She turned away from him and walked to the sofa. "I'm sorry, Patrick. That was a lousy thing to do to a friend." She thought about the dancing together, the funny conversations, the way he'd kissed her as they stood on the dock.

"I guess you got your own back, making me think you wanted her. I don't blame you."

She didn't. How could she? Switching places had been a stupid thing to do. She knew better. She reached for her purse. "I hope you can forgive me," she whispered, knowing tears were merely seconds away.

She'd had her chance, and she'd blown it.

"I knew it was you, Kayla."

"You told me." Fighting for control, she blinked several times.

"I knew it was you," he repeated. "From the beginning. You're the one I touched in the restaurant. You're the one I danced with. You're the one I kissed."

You're the one I want.

He didn't say the words, but she heard them. The purse fell from her suddenly slack fingers. It hit the ground, but she ignored it. "You wanted me?"

His pupils dilated. "Want. There's no past tense in that statement." He motioned to the front of his trousers. "It's hard for a guy to fake interest, or to hide it."

Hot color returned to her face, but this time it was because she was suddenly shy. She didn't dare drop her gaze from his face.

"You never said anything about this. Before, I mean," she added.

"Neither did you."

"But I wasn't sure. We've always been friends. I don't want to mess that up."

He shrugged. "Neither do I."

She cleared her throat. "This is an amazingly awkward moment. What happens now?"

"That's up to you. Do you want me to walk you home?"

That would be the safest course, she told herself. She

and Patrick could put this moment behind them and pick up their old relationship where they'd left it. That made the most sense.

Except she'd already imagined them making love. Her body sensed what it would feel like with Patrick touching her, holding her, being inside her. She wanted him to be the one to teach her what really happened between a man and a woman. Because she trusted him, and because she loved him.

As a friend, of course. A good friend.

She looked at him, then at the front door, and finally at the dark hallway that led to his room. She'd been in there before, helping him put away laundry, or picking out a tie for him to wear when he spoke at a symposium. She'd sat on the king-size bed, even stretched out on it, giving him her fashion advice, along with a reminder that he not forget his ticket.

Safety or seduction?

She closed her eyes and tried to imagine what she would feel like forty years from now. Would she regret leaving or staying? She thought of Sarah and her boxes of memories. Precious, timeworn photos, bits of lace, a frayed teddy bear once loved by her children. Would she, Kayla, want to open her own memory box and know that she could have had this chance with Patrick, but instead had walked away?

The answer was simple.

She stepped out of her pumps and left them in the living room. Without saying a word, she moved past him, down the hall toward his bedroom. Before she got there, she felt his hand on her shoulder.

"Thank you," he whispered, and kissed her bare skin.

She turned to him and held out her arms. He slid close, pulling her toward him, covering her mouth with his.

Paradise found. She'd chosen wisely.

Chapter Ten

Kayla stood by his bed, a trembling, sensual creature, nearly otherworldly in her beauty. Patrick cupped her face. He traced her high cheekbones, the shape of her mouth, her jaw, before stroking her elegant neck.

She watched him steadily, her gaze never leaving his. Her green eyes had softened to the color of emerald mist.

They stood in semidarkness. A lamp in the corner cast a pale glow toward the ceiling. The bathroom light was on, the door partially closed. There was enough light to see by, but not enough to be obtrusive.

He smiled.

"What's that for?" she asked.

"I'm waiting to find out this is just a dream."

She tilted her head to one side. Blond curls drifted over her bare shoulders. "Do you dream about me often?"

They were about to make love; there was no reason for him not to tell the truth. "In the past few weeks, yes."

She returned his smile. "Since the, ah…"

"Kiss?"

"Yeah."

He nodded. "Since the kiss. Everything changed. I'm not sure why. It just got different."

"I agree." She ducked her head, as if she were feeling shy. "I meant what I said, Patrick. No matter what, I want us to always be friends."

Friends and lovers? He'd never experienced that before. Was it possible? "I want that, too. You mean a lot to me. I need you in my life."

She stepped toward him and rested her forehead against his chest. "I need you, too. I know everything is changing between us, but I need to know you'll always be the same."

"I promise. I'm not going anywhere."

He meant the words in an emotional sense, as in, he had no plans to stop caring about her, but as soon as he said them, they took on a different meaning. *I'm not going anywhere, but you are.*

A sharp pain took up residence in his chest. Apparently Kayla felt it, too, because she whimpered softly and wrapped her arms around his waist.

"Patrick."

She spoke his name as a plea. He wasn't sure what she wanted or needed, but the feel of her so close to him forced him to respond with a kiss.

She arched her head back and met him more than halfway. Yielding flesh, warm and sweet, opened to him. He tasted her, felt the tender inner smoothness of her lips, the slickness of her teeth, then began to stroke her tongue.

Once again passion threatened to spiral out of control. She clung to him, her fingers kneading into his back. He touched her everywhere. Hands on her hair, her back, her hips, her rear. He rubbed the cool fabric of her dress, his groin swelling painfully when he found the zipper tab nestled against her spine.

He pulled it down slowly. The dress parted, gossamer silk revealing the warm cream of her skin. His fingers traced a line from her shoulders down her spine, pausing to discover the lacy band of her bra.

Never breaking their kiss, she lowered her hands to her sides. The dress slipped down, pausing at her hips. She wiggled slightly, and the garment was gone.

He rested his hands on her bare waist. His thumbs pressed into her hipbones. Not able to stop himself, he continued the voyage of discovery. Silk panties gave way to smooth thighs. A couple of inches later, he felt the band of her stockings.

He stepped back and straightened. He'd touched her bareness, but the tactile exploration hadn't prepared him for the visual impact of seeing her. A black strapless bra supported generous breasts. Small panties teased him by revealing more than they covered. But it was the stockings that captured his attention.

"I've never seen that before," he admitted, running a finger over the skin just above the band.

She ducked her head. "I don't wear dresses much so I never got used to panty hose. I hate them. These are a lot easier."

The heat inside him grew. He'd wanted her from the moment she opened her apartment door and smiled at him. He'd spent the evening hard. He knew what they were about to do. He anticipated the passionate release he would feel when their bodies joined. Yet, in some odd way, being with her, wanting her, was nearly as satisfying. He didn't want to rush this moment. He wanted to talk and touch and tease, driving them both to the brink of madness, then pulling back. He didn't want their lovemaking to ever end.

She folded her hands over her chest, then dropped her arms to her sides. Her obvious nervousness reminded him that she was nearly naked, while he was fully dressed and staring at her.

Moron, he muttered silently to himself as he took her hand and led her to the bed.

As she settled onto the mattress, he sat next to her. He quickly removed his shoes and socks, then pulled his shirt free of his trousers and unbuttoned it. Then he smoothed her curly hair off her face.

"You okay with this?" he asked.

"Yes."

"Good." He smiled. "Let's deal with the logistical stuff first." He pointed at the nightstand. "I have protection with me, and I plan to use it."

She bit her lower lip, then nodded. "Thank you," she whispered.

"No problem." He bent close and licked her shoulder. "Anything you hate doing?"

"Uh, not really." A tremor rippled through her.

"Do you need me to spank you or call you a bad little girl?"

She pulled away and stared at him. Shock widened her eyes. Bright spots of color blossomed on her cheeks.

He chuckled. "I'll take that as a no."

"You spank women?" She sounded stunned.

"By hand or with a paddle?"

Her mouth dropped open.

He put his finger under her chin and pressed. "I'm kidding, Kayla. I've never spanked anyone. We're both a little nervous. I was trying to distract you."

She exhaled sharply. "You did a great job. I can't believe you asked that. In fact, I—"

He reached behind her and unfastened her bra. It fell to her lap. She stopped speaking with the suddenness of a television going out during a blackout. The next sound she made wasn't actually a word. It was more of a sigh as he pressed her onto the mattress and touched his mouth to her right breast.

She tasted of promise and sin. Sweet and intoxicating. He circled her taut nipple, discovering the pebbly texture, the heat, the smoothness of her curves.

He shifted his weight so that he was kneeling over her, then moved to her other breast. She arched into his caress. With his hands, he began to discover her—the strong yet delicate collarbone, the shape of her upper arms, the tiny mole on the left side of her chest. He counted her ribs, felt the faint lines of scars from her accident years ago, circled her belly button, rubbed her hipbones, then brushed across her panties.

Her body stirred restlessly. She grabbed and released the comforter beneath her. Her eyes closed, her mouth parted.

Over and over he lavished attention on her breasts. He licked the sensitive undersides, blew air across her nipples. He learned every millimeter of the valley between, gently nibbled at the place where the curves began.

When he couldn't stand it anymore, he stretched out beside her and kissed her mouth. Apparently he wasn't the only one aroused by what he was doing. She cupped his face and parted her lips. When he entered her, she suckled him. Fire flared inside. Had she touched his arousal at that second, he would have exploded without warning. Every muscle tensed; control slipped. He had to consciously force himself back from the edge.

He broke the kiss and stared into her eyes. "You're amazing."

"I'm okay," she said.

"Perfect."

She closed her eyes. "Never perfect."

He started to ask why, then remembered the scars. Did she really think they mattered?

"Perfect," he repeated forcefully, and placed his hand on her belly.

He outlined the pattern left by the barely visible marks. She flinched at his touch, so he gently kissed her. As he circled her mouth with his tongue, his fingers danced over the marks that shamed her. He concentrated on touching her with all the caring and passion he contained. He wanted his body to speak to hers, silently saying the right thing so she would believe.

One scar dipped below her panty line. He slipped the scrap of silk down her legs and tossed it on the floor. The white line disappeared into the dark curls at the apex of her thighs.

Returning his mouth to hers, he parted his lips and waited for her to enter. When she did, he sucked her tongue and felt sudden tension stiffening her. Intent on following the scar, he didn't realize how far he'd strayed until his fingers encountered unexpected heat and warmth.

He'd wanted to take longer, but the temptation was too great. He circled through the curls until he found the center of her being. Slowly, gently, taking his cues from her subtle reactions, he touched her there. Over and over. Her legs parted, her mouth pressed hard against his, her hands clung to him.

He listened to the increase in her breathing, felt the climbing temperature of her skin. Muscles tensed and contracted, time had no meaning. She drew nearer; he went faster, not pushing, but assisting.

Gasping for air, she broke the kiss. Her gaze met his.

"Perfect," he murmured.

"Yes, you are," she answered, then closed her eyes and arched her back.

He stopped moving his fingers. For a heartbeat, she hung suspended.

"Patrick!"

Her cry filled him with an intense pleasure he'd never known. He touched her lightly, quickly, circling her as her body shuddered in release.

He took her in his arms and held her as she recovered. When she slipped a leg between his and began kissing his chest, he knew he wouldn't be able to hold back much longer.

"I want you," she said, finding and licking his nipples.

Her hair brushed against his skin. The combination made control impossible.

He sat up and jerked off his shirt. His pants and briefs followed. When she reached for his arousal, he grabbed her wrist and kept her from touching him.

"You can't," he said, feeling like a sixteen-year-old. At her quizzical gaze, he added, "I'm really close."

She put her hand on his thigh and grinned. "How close?"

The pressure of her fingers on his leg made his hardness surge upward.

"My," she said, sounding impressed. "I see what you mean."

He grunted in response and pulled open the nightstand drawer. While he opened the package of protection, she moved behind him and pressed against his back.

"Thank you," she said. "For everything. For being

wonderful and a great lover, and for making this exactly what I wanted it to be.''

He slipped on the condom, then turned toward her. ''Hey, it's not over yet.''

''I know.'' She touched his face. ''I just wanted you to know how I felt.''

Some unidentified emotion tugged at his heart. He didn't dare analyze it. Not now. Usually, he was able to hold a piece of himself back when he made love. He didn't have to give it all. With Kayla, it was different. They connected in a way that terrified him, yet made him never want to be apart from her. What the hell did it mean?

She stretched out on the bed and tugged at his hand. ''Don't look so serious. This is supposed to be fun.''

He moved between her legs and dropped a kiss on her belly. ''Yes, ma'am.''

He stroked between her legs, savoring the heat and the moistness. She parted her thighs wider, closing her eyes as he touched her still-sensitive center. From there he moved down to the place that would accept him. Every part of him clenched in anticipation.

For a moment, the magnitude of what they were about to do stopped him. He believed that, no matter what, they would always be friends, but this one act would change everything forever. It was a risk. He had to take it or not, and had to make that decision without knowing the potential price.

''Hey.'' She glared at him. ''Don't get weird on me, okay? There's no way I'm going to spank you or call you a bad little boy.''

He grinned. ''Just one little swat?''

''Patrick!''

''Okay, okay. I'll behave.''

''Oh, don't do that, either.''

They stared at each other. The humor faded, leaving only desire. He looked at her face, her breasts, her belly, the scars, then at the place that would accept and pleasure him.

"Now," she pleaded, and raised her hips slightly.

He entered her slowly. She was tight and wet, an unbelievable combination. He paused halfway and reached down to part her a little to make it easier. At his touch, she jumped.

He glanced at her. Her eyes were tightly closed, her face was fierce with concentration. Not passion, though. He noticed the tension in her arms and legs.

"Kayla?"

"Please, Patrick. Don't stop."

He moved in a little more. Slowly. As if waiting for some kind of resistance. As if—

He swore silently and started to withdraw. Her eyes flew open, and she grabbed his left arm to hold him in place. "No! I want you to do this."

"You're a virgin."

The statement hung between them. He waited for her to deny it, prayed she would. He wasn't all the way in, but he suspected he would have already felt the physical proof. There wasn't any, just a sixth sense inspired by her reaction to the intimate act.

She took a deep breath. "Make love to me. I want you. I want you inside. I want to feel you in me. I want to know what it's like."

"I've never been with a virgin before."

"Then we're even. I've never been with a man. At least not all the way."

A thousand questions filled his mind. Why him? Why now? Why was she still innocent? Why hadn't he guessed before?

There were no answers. There was nothing but the pleading in her eyes and the painful arousal between his thighs.

She braced her hands against the mattress and pushed her hips toward him. Slick tightness surrounded him, making him moan. She tilted her hips and made the decision for him.

He moved in and out slowly, cautiously, determined not to hurt her. The questions disappeared as pleasure took over. He had enough awareness left to slip one hand between them and touch her center. He couldn't return the gift she offered, but he could make sure she enjoyed the experience.

Her body quickened around his. He thrust faster, feeling her muscles tense as he continued to stroke her. This time, though, he recognized it as coming from desire, not apprehension.

Gritting his teeth, calling on every trick, every ounce of strength, he held back until she called out his name and her body convulsed. He plunged inside and let her contractions take him on a journey so incredible, so unique, it was as if he'd never made love before, as well.

Kayla exhaled softly and rested her head on Patrick's shoulder. His steady heartbeat soothed her, adding to the lethargy creeping through her body.

She'd played around with other men before. While she hadn't gone all the way, she'd experienced physical release. But this was different. Every part of her felt complete, as if a missing piece of her had been found. Contentment swelled up inside her, making her want to lie in his bed, in his embrace, forever. The slight ache between her thighs only heightened her awareness that something wonderful had happened.

Making love had been better than anything she'd imagined.

Patrick stroked her head, running his fingers through her curls, tracing the curve of her ears, brushing the underside of her jaw. As their legs tangled together and his touch soothed her, she wanted to purr like a well-fed cat.

They had been such good friends that she supposed she should have worried that their becoming lovers would change everything between them. Perhaps it had, but not in a bad way. If anything, their connection was stronger. She looked inside, wondering about fear, but couldn't find any.

"Kayla?"

She hovered at the edge of sleep, but his voice called her back. "What?"

The hand on her hair stilled. "Why me?"

Why Patrick? The question was reasonable. Why, after years of holding back, of not trusting someone else with her innocence, why had she given it to him?

"I knew you'd make it right," she said. "In this day and age, it's sort of silly to sleep with just anyone, so I never did. Plus, I always worried about the scars. They've sort of faded, but they're still there. I always imagined having to answer a lot of questions, which I didn't look forward to. You already knew everything."

She paused and raised her head to look at him. Blue eyes met her gaze. She rubbed her fingers against his mouth. "I knew you'd make it special and right. I trusted you." She gave him a quick smile. "I hope that's okay."

He kissed her fingertips. "It's more than okay. I was pleased, if a little surprised. It never occurred to me you were a virgin, but once I realized it, I couldn't figure out why you hadn't saved yourself for a prince."

His voice teased, but there was something cautious in

his expression. Something that warned her that her response would matter to him.

She wrinkled her nose. "Princes have virgins all the time."

"You know that for a fact?"

"I suspect it to be true. A prince wouldn't care, you would."

He wrapped his arms around her and held her close. She lowered her head back to his shoulder and absorbed the sensations of heat, strength and security. The moment stretched between them, a moment when her heart opened and waited. *She* waited, too. Waited for words to fill the silence.

She didn't know what those words would be, yet she found herself holding her breath in anticipation. She needed to hear them, to believe them. They would change her life forever.

He stroked her hair again. "Kayla, I—"

Her body tensed.

"I'm going to miss you when you're gone. I want you to promise you'll always remember this night."

The air left her body in a giant rush. Her heart squeezed painfully, and her eyes filled with tears.

Until he said he would miss her, she'd actually forgotten she was leaving.

But that wasn't what caused her hurt. Instead, it was what he hadn't said. Unspoken words could inflict lethal blows.

"Kayla?" He shook her gently. "Do you promise?"

"Yes," she murmured. "I'll never forget."

How could she? This night had changed her life.

She remembered hearing a song a few years ago. A certain man had come into a woman's life, but too late. She was already committed to someone else. He was, she told him in the song, the first time she'd thought about leaving.

Patrick was the first time Kayla had thought about staying. That was what she'd wanted to hear. Not that he would miss her, but that he didn't want to let her go. That he cared about her.

Her mind shied away from the *l* word. She wasn't ready to talk about love, let alone think it. Neither of them was in love. Except as friends.

It wasn't love that had her thinking about staying, it was the way she felt in his arms. As if, for the first time in her life, she'd come home.

"You can't go to sleep," he said. "Not that I wouldn't love your company, but I suspect Elissa is waiting up to hear the outcome of your experiment."

Kayla sat up and glanced at the clock. It was after one in the morning. "You're right. I should have thought of that myself. She'll be worried."

He kissed her gently. "She's pretty smart. I think she has a fair idea of what happened."

It wasn't until they were dressed and walking her to her apartment that she found herself tongue-tied. What was she supposed to say? Thanks for the good time? I enjoyed the sex? Can we do it again, soon?

Nothing sounded right. She didn't know the rules for post-lovemaking etiquette. She didn't worry that she was never going to see Patrick again. After all, he was her boss, her landlord, her neighbor, and very much a part of her life. He wasn't going to disappear. But would they continue to be lovers? Was it *just* a onetime thing?

As they reached the stairs leading up to her apartment, she almost asked. But at the last minute, she bit back the question. It wasn't fair to ask, when she didn't have an answer herself. She didn't know what she wanted.

In a few weeks, she was leaving for Paris. Could she still do that if she was emotionally and physically involved with Patrick? Could she live with herself if she gave up her dream?

At the top of the stairs, he turned toward her and took her hands in his. He'd pulled on jeans and a T-shirt. Stubble darkened his jaw. He was tall and handsome, and she ached to be with him again.

"Thank you," he said, his gaze intense. "For everything. I—"

Instead of completing the sentence, he cupped her jaw, then kissed her. She parted to admit him, clinging to him, trying to put all her emotions, the joy, the confusion, the questions, into that one kiss.

When he pulled back, he nodded ruefully. "Me, too," he said, and she knew he understood.

The front door opened. Elissa leaned against the door jamb and yawned. "Hi, guys. I heard you coming up the stairs. I'm not interrupting, am I?"

"No." Patrick smiled at her.

Elissa raised her eyebrows. "Then everything worked out?"

"Absolutely."

"Good." She looked at Kayla. "Want a couple more minutes of privacy?"

Kayla shook her head. "Night, Patrick." She kissed him on the cheek and stepped inside.

He gave her a wave and started down the stairs. She watched him until he reached his house and disappeared from view. Only then did she realize tears were trickling down her cheeks.

Ten minutes later, she curled up in a corner of the sofa. She tucked her bathrobe around her feet and sipped at the herbal tea Elissa had made.

Her sister plopped onto the love seat and grinned. "Okay, I want details. Start with the moment he picked you up. And talk slowly. I want time to imagine everything."

Kayla drew in a breath and let it out. "We... There was this restaurant by the ocean, and we danced. I thought he thought I was you and, oh, Elissa, I'm so confused."

She squeezed her eyes shut, determined not to keep crying.

Elissa was instantly at her side. "Honey, I'm sorry." She put her arm around her and pulled her close. "Hush, Kayla. You don't have to tell me anything."

Kayla wiped away her tears. "I want to. I don't mind talking about him. I, we, I'm not sure what happened or what it means. I don't want to feel differently than I do about him. I want it to be okay. I thought it was, but now that he's gone, I'm not so sure."

Her sister patted her shoulder. "The problem is that you're the only one who hasn't figured out how you feel about Patrick."

Kayla didn't like the sound of that. "What do you mean?"

Green eyes, exactly like her own, opened wide. "Kayla, you're in love with him. If not completely, then almost."

Love? No. Not that. "We're friends," she said firmly. "We have been for years. If you're talking about that kind of love, then okay, I agree with you. But romantic love—no way."

"Why is it so difficult to imagine?"

Kayla set her tea on the coffee table and pulled her knees to her chest. "It just is."

"Fine. If you're not in love with him, why are you so upset?"

"I'm not upset!"

Elissa stared at her with knowing eyes.

Kayla grimaced. "I'm a little upset. We made love, and we've never done that before." She didn't bother mentioning *she* hadn't done that before, either. "I don't want it to change everything, but I think in my heart I know it will."

"He loves you."

"No. He doesn't. He can't. Not now." She rubbed her temples. "I'm leaving, Elissa. After we turn twenty-five, I'm off to Paris. I've waited for this for years. I refuse to change my plans. I've earned this trip."

Elissa nodded. "No one's denying that. You're right, you have earned it, and you deserve it. But this isn't about going to Paris, even though that's what you want it to be about. It's about something bigger. All your life you've been waiting for something wonderful to happen. You live in the future and not in the present. I suppose the accident changed everything for you. No one else can understand what you went through that year you were recovering. It was painful to watch your suffering, but not nearly as horrible as it was for you to experience it."

"That doesn't matter now," Kayla said impatiently. "The accident was a long time ago. I've grown up."

"Certainly, but you haven't changed. Inside, you're still twelve years old and trapped in a cast. What on earth is waiting for you in Paris? What could be better than this? You've got a job that you love. People adore you. Kayla, I spend my day wrestling with numbers and a budget. You spend yours making people feel cared about. You change lives."

"You make it sound so dramatic. I haven't saved any-one. I'm not a doctor."

Elissa smiled sadly. "You save their souls. Isn't that more important?"

Kayla shrugged. Her sister made her sound like a hero, but it wasn't true. "Anyone can drive dogs around to visit seniors, or sick kids."

"Sure, anyone can, but who else bothers?" Elissa leaned forward. "You have two sisters who love and re-spect you, a wonderful man who's crazy about you. If you want to go to Paris, then go. But realize that dream has a price. You're leaving a lot behind, and there's no guarantee it's going to be waiting for you when you get back home."

"You guys will be here," Kayla said, trying not to imagine her life without Patrick. Even so, she could feel the bone-chilling coldness of an empty world.

"Stubborn brat, of course *we'll* be here, but that's not what we're talking about. Listen to me, Kayla. Life isn't a dress rehearsal. It's the real thing. If you don't learn to live in the present, if you don't stop ignoring what's right in front of you and constantly reaching for an impossible dream, you're going to wake up and realize you missed out on everything you could have had. And you'll have no one to blame but yourself."

Kayla didn't like what her sister was saying. "I know you think you're helping, but—"

She broke off when she saw tears in Elissa's eyes. Her sister turned away, but not fast enough. Now it was Kay-la's turn to offer comfort.

She touched Elissa's arm. "Cole," she said softly.

Elissa nodded. "Thinking about you with Patrick brought it all back. You'd think after all this time I could let it go."

Kayla remembered her sister's brief marriage to Cole

Stephenson. The hotshot young attorney had swept Elissa off her feet and taken her to New York. Elissa had been barely twenty, so in love she left her sisters and college willingly. Less than a year later, she'd returned. She never talked about her marriage, but Kayla and Fallon had seen the shadows in her eyes and the pain behind her smile.

"You're not over him?" Kayla asked.

Elissa shook her head. "I want to be. I should be. The fire burned so hot between us. Too hot. It burned itself out. Something like that isn't easy to let go." She wiped her face and managed a crooked grin. "Sorry. This isn't supposed to be about me. You're the one with the problem."

"I'm fine," Kayla said. "I just need to think this through. A lot of what you told me makes sense. I do need to live in the present and not the future. But does that mean giving up my dreams?"

"Not if you're sure your dreams are what you really want, and not some leftover fantasy from your childhood."

Was Paris a fantasy? Part of the fantasy of being swept away by a handsome prince? If love wasn't like a tornado, then what was it?

"I don't know what to do," she admitted, feeling helpless. "Which path is right for me?"

Elissa kissed her cheek. "Only you can answer that."

Chapter Eleven

Patrick and Kayla stood at the edge of the construction site.

"I can't believe how quickly everything is moving," she said, pointing to the metal-reinforced framing growing out of the concrete foundation.

Patrick nodded. "The contractors know this is a grant-funded project, and I think they're scared the money might dry up. They want to get the work done fast, which works in my favor. We're going to be up and running by the end of the year."

She flashed him a smile. "You must be excited."

"There are a lot of details to work through."

He wondered if he sounded more enthusiastic than he felt. He hoped so. This research facility would be the fulfillment of an important dream. In time, he would appreciate how lucky he'd been to find grant funding. Over the next few years, he and his team of experts would make medical discoveries that would impact animals' lives. He'd been on the cutting edge of that kind of work in college, and he'd missed it.

So he'd done everything he'd planned.

But without Kayla, his world felt empty. She wasn't gone yet—in fact, there were still a few weeks left until she left for Paris—but every day brought new proof of her upcoming departure. He didn't want to think about her leaving, but he couldn't seem to focus on anything else.

They stood next to each other, leaning against the clinic's van and watching the large equipment move heavy metal beams.

He glanced down at her and realized she'd been quiet for a couple of minutes. "You okay?" he asked.

"No."

The quick reply surprised him. He turned his back on the lot and stared at her. For the first time in several days, he really looked at her.

Shadows bruised the delicate skin under her green eyes. Her mouth was pulled straight, and the set of her jaw was faintly defeated. Although her golden hair was as shiny and curly as ever, instead of wearing it loose, or in one of her fancy braids, she had it pulled back in a simple ponytail. There wasn't any one thing that was so different, it was all of her.

"What's wrong?" he asked.

She shrugged. "Gee, Patrick, you're a smart man. You figure it out."

He didn't like playing games, and he certainly didn't like it with her. "Kayla, tell me what's going on."

She crossed her arms over her chest. Different expressions skittered across her face. He tried to gauge her mood. She wasn't angry—resigned, maybe? Disappointed?

At last she raised her gaze to his. Pain dilated her pupils.

"It's been two weeks. Why haven't you asked how I was until now? You've been avoiding me, as if you wanted to pretend it never happened. How do you think that makes me feel?"

Her accusations caught him low in the belly. Guilt flared. Familiar guilt, because he'd known what he was doing, even as he stayed away from her, and it had made him feel like slime.

"I'm sorry," he told her. "You have every right to be angry and upset with me. I've acted badly."

She bit her lower lip. "Gee, I thought hearing you say that would make me feel better, but it doesn't."

The construction machinery fell silent. He glanced over and saw that a food truck had pulled up on the opposite side of the site. The men used the opportunity to take a break.

"Why?" she asked.

A single word; on the surface, a simple question. Yet he knew the real meaning behind the word, and what she was really asking.

Why did you make love to me? Why did you hold me that way, then avoid me? Why aren't you talking to me? Did I make a mistake by choosing you to be the one? Don't I mean anything to you? We're supposed to be friends, but this isn't how friends treat each other.

"I'm sorry," he said quietly, forcing himself to look at her. "I never meant to hurt you."

"What *did* you mean to do?"

"I wanted to make it okay between us." He figured he could risk a little honesty, but not too much. He had to keep control of himself, so he didn't blurt out that he'd withdrawn from her because the alternative was to fall in love. To want to hold on to her forever. That wasn't an option. She had her plans, and he cared about her enough to want her to get exactly what she wanted and deserved.

"Is this okay?" she asked, motioning to indicate the distance between them.

"No." He reached out to touch her shoulder, then withdrew his hand. He didn't dare touch her. It hurt too much. It reminded him of what he had had once and would never have again.

"You're sorry we made love." Her voice was flat.

"Never," he answered quickly. "I'm honored that I was your first."

She half turned away, staring out toward the city. "No, you're not. It's a responsibility that you didn't want, and now you don't know what to do about it."

He tried to speak, but she cut him off with a wave of her hand. "You don't have to *do* anything," she said. "That wasn't the point. There are no strings attached. We were friends before, and I thought we could still be friends after."

"We are." Yet, even as he spoke the words, he knew they sounded lame.

"Oh, yeah. Best friends." She hunched forward. "If I could take that night back, I would. I'm sorry we made love."

Her words sliced through him like a gleaming blade. He felt the physical cutting, but the pain took longer to kick in. When it did, it nearly drove him to his knees. He had to hold on to the side of the van to maintain his balance.

"Don't say that," he told her. "Don't regret it, please. That night was wonderful for me. I'll never be able to forget it. Or you. No matter what."

She threw herself at him. "Oh, Patrick, I didn't mean to say that. I don't regret anything we did. I loved being with you. It was magic. I just—'' She sniffed. ''I felt so confused, and I was afraid to talk to you.''

''Don't be silly. You can talk to me about anything.''

Her arms wrapped around his waist, and she pressed her face against his chest. He raised his hand to stroke her hair, then pulled away. He couldn't do it; he couldn't touch her. Not knowing she was leaving.

''We'll always be friends,'' he promised.

She nodded, then raised her head. Confusion made her mouth tremble. ''You're not hugging me back.''

He knew he didn't dare explain why. The truth would only make them both uncomfortable. So he settled on a cheap way out.

''That's because I have something to give you,'' he said, stepping back and opening the driver's side door. From under the seat, he pulled out a long, thick envelope. ''This came for you today, before we left.''

She debated whether or not to let him distract her, then finally reached for the envelope. ''If this is another shot list, I'm not interested.''

''I don't think that's it at all.''

She tore open the back and pulled out a dark blue passport. Her breath caught. She flipped it open and stared at her picture, then fingered the blank pages.

In his mind's eye, he could see those pages filled with stamps from countries she'd visited. She was about to enter a world that held no place for him. She wanted to discover new adventures, he wanted to put down roots.

She turned it over in her hands. ''It's so real.''

''I guess you're on your way.''

''Paris, here I come.''

Her smile dazzled him. He forced himself to return it, when inside, his soul blackened and his heart turned to glass before shattering.

In that moment, with Kayla clutching her passport to her chest and chattering about all the things she would do, he finally got it.

He'd avoided her for nothing. He'd hoped to protect himself from the pain, but it was too late. It had probably been too late the first day he met her. It didn't matter that she would only ever think of him as a friend, it didn't matter that she was leaving and he might never see her again. It didn't matter that he'd tried to avoid this his whole life.

He loved her.

He'd thought he'd played it safe. He'd wanted a sure thing if he was going to risk love at all. Now he realized he didn't get to choose who or when. When love arrived, it did so without warning, without worrying about convenience or potential heartbreak.

He loved Kayla with all his heart, and now he had to let her go.

She flipped through the pages again. "It's happening. This feels strange. I know I've planned for it and everything, but I think in some part of my brain, I figured something would stop me."

"Don't tell me you're having second thoughts," he teased, pleased that he sounded completely normal. No matter what it cost, he would never let her know how he felt. He would never be responsible for the death of her dreams.

"Not exactly." She glanced at him, then away. "Things are a little different, that's all. Sometimes I wonder if the idea of going to Paris is going to be better than any actual trip."

It was, he realized, the perfect opening. He could tell her how he felt and ask her to stay. She might even agree. But then what? Would his world be enough for her? How long until she got restless? Until she felt the need to search out that tornado she talked about? His love for her had come upon him slowly. He didn't doubt its validity, or that it was forever, but would she believe that? He'd never once swept her away. It didn't matter that he believed tornadoes to be destructive. Kayla didn't want ordinary. She wanted the fairy tale and Prince Charming.

If her path led her back to him, then he would confess all. But he believed she needed to experience her dreams before she could make a decision about what mattered most. Her happiness was more important to him than his own.

Which probably made him a damn fool.

Loud motors started, drawing Kayla's attention to the construction. "You're going to be so busy with the research center, you're not even going to notice I'm gone."

"I'll notice."

She laughed. "Patrick, by the second week, you won't even remember my name."

He knew it was wrong of him, but he wished her statement was true. Unfortunately, he would remember. It would take more than three lifetimes to ever forget Kayla.

"There's this teacher…" Allison said, pausing to pat Rhonda on her head before turning her attention back to Kayla. "She came to see me and said there's these videos I can watch, so I'll keep up with my friends." Her nose wrinkled. "I'm glad, 'coz I didn't want to get left behind in school."

"I know what you mean," Kayla said. "When I was recovering from my accident, my sisters visited me every day and helped me with my lessons. I didn't want to get left behind, either."

Talk about adding insult to injury, she thought, recalling

those difficult months. As if surviving the accident and rehabilitation weren't bad enough, to be left a grade behind in school would make the situation intolerable. She remembered overhearing a conversation between an instructor and her mother. The instructor had been concerned about Kayla's "social" skills not keeping up, either. What the woman had never understood was that interacting with hospital employees, dealing with pain, physical therapy, adjusting to physical limitation, enduring the dark, endless nights alone, had forced her to grow up faster than any child should. She'd had no trouble socially adjusting with her peers. If anything, she'd passed them by.

Rhonda hopped over Allison's chest and landed on the other side of the bed. She tugged at a ribbon in the child's hair, pulling it loose, then racing to the end of the mattress. Once there, she dangled it and wagged her tail.

Allison laughed. "Silly dog. Bring that back to me."

Kayla had seen them play this game countless times before. As she watched the dog interact with the little girl, she had the oddest feeling that Rhonda really understood Allison's limitations. She played gently, darting away, but always quickly returning, as if she knew Allison couldn't come after her. Even when Allison's parents and older brother visited, she would run and chase balls with them for a few minutes, then spend the rest of the time on Allison's bed.

"I saw your show on cable," Allison said. "I think I know which one was you."

Kayla leaned forward in her chair and held the girl's hand. "What was the show about?"

"The cook left, and there was no one to make dinner. Mrs. Beecham tried, but she doesn't know what little kids like to eat."

Kayla grinned. "We had so much fun filming that one.

Remember the food fight everyone got into in the kitchen?''

Allison nodded.

"That was real. We spent hours on that one scene. By the end of it, everyone was covered in pudding and flour and green beans.''

"Were you the one scooping the pudding out and throwing it at the boys?''

"Yup. And I was in the scene with Mrs. Beecham when we tried to make toast in the big oven and everything caught on fire.''

Allison shook her head. "I didn't know that was you. 'Sally McGuire' is on every night, so I'm going to keep watching it.''

"I hope you enjoy it. That was a long time ago.'' She stroked Allison's bangs off her forehead. While she and Rhonda were visiting, she made it a point to touch the child as much as possible. Kayla remembered feeling isolated when she was in a body cast. There hadn't been much of her skin showing, and everyone had seemed nervous about getting too close.

Rhonda returned the ribbon and flopped down next to Allison, resting her head on the girl's shoulder. Allison bent her neck so her cheek rested against Rhonda's soft fur.

"I'm gonna be moving soon," Allison whispered.

Kayla wasn't sure if she didn't want Rhonda to hear, or if the thought of going to another facility frightened the girl.

"I'd heard," she said. "You're doing really well, and the doctors want you to have more physical therapy. You're going to like the new place. It's closer to your family, there are going to be other children around, and—"

A single tear trickled out of the corner of Allison's eye.

Kayla leaned close and brushed it away. Then she hugged the child as best she could, bending toward her and cradling her head.

"Honey, I know you're scared. Since the accident, everything new is frightening. You've been so brave and strong, but it feels like you're never going to get better." She rocked gently. "You feel like you're going to be broken forever, that you'll never have any friends, that you'll never run again, or even walk, and that you'll never be pretty."

Hot tears dampened Kayla's T-shirt. She ached for Allison. She knew the difficult road to recovery better than anyone.

"I j-just want to be like i-it was," Allison said, between sobs. "I d-don't want to go away. I w-won't see you anymore."

Kayla's eyes began to burn. She'd barely avoided crying that morning, when she was with Patrick. Apparently she wasn't going to be able to avoid tears much longer.

"I'm not going to forget you," she said fiercely. "I swear. I'll write you, and you can write me back."

"But I can't write," Allison moaned. "I can barely hold a pencil, and there's nowhere to put the p-paper." The additional problem unleashed more tears.

Kayla kissed her forehead. "You can dictate letters to me. Make your brother be the one who has to sit here and write everything down."

The crying slowed. "I don't think he'd want to do that."

"I think your parents might insist. Did your older brother used to tease you when you were younger?"

Allison nodded solemnly.

"Wouldn't this be a great way to pay him back?"

A smile tugged on the corner of the girl's mouth. "He broke a couple of my dolls, too."

"Well, then, you're going to be able to make him write a lot of letters."

"Maybe every day," Allison said, warming up to the possibility.

What Kayla didn't tell her was that Allison's brother was suffering from guilt. The uninjured siblings often felt left out and ignored. They wanted parental attention, but felt guilty for that, because they weren't the ones in the hospital. By spending time together, brother and sister would have the chance to get close to each other in a way that wouldn't have been possible without the accident. If things went well, that bond would last them a lifetime.

Kayla straightened. Rhonda moaned at Allison's distress and licked away the rest of her tears. The girl giggled.

"That tickles, Rhonda. But thank you for caring."

Kayla glanced at her watch. "Your mom's going to be here any minute, so I'm going to go out in the hall and wait for her. We've got a couple of things to talk about."

Allison wrinkled her nose. "You gonna tell her I cried?"

"Nope," Kayla said, then kissed her cheek. "That was just between you and me."

Kayla stepped into the hallway and saw that Allison's mother had already arrived. The tall, slender woman had passed her thick raven hair and blue eyes on to her daughter. In about four years, Allison was going to start breaking hearts.

Sheila Kay looked up from the magazine she was reading and smiled. "The nurse told me you were with Allison." She patted the vinyl sofa. "Have a seat and tell me what's going on."

Kayla settled next to her. "I heard she's being moved to another facility."

Sheila nodded, then named the place. "It comes highly

recommended. There are children there, and we want her to have a chance to make friends. I worry about her being so isolated. Plus, it's closer to home, so her father can visit more often.''

"I think it's a great idea." Kayla touched her arm. "Don't worry. No one judges you for wanting the best for your daughter."

"I know. It's just she's upset about the move. And she's not going to be able to see you anymore. That's going to be hard on her."

Just one more relationship she was leaving behind, Kayla thought grimly. "Even though I never discussed my travel plans with Allison, you and I have talked about them. I would have been leaving you in less than a month, anyway. I think it will be easier if she goes first. The new experiences will give her something to think about."

"I hadn't thought of it that way," Sheila said. "It makes sense. I keep thinking how hard this is for me, then I realize it must be so much worse for my little girl. I just want to hold her until she's better."

"She wants that, too. The time will go quickly. Then she'll be up and walking, and this will just be a bad dream." Kayla thought about the scars on her body, scars that Patrick had touched so tenderly. He'd made her feel perfect, as if those marks didn't matter. She sent up a quick prayer that Allison would find someone as wonderful. And that she would have the good sense to hang on to the guy.

"This is a lot to ask, but I was wondering…" Sheila's voice trailed off. Her gaze darted around the hallway before settling on Kayla's face. "About Rhonda. We'd like to adopt her for Allison. Is that possible?"

Kayla hugged the other woman. "Yes. I think it's a great idea."

"Really?" Sheila asked. "She doesn't belong to anyone?"

"No. Rhonda was abandoned. I've brought her here to be with Allison, and I'd planned to take her to visit the seniors, but I never got around to it. I think she already considers herself Allison's dog." Kayla straightened. "You want to take her home with you today?"

"That would be great. Oh my gosh! What do we feed her? Do we take her for walks? I haven't had a dog since I was Allison's age."

"It's easy," Kayla told her. "The most important thing is for Rhonda to be with people who really love her, and you guys have that one down. I'll give you written instructions for everything else."

Sheila sprang to her feet. "I have to tell Allison. She'll be so thrilled! Do you mind waiting for a couple of minutes?"

"Not at all."

Kayla watched the other woman enter Allison's room. She smiled to herself. At least part of her day had turned out exactly right.

Kayla opened the kennel door. Elizabeth stepped out and led the way to the grooming table.

"Good girl," Kayla said as the collie jumped into place.

Kayla collected brushes and combs, then turned on the radio. Soft country music filled the small room at the back of the clinic.

Elizabeth's long coat required frequent grooming, but Kayla didn't mind. She found the work relaxing, and after what she'd been through, she needed this. She knew giving Rhonda to Allison and her family had been the right decision. The dog deserved a great home, and Allison needed a friend. But Kayla had grown used to Rhonda's sweet face. She would miss her.

"Of course, I'm going to miss all of you when I'm gone," she muttered.

Elizabeth gave her an inquiring look, and Kayla stroked her silky ears. "Sorry, girl. Just moaning about nothing in particular. Ignore me."

There was a polite knock at the door. Kayla stuck out her tongue. There was only one person in the clinic who would bother knocking when she groomed a dog.

"Come in," she called, making a serious effort to keep the annoyance from her voice.

As expected, Melissa Taylor glided into the room. Despite the late hour—it was after six—the vet looked as if she'd just stepped out of her bathroom. Long auburn hair curled around her shoulders. Makeup accentuated large, well-shaped eyes. Kayla vaguely recalled showering that morning. She'd even used mascara. Nearly twelve hours later, her clothes were covered with hair, she smelled like dog, and any hint of beauty products had been erased by time, sweat and enthusiastic doggie kisses.

Either Melissa kept a stash of cosmetics and clothes in her car or she had a secret Kayla had yet to discover.

Melissa pointed to the collie. "Elizabeth, right? You take her to visit seniors?"

Kayla forced a smile. "Two correct answers."

Melissa smiled in return, exposing perfect teeth. Had she worn braces as a child? Kayla hoped so. The big ones, with rubber bands and a head brace. Of course, with her luck, Melissa had been born beautiful.

Melissa approached Elizabeth and let the dog sniff her hand. When she'd been accepted, she petted the collie.

Kayla didn't bother watching. Whatever personal reasons she might have for disliking Patrick's new vet, she couldn't fault the woman's treatment of the animals. She handled them well, knew how to calm them, and was a skilled surgeon. No wonder Patrick had hired her. The fact that her body was so incredible it looked airbrushed didn't have anything to do with it.

But it was still darned annoying.

"What can I do for you?" Kayla asked, when it became obvious that Melissa had something to discuss but was nervous about bringing it up. The tight knot in Kayla's stomach gave her a good idea about the subject matter. Oh, well. The day had been painful from the beginning.

"I have a question," Melissa said, not quite meeting her gaze. "Girl talk, really. But it's personal."

"Uh-huh."

"If that makes you uncomfortable, we don't have to discuss it."

Kayla leaned against the grooming table and folded her arms across her chest. Elizabeth sat down to wait patiently. "You want some information?" Kayla asked, even though she knew the answer. There was no point in playing stupid. Might as well get it over with. "I assume this is about Patrick."

"Well, yes." Melissa cleared her throat. "I know the two of you are friends."

"Good friends," Kayla put in before she could stop herself.

"Right. Good friends. And as his good friend, I thought you might know if he was involved right now. You know, dating someone important."

The only sign of Melissa's nervousness came from the way she tossed her hair over her shoulders. A subtle clue, but enough of one for Kayla to see that the other woman wasn't asking casually. Had she taken the job hoping to reach the point where she and Patrick would send out

Christmas cards signed "Dr. and Dr. Walcott wish you all the joyousness of the season?"

Six months ago, the thought of someone being that interested in Patrick would have thrilled her. She'd only wanted his happiness. Now, while she still wanted his happiness, she wasn't sure the word *thrilled* described her feelings about him dating someone else.

Melissa wanted to know if Patrick was dating someone important.

Kayla remembered the night they'd made love, the warmth of his arms around her, the passion they'd shared. She thought about being near him, with him. Then she remembered back just a few hours, to that morning, when they'd been at the construction site. Despite everything they talked about, despite their once having been lovers, he hadn't even hugged her.

She looked at the beautiful redhead. "No," she told Melissa. "Patrick isn't dating anyone important at all."

Chapter Twelve

"You don't have to do this," Patrick said as Kayla smoothed the wallpaper into place. "I could hire someone."

She stepped back to admire her work. The paper was perfectly straight; the subtle pattern, cream with tiny flecks of blue and tan, gave texture and depth to the wall.

"No way. I started this project, I'll finish it. Besides, with everything going on, you won't have time to hire anyone. If I don't finish this, five years from now your living room will still be in a state of shambles."

She smiled as she spoke, trying to act as though everything was all right between them. As though they were just good friends getting together to work on a project. Obviously, she was doing a great job, because he patted her on the back and went to grab them both a soda.

She watched him go, trying not to notice the way his shoulders filled out his shirt and his butt filled out his jeans. She'd always thought he had a nice body, but since becoming intimately familiar with the length and breadth of him, she found it difficult to focus on anything else.

Time slipped through her fingers like shiny marbles, and there was nothing she could do to hold it back. Her twenty-fifth birthday was in three days, her trip to Paris a week after that. She'd thought…or hoped…that she and Patrick would be able to reconnect. Especially after their talk a few days ago at the construction site.

But they hadn't. He treated her as he always had. As if she were a combination of best friend and kid sister.

Maybe she was at fault. After all, hadn't she been the one to change the rules? If she hadn't gone on that date with him, if they hadn't made love, everything would be okay.

Patrick returned with the drinks and the wrapped sandwich she hadn't been able to finish earlier. She settled on the floor and unwrapped the plastic. He sat next to her and opened a bag of chocolate cookies.

"I like it," he said, glancing up at the wall they'd already finished. "The pattern is better than that floral junk the previous owner had used."

"That's what you get for buying a house from a little old lady with a thing for flowers," Kayla teased, remembering the pink sinks in the bathrooms and the dusty-rose flooring in the kitchen. Patrick had replaced both the first month he lived there.

He motioned to the remaining blank space. "We're not going to finish it tonight."

"Probably not, but it won't be much longer. Now that the old stuff is off and the walls are prepared, it will go fast."

As he talked about buying new furniture, which she knew he would get around to doing in the next millennium, bits of their past washed over her. Time they'd spent together, things they'd done. Since graduating from college, she'd spent more time with him than with anyone else. She knew her sisters better, but they lived in other parts of the state.

So many memories, so much caring and respect. Had it all been ruined by a single night of passion? She didn't want to think so. She couldn't regret being in his arms. For as long as she lived, she would carry with her the recollection of that night. No one else could have made her first time more special, more right. Having to do it all over again, she wouldn't want to do anything differently. Yet if the price of passion was their special friendship, would she have a choice?

Patrick picked up his soda and motioned to the wall. "I should have hired you to decorate the research facility."

"No thanks. I'm strictly an amateur. Besides, I don't think the scientists are going to notice wallpaper and paintings. They'll be too caught up in what they're doing."

Instead of smiling, he looked away. "I hope so."

She shifted toward him. "What does that mean?"

He shrugged. "Nothing, really. I guess I'm a little nervous about the whole thing."

"But this is what you've always wanted."

"I know." He stared at her. "In my head, I can see it all happening. I have these great plans for continuing research I started before. If we're lucky, we'll make progress and do some good."

"You will," she said, and placed her hand on his arm. "You're the best, Patrick. You have vision, and the guts to go after what you want."

"Turning vision into reality isn't guaranteed."

"I believe in you."

He covered her hand with his own. "Thanks. That means a lot. You don't give your support lightly."

"You'll always have my support. And anything else you need."

She made the comment lightly, but he didn't seem to catch the humor. To make matters worse, he pulled his arm toward his side, dropping her hand to the floor.

"I have something for you," he said, leaning to his left as he pulled something out of his right rear pocket.

She wasn't fooled by the casual action. Patrick had deliberately physically disconnected from her. A band tightened around her chest. What had happened to them? Was it over forever?

"Here." He handed her a piece of paper.

She opened it and found a list of names and cities. Next to each was a phone number. "I don't understand."

"These are a few people I know over in France." He pointed to the top two names. "Luc and Michael both live in Paris. I called them and told them you were a friend of mine and that you would be visiting. If you need anything, they'll be happy to help you. Luc especially. Watch out for him. He's a practiced heartbreaker. Not exactly in the same league as a prince, but the family owns a château somewhere in the South of France. Michael's married. I've never met his wife, but she's supposed to be nice."

Kayla frowned. "I'm still confused. How do you know these people?"

"I've met them at the various symposiums I've been to. I also have a couple of friends in England and Italy. If you decide to go there, let me know, and I'll put you in touch with them."

Light brown hair fell over his forehead. His white T-shirt enhanced his tan and brought out his blue eyes.

She'd stared at his face thousands of times. She could draw it from memory.

And yet she didn't know him.

Oh, she knew facts about his life, but she didn't really know *him*. Patrick traveled to different symposiums and lectures several times a year. He often talked about the people he'd met there. People from other countries. She knew he kept in touch with several of them through the Internet and occasional phone calls.

Still, the list of names shocked her. Patrick, whose difficult childhood had made him want to put down roots, had seen worlds she'd only dreamed about. He'd visited places, talked with strangers, made friends and invited them into his life.

"Thanks," she said, setting her untouched sandwich on the floor, folding the paper and tucking it into her shirt pocket. "I'm sure I'll be fine, but it's nice to know there's someone I can contact if I need something."

"You'll have a great time," he said, and ate another cookie.

"It's going to be weird being away from everyone."

"You won't miss anybody. There's all of Paris to see, and besides, you'll be too busy with your princes."

"Yeah." Princes. That wasn't likely to happen. And she didn't care. Frankly, Luc's château or Prince Albert's fortune weren't as appealing as she would have thought. She was perfectly comfortable right here in Patrick's living room.

"You're going to be busy, too," she said, knowing she was about to make the situation worse, but not able to help herself.

"With the research facility."

"And with your new employee."

He raised his eyebrows.

"Melissa is attracted to you," she said, her voice teasing. Maybe she should consider a career on the stage. She was able to sound completely normal, as if the situation didn't bother her in the least. Yet the pain inside was so bad, she half expected to faint.

Patrick shrugged off her declaration. "Not interested."

"But she's a redhead. Aren't they your favorite?"

He stared at her. "I told you they weren't. Or don't you remember?"

His serious expression made her want to cry. Of course she remembered. She remembered everything about that night. What they'd talked about, how they'd danced together, the kiss on the dock outside the restaurant.

"I—" She didn't know what to say.

Patrick finished his soda and set the empty can on the floor.

Silence filled the room. The air thickened with tension. Kayla wanted to run away, but she didn't have the strength to move. They both remembered. In the stillness, memories crowded around them.

She longed for him, to be in his arms again. Her body heated. Tonight, they could be together. Tonight, they could relive the perfection and make it right between them. Here, in this house, where they'd spent their best moments together.

She reached her hand toward him. "Patrick."

Either he didn't notice, or he didn't care. He stood up and placed his hands on his hips. "We should get back to work."

Somehow she stumbled to her feet and reached for the roll of wallpaper. Only when she attempted to focus on the subtle pattern and couldn't did she realize her eyes had filled with tears.

As she blinked them away, she tried to figure out what

was wrong. So Patrick didn't remember the past the same way she did. It wasn't the end of the world. It wasn't as if she were in love with him.

Love. The word hovered in her mind. Elissa claimed she, Kayla, was already in love with Patrick. Kayla wasn't so sure. All she knew of romantic love was what she'd seen, read and been told. Mrs. Beecham had sworn love was a tornado that swept away everything in its path. Patrick said tornadoes destroyed. Who was right?

But if she didn't love him, why did she hurt so much?

"Do you want me to measure for the next piece?" he asked.

She looked at him, then at the wall. "No," she said. "I don't think I can do this anymore."

She wasn't talking about the wallpaper, but he didn't get that.

"I can finish it up myself," he told her. "No problem."

"You don't have to. I can help. Just not tonight." She walked to the door. "I—"

He followed her. "You look tired, Kayla. Get some sleep."

Even as she told herself she was making a mistake, she turned and hugged him. She pressed her body tightly against his, letting all her feelings flow through her into him. Surely he would understand and respond. He had to.

As her arms held him close and her hands stroked his back, she registered that he didn't return the embrace. Shock immobilized her. It wasn't until he gently put her away from him that she was able to move.

She dashed out the door and along the driveway. Tears streamed down her face. Even as she raced up the stairs to her apartment, she listened for a voice that didn't speak. Despite her fervent prayers, he never once called for her to come back.

* * *

Kayla finished pouring the champagne and glanced at her sister. Fallon held the phone to her ear and listened.

"Yes," she said. "Okay, that's great. I'll tell them. We really appreciate everything. Uh-huh. Oh, thanks. Yes, I'll pass along your best wishes." She hung up and grinned. "That's it. The money is released and has already been wired to our banks. It's done!"

"Finally," Kayla said, feeling her mood lighten for the first time in days. She passed out the fluted glasses.

Elissa took hers. "What else did Mr. Applegate want? He kept you for a long time."

Fallon sank back into the sofa and kicked off her loafers. "The usual. If we have any questions, he will be happy to help us personally. Oh, and birthday felicitations to all of us."

"*Felicitations?* There's a word you don't hear often enough." Kayla raised her glass. "Happy birthday."

Her sisters echoed her toast and they all tasted the champagne.

Fallon wrinkled her nose. "While it's nice..." she said, her voice trailing off.

Elissa grinned. "I was thinking the same thing."

"Me, too." Kayla took another sip. "For the first time in our lives, we splurged and spent two hundred dollars on a bottle of champagne. And we all like the twelve-dollar stuff better."

Laughter filled the room. Kayla stared at her sisters, then at the silly decorations on the walls and ceilings. Balloons floated everywhere. She'd hung crepe paper and banners. Party favors more suitable for a six-year-old's birthday littered the coffee table.

She felt as if she were seeing light for the first time in days. She'd been walking around in a fog of pain and confusion. Even though she hadn't come to terms with whatever was happening between Patrick and herself, even though her reaction and her feelings still confused her, she was done with the suffering. Her sisters were with her for a week, until she left for Paris. She was determined to enjoy their time together.

"Are we going to rent romantic movies and sob?" Fallon asked.

"Of course." Elissa glanced at Kayla. "Aren't we?"

"Sure. It's a tradition. I have tons of popcorn and soda. I've collected take-out menus from every restaurant within ten miles. Wednesday there's a great sale at our favorite department store."

"Heaven." Elissa sat on the floor by the sofa. Her long, flowing skirt covered her feet. With her ruffled blouse and her hair piled on top of her head, she looked like a nine-teenth-century woman come to life. "Maybe I'll buy a few things."

"Jeans," Kayla said. "You don't own any."

"I do so. I have at least one pair." Elissa frowned. "Somewhere."

Fallon brushed her tailored trousers. "Why does it have to be jeans? Just regular long pants would be nice."

"Maybe *you* should buy something with ruffles," Kayla teased.

Fallon rolled her eyes. "I'll do that the day you wear a business suit."

Kayla stretched out on the love seat and propped her feet up on the armrest. "Remember those hideous matching dresses Mom put us in all through elementary school?"

"All frilly skirts and puffy sleeves." Fallon shuddered.

"In pink and peach and cream," Kayla added.

Elissa stared at them both. "They weren't so bad."

Kayla leaned down and grabbed some confetti from the floor, then tossed it at her sister. "Bite your tongue."

Elissa ignored her. "I'm glad we didn't go away to celebrate our birthday."

"Me, too," Fallon said. "What if the money hadn't been released? We would have been stuck with an expensive vacation and no way to pay for it."

"Practical as ever," Kayla told her. "But the money has come through, so there's no excuse for backing out of our Christmas plans."

"I'll be there." Fallon made an X over her heart. "The Caribbean over the holidays. Sounds heavenly."

"I want to go, too," Elissa said. She glanced at Kayla. "Are you still going to Africa in the spring?"

Kayla sipped her champagne. "I don't think so. My travel agent sent me the shot list."

"Did you faint?" Fallon asked.

"Almost. So I was thinking about something a little safer. Maybe a cruise."

"That's what I want to do." Fallon leaned forward and rested her elbows on her knees. "I've been thinking about the money. I'm going to give some of it to charity, and I'm going to put some of it away for the future. The rest is for me. I toyed with the idea of getting a new car, but I think I'd rather do a little traveling."

"You could come to Paris with me," Kayla said, thinking the trip would be better with one of her sisters along.

"I can't. Classes start in late August, and I'm committed to that until mid-December. Then I'll be off for a year. Maybe we can do something in spring."

"That would be nice." Spring seemed so far away. Who knew what would have happened by then? Right now, even her trip to Paris felt surreal. She suspected that by the time she got back, everything would have changed.

What would happen then? Would she pick up the pieces of her life? Was that even going to be an option? No doubt Melissa would succeed in her quest for Patrick's attention.

Don't think about it, she told herself. Not today. She would mourn Patrick later.

"I'm going to cut the cake," Fallon said. She put her champagne on the coffee table and walked to the kitchen. "What kind is it?"

"What do you think?" Kayla asked.

"Double chocolate with fudge filling and icing?" There was a hopeful note in her voice.

"What else?" Kayla glanced at Elissa. "You're being awfully quiet."

Elissa shrugged. "Just thinking."

"About the trust fund?"

Her sister hesitated, then nodded. "I know you two think I'm crazy, but I just can't help it. All that money scares me."

Fallon stuck her head around the kitchen wall. "What are you talking about? Speak up, I can't hear."

"Elissa's still scared of the money," Kayla called.

Fallon stepped into the living room and stared down at Elissa. "Get a financial planner, put it in another trust fund, buy yourself a dog, but please promise me you won't write a check and just give it all away. This is yours, Elissa, as much as it's mine or Kayla's. We earned this money working on that damn show, week after week." She tossed her head, sending blond curls tumbling down her back. "Make plans for the future."

Elissa grimaced. "I promise I won't write a check and give it away all at once."

"And that you won't give all of it away in pieces," Fallon said.

"Agreed. I'll keep some for a rainy day."

Kayla leaned over and patted Elissa's shoulder. "Don't be so afraid of it," she said. "It's just paper, or numbers on a bank statement."

Elissa nodded, but Kayla knew she was more interested in not upsetting the happy mood than in agreeing. Ever since they starred on "The Sally McGuire Show," Elissa had believed money was the root of the family's problems. In her mind, fighting over the girls' earnings had caused their parents' divorce. Their father had lived an extravagant life-style he couldn't afford. In the end, it had killed him, when he lost control of his expensive sports car and plunged into a canyon.

"I miss him, too," Kayla said softly.

Elissa gave her a grateful look. "I've been thinking about him a lot."

Fallon walked to the love seat and nudged Kayla's legs out of the way. "Me, too," she said, sinking onto the cushion. "It's tough now, and around the holidays."

For a second, nobody said anything. Then Elissa spoke. "She didn't call."

It was a statement, rather than a question. The "she" was their mother.

Kayla smiled ruefully. "It's pilot season, girls. What did you expect?"

"Pilot season," Fallon said, in the same tone Kayla would expect her to use to announce she had lice.

"I remember those days," Elissa said. "The waiting, the auditions."

Pilot season. "I don't want to remember," Kayla said. "It was awful."

Late spring and early summer meant the networks were casting their new fall television shows. Hopeful children came in from all over the country. The yearly pilgrimage had been more nightmarish for the triplets, because when it wasn't pilot season, their mother took them on movie and commercial auditions. Free afternoons were quickly filled with singing and dance lessons, not to mention the occasional acting class. If they'd been interested in entertainment as a career, they might have enjoyed the processes, but none of the sisters had done anything but endure.

"How old are the twins?" Fallon asked.

"Six," Kayla answered. "Plus Clarice is nearly eight, Andy is ten." Three half sisters and a half brother the triplets had never met.

"Mom sure didn't waste any time," Elissa said. "She was remarried and pregnant within a year of the divorce." She sighed. "I hope those kids enjoy the business more than we did."

Their mother had been furious when the girls refused to continue on television. She'd been determined to "make it" with a new set of children. Kayla hoped she was successful. It must be difficult to spend one's whole life chasing an impossible dream.

"Enough," Elissa said, and stood up. "We're here to celebrate, not dwell on the past. We're young, we're healthy and attractive, and now we're rich." She grinned. "Sort of."

"Comfortably well-off," Fallon said.

Kayla motioned to the kitchen. "I need chocolate cake or I'm going to die."

"Coming right up." As Elissa walked in that direction, there was a knock on the door. She unfastened the lock and pulled the door open. "Patrick. This is nice." She looked over her shoulder. "Patrick's here, and he has gifts. I think we should let him in."

Kayla scrambled to her feet, brushing at the front of her jeans and tugging on her T-shirt. She hadn't thought they would have company today, so she hadn't bothered with makeup or fixing her hair.

"By all means," Fallon said, also standing. "I've wanted to meet Kayla's friend for a long time."

Patrick grinned engagingly at the women. Kayla stared at him, hoping their eyes would meet, but he seemed to pass over her.

"I don't want to intrude," he said. "I have a few things for the birthday celebration, then I'll leave you ladies alone."

"Don't even think you're intruding," Elissa said, taking his arm and pulling him into the apartment. "We'd love the company. We're going to be together for a week, so there's plenty of time to catch up." She touched the roses he held in his arms. "Do you need some help with these?"

"Absolutely." He shifted them in his arms, then held out a dozen paper-wrapped peach roses. "Happy birthday."

Elissa clapped her hands together. "You shouldn't have, but I won't refuse them." She took the roses and inhaled their fragrance. "What a sweetie. Thank you." She raised on tiptoe and kissed his cheek.

Fallon was next. "We haven't been introduced," he said, handing her a dozen red roses. "I'm Patrick Walcott."

Fallon also kissed his cheek. "I like your style," she said, smiling. She glanced at Kayla and winked. "Okay, now I get it. You've kept him hidden away all these years because you knew we'd try to steal him from you."

Patrick grinned. "I'm yours for the taking."

Blond eyebrows arched. "That's not what I heard."

Kayla didn't want to think about how much Elissa had told Fallon. The sisters didn't have a lot of secrets between them. It wasn't that she minded them knowing, it was just that things were so unsettled between Patrick and herself right now. She didn't want either of them to be embarrassed.

Patrick stepped in front of her and held out the last dozen roses. They were exceptional, with creamy petals touched with peach at the top. Their scent enveloped her. Yet, for all their beauty, she couldn't stop looking at him.

He wore a suit and tie. She'd known he had a meeting with several of the scientists that morning. No doubt he had appointments at the clinic, too. She hadn't expected to see him, especially after how they'd parted last week. But she was glad he'd made the time to stop by.

"Thank you," she said quietly. "You're very thoughtful to remember all of us."

"You three are the only triplets I'm ever likely to know. Of course I want to help you celebrate such an important birthday." He turned to Elissa. "Did the money come through?"

She nodded.

He patted Kayla's shoulder. "So you're off to Paris. Good for you." He moved away before she could follow her sisters' lead and kiss him.

Patrick sat on the sofa. The roses were safely put away in vases and pitchers. Elissa brought him cake, Fallon showed him what they were drinking and offered champagne.

"I'd love a glass." He pointed to the bottle he'd brought with him. "I guess this is a pitiful offering."

Fallon glanced at their expensive champagne, then reached down and grabbed his. "To be honest, we like this stuff much better. I guess we don't really have millionaire tastes."

"Yet," he said.

Fallon leaned close. "None of us has a million dollars.

Does that upset your plans to marry Kayla for her money?"

"Absolutely. I'm crushed."

They shared a smile.

Patrick had been prepared for the three women to look exactly alike, but the reality was more disconcerting than he'd imagined. Even without the difference in clothing, he would have been able to pick out Kayla. He was so familiar with her face and the way she moved that he could spot her without effort. Elissa and Fallon were more difficult. Had they been wearing the same clothes, he suspected, he would have easily confused them.

He leaned back against the sofa. Kayla sat on the love seat, as far away from him as possible. He didn't blame her.

Even after Fallon had poured his champagne and Elissa had passed out cake to everyone, Kayla didn't join in the conversation. She sat quietly observing, occasionally giving him questioning looks. His actions over the past couple of weeks had confused her, and she wanted to know what was going on.

He wanted to tell her the truth. He wanted her to know that he had to avoid her, for both their sakes. If they got emotionally involved now, it would make her leaving that much more difficult. Better to keep apart, to at least pretend to be friends.

But he couldn't speak the words. He knew in his heart he would be too tempted to say it all. To tell her that it was too late for him. He already *was* emotionally involved. Without wanting to, he'd fallen in love with her.

What would happen if she knew the truth? Would she smile pityingly at him? Would she get uncomfortable and awkward? Would she try to respond in kind, only to have the lie lodge in her throat? Would she feel guilty?

He didn't want any of that. Better that she be angry for a while. When she was over it, and when his pain of loving but not having had subsided to a manageable ache, they could go on as before. Friends.

At least if they stayed friends, he would never lose her completely.

Fallon and Elissa kept him entertained with stories from their childhood. In many of them, Kayla was the star. She didn't seem to mind the teasing, laughing with her sisters, but she still didn't say much.

He found it difficult to pay attention to what was being said. He just wanted to sit there and stare at Kayla, memorizing everything about her, absorbing her so he wouldn't be so lonely when she was gone.

After about a half hour, he stood up. "I hate to eat and run, but I've got appointments at the clinic in about forty minutes."

Fallon and Elissa walked him to the door. "It's been wonderful," Elissa said. "We're here for the whole week. It's an extended slumber party. So come by again. We'd love to see you."

Fallon gave him a quick hug. "She's right. We're planning a session of truth or dare tomorrow, and I'm sure you don't want to miss that."

He could imagine a few dares he would like to make, but didn't think that was what Fallon had in mind.

He waited for a second, but Kayla didn't join them. No doubt she wanted to avoid another rebuff.

"Kayla, would you mind seeing me out?" he asked.

She looked startled, then rose to her feet. Elissa and Fallon stepped back to give her room, then retreated to the kitchen. He moved out onto the porch, and she followed him.

The late-afternoon sun was drifting toward the western

horizon. When she joined him on the small wooden porch, he pulled the front door shut behind her and leaned against the railing.

There wasn't much room, so she was forced to stand close to him. He watched emotions chase across her face. Apprehension, determination and a few others he couldn't identify.

"I want the chance to say happy-birthday in private," he told her.

"Great. Thanks." She reached for the door handle.

He wrapped his fingers around her wrist to stop her. "Don't go in yet. There's something else."

Her gaze lifted to his. The wariness there made him want to confess all and beg her forgiveness. But he couldn't do that. It wasn't fair to either of them. Or was he just taking the coward's way out?

He released her, reached into his jacket pocket and pulled out a gift. The box was nearly square, although not as tall as it was wide. A pale silver ribbon crisscrossed over foil paper.

"You already gave me roses," she said, not taking the present.

"This is special." Like you. But he didn't say it.

She took it and tugged off the wrapping. Inside was a gray jeweler's box. She lifted the cover and gasped. The wrapping paper and ribbon fell from her fingers, and she nearly dropped the box. As she caught it, she pulled out a bangle bracelet—an oval of gold with inset square-cut diamonds.

She turned the bracelet over in her hands, staring at it. "I can't accept this," she whispered. "It's too lovely."

"I want you to have it. Something to remember me by."

Before she could object, he took the bangle and opened the clasp. He slid the piece over her hand and settled it around her wrist. When the clasp closed, the bracelet fit perfectly.

Before he could stop himself, he cupped her cheek. "That's the deal, kid. As long as you wear this, you're not allowed to forget me."

"I could never do that. You're a part of me."

She raised her head. His gaze locked on her mouth. He could think of nothing but kissing her, tasting her, holding her close.

He set the box on the railing and reached for her. She came willingly, choking out a sob that tore at his heart. They hugged each other close, gripping tightly, as if they feared being torn apart.

"Kayla, I've missed you," he whispered into her hair.

"I've been right here."

"For now."

She started to step back to look at him, but he didn't release her. He didn't want her to see his face and know what he was thinking.

"What does that mean?" she asked.

Instead of answering, he pressed his mouth to hers.

Their lips touched gently, brushing against each other. Neither tried to deepen the kiss. Passion burned hot, yet this chaste contact was enough. He knew that if he did more, he would have to be with her. Not just for tonight, but for always.

"Patrick." The word whispered against his cheek.

He dropped his hands to his sides and turned to the stairs.

"Stay," she said. "You'd be welcome. My sisters are dying to get to know you."

"I have to get to work."

"Then come back after the clinic closes. We'll still be here."

He shook his head. She didn't know what she was asking. "I can't."

"Why?"

He climbed halfway down the flight, then glanced back at her. Her golden curls tumbled over her shoulders. Her old jeans and T-shirt outlined her body, and the vision tempted him. *She* tempted him. The sun dipped lower, catching a finger of light on one of the diamonds in her bracelet.

She clutched the railing. "Why can't you come back?"

He had no strength to lie. "Because it hurts too much."

Chapter Thirteen

Someone was pounding on the front door. Patrick glanced at the VCR clock and saw it was barely past seven in the morning. As he tossed the newspaper on the sofa, he stood up and headed for the door.

Kayla, he thought with one part anticipation, two parts dread. If she'd come looking for an explanation of what he'd told her yesterday, she wasn't going to get one. If she'd come to tempt him, he was weak enough not to resist.

But when he opened the door, the tall, golden-blond, green-eyed beauty on his porch wasn't Kayla.

"I know it's early," Elissa said, and shrugged. "Kayla mentioned you wouldn't be leaving for the clinic until eight-thirty. I was going to wait for another hour before I bothered you, but when I saw you come out and get the paper, I knew you were up."

"Come in," he said, stepping back and motioning her

inside. What was she doing here? Something about the set of her shoulders and the determination in her gaze told him this wasn't just a social call.

"I've made coffee," he told her.

She shook her head. "I've had some, thanks."

As she sat on the sofa, he took in her neat braid and the pale blue sundress that fell nearly to her ankles. He rubbed the stubble on his jawline and glanced down at his old shorts and torn T-shirt. "I wasn't expecting company."

"I know. Sorry."

He pushed the loose newspaper onto the floor and settled at the opposite end of the couch. "Why do I think I'd feel better if you actually looked sorry?"

She gave him a faint smile that faded quickly. "You want to know why I'm here."

"That's a start." Although he had a fair idea. He and Elissa only had one thing in common.

"It's about Kayla," she said.

"Okay. What about Kayla?"

Elissa angled toward him. She pressed her knees tightly together and rested her hands on her lap. "You're breaking her heart."

He'd expected a lot of accusations, but not that one. If anyone's heart was on the line in this situation, it was his. "You're exaggerating," he said. "Kayla may be a little confused by some of my actions—"

She cut in before he could finish. "Confused? You gave her a beautiful birthday present, yet instead of being happy she spent the rest of the day fighting off tears. When I asked her why, she didn't want to say. Finally she admitted you were ignoring her."

"I haven't been ignoring her. I came by yesterday."

"That's not what she meant, and you know it." Elissa's eyes darkened to the color of emeralds. Her shoulders straightened, as if she were preparing to fight to protect those she cared about. "Kayla was a virgin when you made love. I can't believe how you're treating her. I thought you were a decent guy, but obviously I was wrong."

Her words caught him off guard, like an unexpected slap. The sting lingered as he wrestled with conflicting emotions. He knew he'd been distant with Kayla, but his intentions were honorable. At least that was what he told himself.

Elissa sighed. "By the look on your face, my comments aren't that far from the truth. And before you ask, the answer is no. Kayla didn't discuss the details of what happened that night. It was easy to figure out you two had been intimate. As for the other thing—" She waved her hand in the air.

Patrick assumed "the other thing" meant Kayla's virginity.

"I was guessing about her innocence," Elissa continued, confirming his thoughts. "The look on your face tells me I was right."

"Why did you think she was innocent?"

"Because she's always been a little wary of romantic relationships. She holds men at arm's length. Not in an obvious way. She's friendly and spends a lot of time with them, but doesn't really allow them to get close. At least not physically. I've never been able to figure out why. I think some of it has to do with her accident. She realizes, more than most, how quickly life can change. Maybe she wants to avoid being vulnerable. And then she'd got that silly idea about love being a tornado. She wants to be swept away."

He nodded. Elissa was right. "There's also the scars."

Delicate eyebrows drew together. "What?"

"The scars from the accident. She feels self-conscious about them."

"She still has scars?"

"On her stomach and chest. The tops of her thighs, too. They're faint, but there."

Elissa relaxed slightly, leaning against the back of the sofa. "I never knew. I saw them when we were still kids, but I assumed they'd faded away. Scars. Fallon and I should have thought about that. No wonder she felt self-conscious about going to the beach. She always wore a one-piece bathing suit and shorts. I figured she was shy."

She looked at him. "As triplets, you'd think we'd be better at guessing her secrets."

"The accident changed everything."

"I know. When Kayla was injured for a year, it's almost like the three of us disconnected a little. I regret that." Her mouth twisted. "So she hasn't shown the scars to us, but she let you see them."

And touch them and kiss them, he thought, remembering how lovely she'd been. Those faint white lines on her skin had simply made her unique. They were as much a part of her as her smile, or the way she spoke his name. He treasured her trust.

"Do you care about her?" Elissa asked.

Easy question, difficult choice of answers. He could take the cheater's way out and say of course he did—they were friends. He could make up some story about people having different needs at different times in their lives. Or he could tell her the truth.

He chose the latter. "I love her."

Elissa's eyes widened. "I didn't expect that."

"Neither did I. But now I do, and I can't make those feelings disappear."

"I don't understand," she said. "If you love her, why

are you ignoring her? She said she tried to hug you a couple of times, but you didn't respond. I thought you'd decided being lovers had been a mistake. Obviously that's not the reason.''

He shook his head. "There's no way I can regret what happened between us that night. I'll keep those memories forever. But I can't risk making the situation worse. Kayla has already decided what she wants, and it's not me. If I told her how I felt, she would be confused. Because I love her, I want to make it easy for her to walk away.''

She leaned forward and touched his knee. "I can't decide if you're the most noble man I've ever met, or a fool. I want to say you're a fool. I want to make you tell her the truth, but in this situation, I think you're making the right choice.''

He hadn't expected validation. Instead of making him feel justified, her words left him with the sensation of being trapped in an underground prison. There was no light, no relief, no chance of escape.

"Life is about timing,'' she said. "This is Kayla's time to live her dreams. Maybe, when she's met her prince, she'll realize there's someone just as wonderful waiting at home.''

Or maybe she won't, he thought, swallowing hard. Either way, as long as Kayla was happy, he would survive.

She gave him a sad smile. "I fell in love once. To someone I'd known for a long time. When the three of us were still doing 'The Sally McGuire Show,' we 'adopted' an orphanage, visiting the children there, writing letters, sending gifts, that sort of thing. One boy, Cole, used to talk to me. He was five years older than me and, at eleven, I was thrilled a sixteen-year-old boy would even notice me. We started writing to each other and became friends.''

She kept her gaze fixed on him, but he sensed she'd left

the room and was instead caught up in the past. "We started dating when I was seventeen. For me, it was love at first sight. The second I saw him standing on the doorstep, smiling at me, I knew he was the one. But he was older and concerned, so he took it very slowly. We were married when I was twenty."

"It didn't work out?" he asked.

"No." She shook her head. "I accept most of the blame. I was away from home, I missed my sisters and my friends. I—"

She gave him a rueful smile. "Sorry. I'm sure you're not interested in the details. The point is, it wasn't our time. We both loved each other, but love turned out not to be enough."

"It's not time for Kayla and me, either," he said. And even if it was, he didn't know if she loved him. She cared. Obviously. But caring wasn't love. He suspected her feelings were a result of their physical intimacy and not because she'd discovered a new emotional depth to their relationship. In time, she would see that and let the memories of their night together fade until they blurred, like words from an old newspaper.

"I agree it doesn't appear to be your time, but neither of us can know for sure. A minute ago, I told you keeping your feelings from Kayla was right. Now I'm not so sure. If you let her go without telling her you love her, you're asking her to make a decision without all the facts. Telling her you love her isn't the same as asking her to stay."

She had a point. "I wouldn't want to pressure her."

"Are you concerned about pressure or getting rejected?"

"Both."

"At least you're honest."

"It's easy to tell you the truth. There's no risk."

She smiled at him. "There's a little one. I could tell Kayla everything we've talked about."

"You won't."

"Thanks for trusting me."

He touched her shoulder. "You have one very special sister. I doubt you're all that different from her."

"If you trust me to keep your secrets, can't you trust me enough to take my advice? At least think about telling her your feelings before she leaves."

He didn't want to think about Kayla leaving at all, let alone what he would say to her when the moment came.

"Please?" Elissa asked. "For Kayla's sake?"

For Kayla's sake, he would do anything. "I'll consider it," he promised.

"And I'll write you every day," Allison said, sniffing.

Kayla tried to smile. "That's a big commitment. How about every week, instead?"

"Okay." The little girl wiped away her tears. "My mom said you're leaving, too. On vacation. Are you gonna send me postcards from Paris?"

"Of course. Lots of them."

Allison was leaving for her new rehabilitation facility later that afternoon. Kayla had wanted to stop by to say goodbye.

"Is it pretty there?" Allison asked.

"Very pretty. There are lots of old buildings and museums, little cafés and wonderful stores."

"Oh. I guess it's nice, but I'd rather stay here and play with the dogs. Won't you miss them?"

"Very much. But I'll be back."

"Then you're gonna start visiting kids again?"

That part of her future hadn't been decided. Kayla wasn't sure what would happen when she came back. She hadn't yet decided how long she would be gone. After Paris, there was the triplets' Christmas plans for the Caribbean. In the spring—she wasn't sure. As much as she might want her old job back, she doubted Patrick would offer it to her. Too much had changed; they would never go back to the way things had been just a few months ago.

"I'll never visit a kid as special as you are," Kayla said, and hugged Allison. Her eyes began to burn. She'd wanted to avoid crying, but that seemed unlikely. Leaving was a lot harder than she'd imagined.

"When I grow up, I'm going to be just like you," Allison said, her voice muffled.

"No, honey. You're going to be your own person, and that's the way it's supposed to be."

Allison nodded. "I want to be a doctor who takes care of kids like me."

"You'll be a great doctor."

A nurse stepped into the room. "I hate to interrupt, but we have to get her ready to travel."

"I understand." Kayla kissed Allison's cheek, then straightened. "I'll write."

"Me, too."

"Be good to Rhonda."

"I promise I'll love her forever." Allison's gaze was so intense, and she spoke so earnestly, Kayla had no trouble believing her.

"I know you will. Bye." She waved, then walked out of the room.

Once in the hallway, she leaned against the wall and squeezed her eyes shut. The action didn't help. Tears flowed down her cheeks faster than she could brush them away. She heard footsteps.

"Give me a second," she said, her voice thick with emotion.

"I'm in no rush."

She couldn't judge Patrick's feelings from his voice. Not that looking at him would help at all. Lately, he'd become a stranger.

She gulped back a sob and struggled for control. "Did you see Allison's mother?"

"Yes. Rhonda is doing fine and enjoying all the attention. They have an appointment to bring her into the clinic at the end of the month, just to make sure she's adjusting. But I don't think there's going to be a problem."

She sniffed and wiped her face again. "I'm sure you're right. A family is just what she needs."

The tears had stopped, and she risked opening her eyes. Patrick stood a couple of feet away, his attention focusing on the nurse's station at the far end of the corridor. She didn't know if he was being polite and giving her privacy, or if he just didn't care.

She studied his face, the shape of his head, his body. She'd been so sure she knew everything about him. What had changed?

"Stay."

"I can't."

"Why?"

"Because it hurts too much."

Their brief conversation played over and over in her head, as it had ever since her birthday, last Monday. Why had he said that to her? What hurt? Being with her? Being around her? Had she done something horrible? Had he grown to hate her that much?

He glanced at her. "Feeling better?"

She nodded.

"Then let's go," he said lightly.

He started down the corridor, but she didn't move. He retreated to her side. "What's wrong?"

She stared into his blue eyes and wondered what he was thinking. "Does any of this matter?" she asked.

"What are you talking about?"

"Me. Us. You're a stranger. I don't know how or why, but you've gone away."

Impatience pulled his mouth straight. "You're exaggerating. You're the one going away. I'm simply trying to make that easier for both of us."

"By ignoring me?"

He crossed his arms over his chest. "I'm not ignoring you, Kayla. I'm here, aren't I?"

She wanted to step toward him, to hug him close and be hugged in return. But despite the kiss they'd shared on her birthday, she remained wary. He'd rejected her before. She wasn't sure she could handle his coldness again.

"Here but not here," she said, and dropped her gaze to the floor. "This is hard for me, Patrick. It hurts." She wasn't sure if she was describing missing him, or leaving. It didn't matter—both were painful. "Don't you care anymore?"

"Of course I care." *I love you.*

She didn't actually hear the words, but for a moment they seemed to echo in the room. Something shifted in her heart. Something frightened and hibernating burst into life. It was as if she were seeing colors for the first time.

Paris, her dreams, a prince, her job, his research facility, their night together, the details and complications, the wonder, all tumbled together. They would work it out. Why not? He loved her. He—

He reached forward and ruffled her bangs. "We've been a part of each other's lives for years. You're the best friend I have, Kayla. I'm willing to admit I've been a little withdrawn, but that's because I'm going to miss you when you're gone. Maybe it's selfish, but it's easier for me if I pull back early.'' He gave her a crooked smile. ''Besides, compared to European royalty, I'm going to look pretty tame, right? I figure three days after hitting Paris you'll be kicking yourself for not visiting sooner. You're going to forget all about me.''

Pain enveloped her like a thick, wet blanket. His words came from a long way off, filtered almost, the sound muffled. But she heard every one of them. The meaning was clear.

He didn't love her. Not romantically. It wasn't supposed to matter, but it did.

''You ready to head back to the clinic?'' he asked.

She nodded, not sure she trusted her voice. If she spoke, she might give something away. She couldn't have said what that ''something'' was; she only knew she must keep it from Patrick.

Poor Kayla, always living in a fantasy world. Poor Kayla, trapped in a hospital bed while other children could run and play. Poor Kayla, with no real career, no boyfriend, no plans for the future except to go to Paris and marry a prince.

Poor Kayla, who got crazy for a moment and thought her best friend might love her. She tried to laugh at the notion, but all that came out was a weak squeak. If he noticed, he didn't say anything.

Patrick didn't love her, and she didn't love him. Why would she? They'd had a great night together, nothing more. Passion had grown slowly between them. It hadn't been like a tornado, so it wasn't real.

Get over it, she told herself. Paris awaits.

The expensive stuff went down easy, Patrick thought as he held the bottle of Chivas Regal up to the light. He wasn't exactly drunk. As long as he didn't try to get up and walk, he would be fine.

He turned his head and looked at the photograph lying on the coffee table in his living room. The picture of his father had been taken twenty years ago. A thin, preoccupied man standing in front of an anemic Christmas tree. Tiny lights glowed in an assortment of colors, making the man's skin pasty by comparison.

"You weren't having a good time then, were you, Dad?" Patrick asked aloud. "You hated the holidays. Hell, you hated every day. And I hated *you* for that."

He brought the bottle to his lips and swallowed another mouthful. "It was like living with someone already dead. You walked through the room just like you were alive, but there were times I swore I could see right through you. I called you a lot of names back then. I thought you were a coward and a loser. I thought you were weak."

His eyes burned as he stared at the photograph. There were so few. The family had never taken many pictures. After Patrick's mother died, his father hadn't seen anything but the past.

"I hated that, too," he went on. "I knew that I wasn't enough. That without her, you had no reason to live. Sometimes I wanted to grab you and shake you, all the while screaming that I was still alive. That I mattered."

He leaned back in the chair and sighed. "I never got it. I never realized how much you loved Mom. I'm sorry about all those things I said and thought. I'm sorry I didn't try harder to get close to you."

His gaze focused on the picture. Maybe it was the alcohol, but he almost felt as if his father could hear him. "I understand now. Life doesn't give you a choice. You can't pick who you're going to love, or when that love is going to strike. And if it's not destined to be, there's not a damn thing you can do except walk through the days, as empty and transparent as a ghost.''

He glanced down at his lap, half expecting to be able to see through his body to the pattern of the chair. His legs were solid.

For now, he thought, taking another swallow. But, like his father, he'd fallen in love with a woman who couldn't stay. And, like his father, he would spend the rest of his life walking from room to room, waiting for the pain to end.

Chapter Fourteen

"How many for dinner?" the hostess asked.

Fallon glanced at Kayla. "Patrick's going to meet us here, right?"

"That's what he said," she answered, trying to sound cheerful. She didn't know anything about Patrick anymore, but she assumed he would at least be coming to her farewell dinner.

"Four," Fallon said. "And we'd like a table by the water."

The hostess nodded and made a note on her clipboard. "There's about a thirty-minute wait," she said, handing Fallon a small square pager. "This will buzz when your table's ready."

"Thanks." The three of them stepped back from the small desk.

"I need to visit the ladies' room," Elissa said. "You two want to wait or come with me?"

Fallon linked her arm through Kayla's. "We'll come with you."

Kayla had spent the past couple of days trying to act normal, but it was getting difficult. With both sisters staying in her small apartment, there wasn't much privacy, and there was even less time alone to think. She kept telling herself that if she could just sit quietly somewhere, she would be able to understand everything that was going on.

But before she could say that she would be happy to wait in the foyer, Fallon was already pulling her along toward the back of the restaurant.

The Empress Café sat on the water. To the left, the bridge to Coronado rose up like a beautiful piece of abstract art. As usual for July, no clouds marred the perfection of the deep blue sky. As the sun crept toward the horizon, the colors would change, but never lose their intensity.

"Just think," Elissa called over her shoulder. "Forty-eight hours from now you'll be in Paris."

"I can't wait," Kayla said automatically, then frowned as Elissa reached the back of the restaurant and turned left. "The bathrooms are to the right," she told her.

Elissa kept on walking.

"They've remodeled," Fallon said, and patted her arm.

"How do you know?"

"The hostess mentioned it."

"I didn't hear her say that."

Fallon arched her eyebrows. "Are you going to be cranky the whole evening? Because if you are, we're not going to pay for your dinner."

They paused in front of an unmarked door. "I didn't know you were considering it."

Fallon grinned. "Mind your manners and you just might be pleasantly surprised."

Elissa pulled open the door.

"This is *not* the bathroom," Kayla said loudly.

"You're so right."

Elissa stepped out of the way, and Fallon tugged Kayla into a darkened room. Kayla resisted, uneasy about the situation. Then her sister released her arm. Lights flashed on and a large group of people yelled, "Surprise!"

Kayla knew her mouth was hanging open, but she couldn't get herself together enough to close it. The large room at the back of the restaurant had been decorated for a going-away party. Balloons swayed from chair backs and table centerpieces. A badly drawn mural of Paris covered most of one wall. On a window facing an amazing view of the ocean, someone had written We'll Miss You, Kayla. Have A Good Time And Kick Some Royal Butt.

The round tables had been covered with red-and-white-checked tablecloths, French music flowed from speakers. But while the decorations were terrific, what really touched her was the group of people smiling at her.

In addition to her sisters were the staff from the clinic, including Jo, Cheryl and Melissa. Kayla ignored the twinge she felt knowing the beautiful vet would be around to comfort Patrick while she was gone. Assuming he was going to miss her.

Mr. Peters, Mrs. Grisham and other residents from Sunshine Village waved when she noticed them. Sarah sat in a wheelchair, a thick lap robe covering her frail legs. There were several families who had adopted pets from her, including Allison's parents, Duchess's owners, and Paul, the former football player. She wondered if his cat still ran his life.

Elissa and Fallon came up and hugged her.

"Okay, so dinner was just an excuse to get you here," Elissa said. "Are you surprised?"

"Very." Kayla couldn't stop looking at the crowd of people. "I can't believe you guys put this all together for me."

Sarah pushed a button on her electric wheelchair and moved forward. "We love you, child," she said, taking Kayla's hand. "We're going to miss you, but we all want you to have a wonderful adventure."

"Thank you." Kayla bent down and kissed her cheek.

"Hey, let's turn off this hokey French music and play some real tunes," Mr. Peters demanded.

"You're a cranky old man," Mrs. Grisham told him, slapping his hand. "We're setting a mood."

"But I saw a jukebox in the corner. We could jitter-bug."

Mrs. Grisham raised dark eyebrows. "At your age?" She laughed. "You'd strain something."

Mr. Peters leaned close to her. "Then we could play doctor and patient."

Mrs. Grisham rolled her eyes, but Kayla noticed she didn't move away or scold him again. Romance at Sunshine Village?

The crowd surrounded her. As she greeted people, Fallon and Elissa explained how they'd planned the party.

"We started about two months ago," Elissa said. "I spoke to Cheryl at Patrick's clinic, and she agreed to take care of collecting RSVPs from the guests."

She continued talking about the logistics, but Kayla wasn't listening. As she shook hands with Allison's parents and nodded as they told her how well their daughter was doing, a part of her brain repeated a single phrase over and over. As if a needle had become stuck on an old record.

Where was Patrick?

She scanned the crowd, but he wasn't around.

When she could escape, she grabbed Elissa and pulled her into a corner. "Is Patrick supposed to be here?"

Elissa nodded. Her eyebrows drew together in a frown. "I don't understand why he's late. I confirmed a couple of things with him this morning, and everything was fine. Maybe there was a last-minute emergency at the clinic."

"I'm sure that's it," Kayla said, even though the knot in her stomach told her it was something else. There was a problem with Patrick. She could feel it.

She thought about phoning the clinic, then figured that if he *was* in the middle of surgery, she wouldn't want to disturb him. So she tried to ignore her concern and get into the spirit of the party.

While waiters circulated with trays of appetizers and drinks, Elissa led Kayla to a chair in the center of the room. Presents had been piled high.

Kayla stared at the proof of her friends' generosity and had to swallow. "You guys are going to make me cry."

"You'll spoil your makeup," Jo warned.

"True."

Fallon handed her a small rectangular box. "Open this first."

Kayla tore off the paper and laughed when she saw the disposable camera inside. "Is this for the party?" she asked.

Fallon nodded. "You can use it tonight, then take it in to a one-hour place tomorrow. That way you'll have photos to remember us while you're seducing Prince Albert."

Kayla raised the camera and took a picture of the entire group. Everyone got into the spirit, suggesting shots, posing for her. Cheryl had a camera of her own and instructed the triplets to line up together.

"Amazing," Sarah said as the women stood next to each other. "They're nearly exactly alike."

"Yes, but I'm prettier," Fallon teased.

"You are not," Kayla and Elissa answered together.

When Cheryl had taken her photo, Kayla watched her sisters move around the room, talking to guests. They didn't know anyone here, yet they were friendly and gracious, and so completely different, Kayla didn't know how people could confuse them.

Fallon, always tailored, always correct, wore a royal blue sheath. The sleeveless dress ended precisely two inches above her knees. Elissa, the true romantic, dressed in pastel pink. A scoop-neck, capped-sleeved, gauzy two-piece outfit hugged her from shoulders to waist before flaring out in gentle pleats to fall nearly to her ankles. The dress swayed when she walked.

Kayla had picked out a simple silk T-shirt and a short straight skirt, both in purple. She hadn't bothered with stockings and wore flats instead of heels. Usually she didn't care about jewelry, but tonight she wore the bracelet Patrick had given her.

Her sisters continued to make sure their guests were comfortable. Kayla watched, realizing that it wasn't just clothing that told them apart. Even their hairstyles identified their personalities. Fallon had a French braid, Elissa piled her curls on top of her head, while Kayla wore her hair loose.

To her, the differences were much more than physical. And those differences were what made them unique.

"There are other presents," Sarah said, pointing to the pile on the floor. "Have a seat and get at it."

An hour later, Kayla was surrounded by crumpled sheets of wrapping paper and a stack of wonderful gifts. She had everything she would need for her travels. From a voltage changer for her blow dryer and curling iron, to a phrase book, to a pillow for sleeping on the plane. There were maps of Paris and France, clever travel kits with sewing supplies and medical goodies, a current French newspaper, a travel-size cassette player with several new tapes, and a beautiful hand-crocheted shawl from Sarah.

The largest gift, a set of luggage, had been opened, although the giver hadn't arrived. For the hundredth time, Kayla scanned the room and wondered what was keeping Patrick.

After dinner, Mr. Peters got his wish. The French music faded, and he picked the first tune from the jukebox. Instead of Glenn Miller, most of the songs were from the fifties and sixties. After pushing the tables aside, most of the guests pulled off their shoes and danced in the center of the room.

"You guys are too young to remember the sixties," Cheryl said, demonstrating the mashed potato.

"So are you," Kayla countered.

"Yeah, but I'm the youngest of six, and I watched my brothers and sisters very closely."

They laughed and danced, arms swinging in the air, hips swaying, feet shifting. A whisper of warmth brushed the back of her neck, and Kayla spun around.

He wasn't close enough to have touched her. From the way he glanced around the room, he hadn't even spotted her yet. But he was here, now, and that was enough.

Kayla started walking toward him. She knew the exact moment he spotted her. His solemn face relaxed into a smile.

"Hi," she said, when she was a few feet away.

"Hi, yourself."

For a second, she wondered if he was going to reject her tonight. She hesitated, rather than offering him a hug. He eased her mind when he held open his arms.

As she stepped into his embrace, he held her tightly against him. She returned his touch, wrapping her arms around his waist and pressing her head against his shoulder. She could feel the steady pounding of his heart.

"Sorry I'm late," he murmured. "Something came up at the clinic."

"Everything okay?"

"Sure."

There was something about his tone of voice. Something that made her want to question him. What was he holding back?

Before she could ask, the record ended and another dropped into place. The room filled with the scratchy sound of a needle on vinyl, and then the opening notes of "Smoke Gets in Your Eyes" flowed over them.

Without saying anything, they began to dance. Their bodies moved together in perfect communication. His heat and scent surrounded her, filling her with contentment. She'd always been at her best when she was with him.

As they circled the room, she glanced at the people around them. A few couples had joined them, including Allison's parents and Mrs. Grisham and Mr. Peters. Melissa caught her gaze, then turned away. Kayla didn't have it in her to feel triumph or pity. Tonight there was no room for petty emotion.

In the security of Patrick's arms, she studied the individuals who brought joy to her world. Sarah, Fallon and Elissa. Elissa waved, then snapped a picture of Kayla and Patrick dancing. She was pleased she would have that moment to take with her.

She thought of all she would be leaving behind this time tomorrow. Her plane took off Sunday evening and arrived in Paris in the early afternoon on Monday.

She thought of the sites she would see, the people she

would meet. After waiting nearly thirteen years, her dream had arrived.

But instead of feeling light with joy, questions weighed on her. Was she doing the right thing? Was she being selfish? Would she have a life to come back to, or would everyone have moved on and forgotten her?

She knew that by "everyone" she really meant Patrick.

The record ended, but he continued to hold her. Another slow song drifted through the room, and they swayed to the sound. Her eyes drifted closed. She tried to imagine herself in Paris, sipping coffee at a café, watching the world walk by.

But instead of the famous French capital, she saw a pair of ruby slippers and a young girl clicking her heels three times.

"There's no place like home."

She held Patrick tighter. Home. Was that where she belonged? Was she making a huge mistake?

They turned in a slow circle, and her gaze fell on the pile of presents everyone had bought her. Her tickets waited at her apartment, she had reservations at a hotel, appointments to meet with Sarah's friend's granddaughter and the people Patrick knew. Everything was in place.

There was no turning back.

Light from the full moon spilled into her bedroom. Kayla tossed back the sheets and sat up. A quick glance at the clock told her it was nearly one. She and her sisters had come home from the party two hours ago and gone right to bed, but she hadn't been able to sleep.

She quietly walked to the window and stared up at the sky. The moon sat high, nearly directly overhead. Its brightness concealed most of the stars, except for those close to the horizon.

The apartment was silent. Elissa slept on a cot in the corner of Kayla's bedroom. In the living room, Fallon rested on the sleeper sofa.

Kayla thought about returning to bed, but she was too restless. In less than twenty-four hours, she would be gone. Her life would change forever. How could anyone sleep?

She grabbed a pair of shorts and a T-shirt she'd left on her dresser that afternoon, then slipped into the bathroom. Five minutes later, her face washed, her hair brushed, she made her way into the living room, then out the front door.

Once settled on the steps, she drew in a deep breath. The night air was cool. She hugged herself, knowing she would be freezing in about twenty minutes, but determined to enjoy the solitude until then.

Memories of the party made her smile. She had good friends, people who really cared about her. She wasn't sure what she'd done to deserve that much support, but she was grateful for it.

She thought about Patrick. Something had been bothering him. He'd left right after they served cake. She'd hoped for another dance, but before she could ask, he was gone.

Patrick. Her gaze settled on his house at the end of the driveway below.

She wished… She shook her head. What did she wish? That they could go back to the way things had been between them? Did she really want that? Or had she secretly been hoping for something more?

"Of course I care."

Those words. They'd stunned her, left her breathless, anticipating something she couldn't even name. He'd created a moment of magic, then made it disappear.

"We're friends."

Friends. While she loved the friends in her life, she hated the word. It confused her—*he* confused her.

A flicker of light caught her attention. She stared more intently and realized a light had been on when she first came out. Because the drapes were pulled, she hadn't noticed. Until Patrick moved in front of it and momentarily blocked the glow.

He was awake.

She was halfway across the driveway before she realized what she was doing. At his front door, she raised her hand to knock, then paused. What was she going to say?

"I'll think of something," she muttered under her breath. "How humiliating can it be? After all, I'm leaving the country tomorrow."

With that, she rapped on the door.

He opened the door and stared down at her in surprise. She returned the stare. He wore nothing but loose shorts that hung low on his hips. His hair stood up in spikes, as if he'd been asleep.

"Did I wake you?" she asked.

"No. I tried to lie down, but I couldn't sleep."

"Me, either." She motioned toward the stairs leading up to her apartment. "I was sitting outside when I noticed you had a light on. I thought you might like some company."

Instead of answering, he pushed the door open.

"Want something to drink?" he asked when she'd settled on one edge of the sofa.

"No, thanks."

There was a tumbler filled with ice and clear liquid on the coffee table. He sat in front of it and leaned back against the cushions.

There was less than two feet between them, yet she felt

as if they were separated by the world. Tension knotted in her stomach, as it had at the party.

"Something's wrong," she said.

He glanced at her and smiled. "I'm gonna miss you, kid. Who else would know what I was thinking?"

"No one. So tell me what's going on."

He shook his head, leaned forward and grabbed his drink. "Just some odds and ends. Nothing for you to worry about the night before you leave."

His voice sounded funny. Was he drunk? Kayla didn't think she'd ever seen Patrick drink more than a couple of beers. She leaned toward him and took the glass. She sniffed, but couldn't smell anything. When she took a sip, she tasted ice water. Obviously whatever was bothering him wasn't that serious.

"What did you think?" he asked as he retrieved the glass. "That I was drowning my sorrows?"

"It crossed my mind."

He set the glass on the table and angled toward her. "Only as a last resort."

His hands lay loose in his lap. She had the strongest urge to reach forward and take one in hers. To touch him. Be near him. Is that why she'd come over?

To distract herself, she said, "Thanks for the luggage."

"You already thanked me."

"I know, but—" She shrugged. "I'd told you which ones I'd thought about buying, and you remembered. That makes the gift more special."

"You're welcome." He leaned his head against the sofa back. "You're going to enjoy Paris. I hope you remember to come back."

To you? she wanted to ask, but didn't.

"I'll be around," she said.

There was only a single lamp on in the room, and that

was in the corner by the front door. They sat in semidarkness. As Patrick shifted, shadows concealed, then exposed, parts of his face and body. She could make out the clean line of his jaw, his shoulders, his left arm. The thick, defined muscles of his chest were visible, as was his stomach. Or maybe she couldn't see them at all. Maybe she remembered them so well, she didn't need light to know what they looked like.

The heat began so slowly, she didn't notice it at first. It slipped down her legs and arms, then up through her torso. Her breasts swelled and ached. That magical place between her legs throbbed in time with her increasing heartbeat.

Did he feel it, too? The need? The tension?

Her gaze sought his. She couldn't read anything in his eyes. Did he want her, or did he simply tolerate her presence?

Touch me!

The voice screamed loudly in her head, yet her lips didn't move. The room was still. She waited, commanding him to move toward her, to take her in his arms as he had at the party. She was leaving tomorrow; she wanted tonight with him. She wanted the memory to carry with her for the rest of her life.

But he did nothing. He simply returned her gaze, waiting. For what? Permission? For her to leave?

When she couldn't stand it, she slid forward on the sofa. She moved deliberately, so that there could be no doubt of her intentions. So that he could stop her at any moment. She didn't want to think about being rejected, but if he turned her away, she would survive.

Her hands cupped his face. Stubble teased the sensitive pads of her fingers. She leaned toward him and pressed her lips to his.

He accepted the caress, but didn't return it. She closed

her eyes and put her heart and soul into the kiss, letting her feelings pour over him. He stirred restlessly, yet neither moved away nor deepened the kiss.

She straightened. "What's going on?" she asked, confusion and frustration adding a sharpness to her tone. "Do you want me to leave or do you want me to beg?"

His eyes darkened to the color of the night sky. He raised his hands to her shoulders, then dropped them back to his lap. "I want you not to have regrets."

Was that all? She smiled. "I could never regret being with you, Patrick. I want this. I want you."

Without warning, he pulled her to him, turned her so that she lay on her back, and then he stretched out half on top of her. His arousal pressed into her hip. His hands were everywhere, touching her arms, her thighs, her breasts.

"Thank God," he said, his voice low and thick with passion. "Thank God."

Chapter Fifteen

He kissed her with the intensity that left her breathless. His lips covered hers, his tongue plunged inside. She raised her arms to wrap them around his neck and draw him closer. She needed more; she needed to be one with him.

As he traced the sensitive places in her mouth, he drew her into a sitting position. From there, they rose to their feet. Still the kiss continued. He pressed against her. Bare legs brushed. Her hands lowered to his shoulders, then his back. He wasn't wearing a shirt, and she ached to feel his skin against hers.

She reached down and fumbled with the hem of her T-shirt. He backed away a little to give her room. Finally, as she tugged up the fabric, they broke the kiss.

They were both breathing heavily. Passion dilated his eyes. ''I want you,'' he said hoarsely. ''Now.''

As she tossed down her shirt, he pulled her toward the

bedroom. She kicked off her sandals, stumbling slightly when a strap caught around her heel.

He bent down and freed her. On his way up, he nibbled on her thigh, then licked her belly. Her muscles contracted at the contact. She had to clutch his shoulders to keep from falling to her knees.

When he'd straightened, they continued toward the bedroom. Patrick unfastened her bra, then tugged at her shorts. She pulled on his, so by the time they'd turned on a lamp and tumbled onto the sheets, they were both naked.

"I don't remember it being like this." She sighed as he kissed her neck, then down her chest. He took her already hard nipple in his mouth and sucked.

"I know," he said, before reaching for her other breast. "I want to take it slow, but—"

"No." She cupped his face and forced him to look at her. "Don't hold back anything."

Their gazes locked. The fire in his eyes heated her blood and made her feminine place dampen with need. She released him and moved her hands to his rear. Once there, she squeezed the tight, round flesh. He arched against her. His arousal bumped her belly, the tender sacs between his legs brushed against her center. Pleasure shot through her.

She parted her thighs, tilting her hips toward him. He repeated the action. The friction teased at her, not enough to take her closer to release, yet more than enough to make her willing to do anything he asked.

When he slipped away, she whimpered in protest.

"Don't worry," he promised. "I know something better to do."

With that, he knelt between her knees. He covered her breasts with his hands, then bent low and kissed her belly button. His fingers circled her nipples, brushing them gently, connecting those sensitive points with the one his mouth approached.

She felt warm breath at the top of her thigh. She knew what he was about to do. She'd read about it, heard friends talk about it, but no one had ever touched her there...not that way.

An intimate kiss. Elissa had once whispered it could be the most perfect pleasure. Kayla couldn't imagine anything more wonderful than what they'd done before, yet she was willing to be proved wrong.

He brought her hands to her center and urged her to part for him. With the protective folds pulled back, she was exposed to him. Her eyes shut tight, and she shuddered in embarrassment. Why would he want to look at her *there?*

"You're so beautiful," he whispered, stroking a single finger along her sensitive flesh. He didn't touch that tiny point of pleasure, instead discovering the rest of her.

As he circled the entrance, she pushed toward him, remembering the pleasure he'd brought her there. He dipped inside, deeper, hinting at what they would do later.

Then, when she'd nearly forgotten about being exposed and how he was going to touch her, he placed his tongue against her.

The moist, gentle contact impacted against her nerve endings. Small explosions went off in different parts of her body. There was no reason for breath or thought, no reason to exist, except for the sole purpose of experiencing the sensations he created.

He licked her slowly, as if exploring a perfect treasure. Her entire being concentrated on that one place and the power he wielded.

When he stroked faster, her body trembled. Involuntary quivers of muscles, an uncontrolled gasp. Her head moved from side to side. She might have said something. Maybe his name, maybe a plea that he not stop. She wasn't sure of anything except the promise of a release so incredible that the anticipation alone was enough to speed her closer.

With one hand, he continued to move inside her. Long fingers pressed up, as if caressing her center of pleasure from both sides. With his other hand, he reached up and cupped her breast. He squeezed her taut nipple, matching the rhythm of his tongue.

She pressed her heels into the mattress, parting her legs wider, straining toward him. She didn't know how long he'd touched her there. Seconds...maybe days. She spiraled higher and higher.

"No!" she gasped. "Not yet. It feels too good."

But she had no control. Even as she absorbed intense pleasure, even as she became one with the heat and the flames, her body betrayed her. Muscles tensed, though she tried to relax them. She fought against the climax. She wanted to go on like this forever.

As if he had read her mind, Patrick stopped. Her body froze. Release was so close, she could feel the first whisper of ecstasy.

Before she could cry out in protest, he began again. Lighter, yet faster, touching everywhere he had before, his tongue creating magic. Completion hovered stubbornly out of reach, taunting her. She surged toward it. Closer. Closer. Closer still.

Then it was upon her. She and the pleasure were one. Every part of her vibrated with wondrous surrender.

As she relaxed, Patrick slipped next to her and pulled up the covers. He shifted so her head rested on his shoulder and her legs tangled with his. She rested one hand on his belly.

An aftershock rippled through her and she smiled. "How'd you do that?" she asked softly.

"I was inspired by my subject."

"Hmm. That was the most amazing experience of my life."

He stroked her hair. "For me, too."

She closed her eyes. Almost of its own accord, her hand slipped lower, through the curls, until she felt the length of him. He was hard and ready, and he jumped against her fingers when she touched him.

Now it was his turn to suck in his breath.

"All this for me?" she teased.

"Everything's for you."

He sounded so intense, she opened her eyes. Passion pulled his mouth straight and tightened the line of his jaw. Lethargy vanished in an instant. She wanted him again.

"Where is it?" she asked, speaking of the protection.

"I happen to have one ready."

She took the condom from him and pushed away the sheet. When he was exposed to her gaze, she caught her breath. The need and strength inherent in his maleness made her feel powerful. He was aroused because they were together. Because of what he'd done to her and what she was about to do to him.

She knelt between his thighs and took him in her hand. After stroking up and down several times, she bent low and licked the sensitive tip.

Her free hand rested on his thigh. She felt his muscles tense with her action. He groaned low in his throat. She licked again, then drew him into her mouth. She suckled him, moving her fingers at a matching rhythm, feeling the passion grow.

"Look at me," he said.

She glanced up and saw that he'd raised himself into a half-sitting position. Her hair tumbled onto his thigh and belly, her mouth embraced his maleness. It was a moment of connection so strong, she knew that whatever happened between them, they would both remember what had once been. It was, she told herself, enough.

He touched her wrist and indicated she should stop. She opened the protection, then slid it over him. Before he could shift her onto her back, she cleared her throat.

"Would you mind if I tried being, um, on top?"

He grinned, then stretched out on the bed. "Be my guest."

She straddled his hips. As she reached down to guide him inside, he did the same. Their fingers brushed. Again they looked at each other. He glanced down, and she followed his gaze. The tip of him pressed into her, their hands overlapped on his arousal. It was all there, the intimate joining of two people. She hadn't known it could be this wonderful.

She sank down on him, feeling him fill all of her. Recently satisfied need flared to life. He grasped her hips and set the pace for their joining. She tossed her head back, letting her hair flutter against her back. She liked being on top, being in control. Her thighs tightened around his hips, drawing him in deeper until he touched her soul.

When his hands clasped hers, she leaned forward, letting him lower her until she rested against his chest. He released her, then reached between them, opening her so that the most sensitive part of her rubbed him with each thrust.

Instant pleasure caught her off guard. She gasped his name, then kissed him.

As their tongues stroked together, she felt him collect himself for his release. Her own body began tensing, heading toward the promise.

"I can't hold back," he growled, obviously struggling for control.

"Don't. Just feel it," she urged, moving faster.

"Not yet." He pushed her upright, then groaned. "That's worse."

She saw him staring at her breasts. They bounced in time with their joining. She cupped them to hold them still.

"Better?" she asked.

"Not exactly."

Then his eyes closed. He surged toward her. As she prepared herself to absorb his pleasure, he reached between them and touched a fingertip to her core. Without warning, she soared into her climax, barely able to register that he followed her. She leaned forward and clutched at his shoulders, rocking and thrusting to drain everything from them both.

Later, when they were back under the sheets, nestled together, Kayla sighed. Their lovemaking had been more than she'd imagined it would be. Better than last time. Would it continue to get better as they learned about each other's secret desires? A voice inside whispered that it would.

A sense of rightness filled her. This was where she belonged. In Patrick's bed, in his arms. In his life.

He'd positioned them so they lay like spoons, his front nestled against her back.

"Kayla?" he murmured, sounding nearly asleep.

"Yes?"

"Stay with me."

Stay. It was what she'd always wanted. Why hadn't she seen that before?

"Yes, Patrick. I'll be right here." She placed her hand on top of his and squeezed.

He pressed a kiss to her bare shoulder. "Thanks. After making love with you, I don't want to sleep alone. There'll be plenty of time for that when you're gone."

His regular breathing told her he'd fallen asleep. She

pressed her lips tightly together and let her tears fall silently onto the pillow.

She'd been prepared to stay for a lifetime, but he only cared about a night. When she first came over, she'd told herself any humiliation or rejection wouldn't be that awful. After all, in less than twenty-four hours she was leaving for Paris.

The pain in her chest deepened. She knew now what it meant, why she'd been so confused lately, what was wrong with her life.

Somewhere between the laughter and teasing, over sodas or sandwiches, after patients or while making love, she'd fallen in love with him.

There was no need to go searching for her handsome prince. He'd been living next door the whole time.

As the tears continued to flow, she wrestled with the fact that he hadn't once indicated he'd had a change of feelings. In his mind, they were just good friends.

The hurt in her chest deepened. She knew it was a problem to be on an airplane when you had a cold or certain illnesses, but how dangerous was it to fly with a broken heart?

Patrick sat in bed and watched Kayla sleep. She stirred occasionally, pushing the sheets as she turned, exposing her naked body to view. Each time she settled, he pulled the covers back into place. He'd long since memorized every part of her.

Physical contentment fought with emotional anguish. He loved her more than he'd ever loved anyone or anything in his life. He hadn't known such depth of emotion was possible. In the past couple of months, she'd become a part of his being, as if her presence had been grafted onto his soul. When she left him, he would mourn her absence with the same passion that he would mourn the death of hope. Like his father before him, he would move silently through his world, enduring, emotionally limping, as though a part of him had been ripped away.

He rose from the bed and pulled on his shorts, then made his way to the living room. Instead of turning on a light, he pulled open the drapes. It was nearly dawn. The start of a new day...the day Kayla would leave.

In a twisted sort of way, he should be grateful. He'd just endured the worst day of his life, and he'd survived. Kayla's departure allowed him to forget what else had happened. Compared to the devastation of losing her, the loss of funding for his research facility would barely warrant a footnote in the story of his life.

The sun rose, slipping above the horizon in slow motion, as if in no hurry to start the day. A *thunk* on his porch informed him the paper had been delivered. Patrick resisted moving for a couple of minutes, then pushed to his feet and went to retrieve it. There was no way he wanted Kayla reading the front page. That would ruin everything.

He opened the front door and saw someone crossing toward him. In the half-light, he might have mistaken her for Kayla. The same body shape, the same hair, the same temper blazing in the same green eyes.

Elissa tugged her robe tighter around herself and glared at him. "What do you think you're doing?" she demanded, then thrust her copy of the newspaper at him. "Have you read this?"

He reached behind him and closed the front door. He didn't want Kayla to wake up and hear their voices. Then she would know what had happened. He would do anything to avoid that.

"Have a seat," he said, settling on the porch's single step.

Elissa continued to glare at him.

"I'll explain everything."

"You'd better." She sank next to him, every fiber of her being vibrating with anger. "She spent the night with you, didn't she?"

He nodded.

Her gaze narrowed. "And you didn't tell her a thing."

It wasn't a question, so he didn't bother answering.

He folded both newspapers together and stared at the still-dark western sky. "I received a phone call yesterday, from the foundation I've been dealing with. A highly placed officer has embezzled millions. He's already left the country, and they're not sure they can recover their money."

"I read that much in the paper. It's why you were late to the party yesterday, isn't it?"

"Oh, yeah." He'd been on the phone, trying to figure out how the news affected him. The answer had been succinct.

"What does the embezzlement mean to you?"

He continued to stare at the horizon, but instead of treetops and sky, he saw the research building as it should have been. He saw the equipment he'd ordered, the scientists working. What could have been a chance to make a difference had turned to dust.

"They're real sorry, but there's no money to give me."

She caught her breath. "Oh, Patrick, I'm sorry."

She placed her hand on his arm. A comforting touch, so like her sister's that it should have eased his pain. It didn't. Elissa was a wonderful person, but she was a poor substitute for the real thing.

"They're going to try and get me alternative funding. It'll take a while, and there's no guarantee it will come through. They might recover some of what was stolen. If it's enough, they'll help me out." He shrugged. "It's been a gamble from the beginning. I knew there were a thousand things that could go wrong."

"But you never expected to lose the money once you had it."

"No, I never expected that."

Life had broadsided him in a couple of different ways. First with Kayla, and now with this. At least he still had the clinic. He would bury himself in work and try to forget.

"Why didn't you tell her?"

"That's easy. Her plane leaves tonight, and I want her on it. If she knew about this, she would want to fix it. That's what Kayla does, she heals the world. I'm not going to stand in the way of what she wants, and I'm not going to be one of her damn strays. So I'm not going to say anything, and neither are you."

For the first time since sitting down, he looked at Elissa, pinning her with his gaze. "I want your word on that," he said.

"Why? What's so wrong with her wanting to fix it? She cares about you."

Cares. It was a start, he supposed. Better than hating him, or having no feelings at all. But he'd wanted everything. Both with the research facility and with her. Better to walk away than to get it half-right.

"I don't want her pity and I don't want her money. You know that's what she'd offer me."

Elissa nodded. "She'd write you a check without blinking." She drew in a deep breath. "Do you know what you're giving up?"

He knew she was talking about more than the research facility. "I'm intimately familiar with the pain I'm going to face." He'd watched his father live through it for twenty years. Walcott men were cursed that way. He knew because history was about to repeat itself.

He turned his attention back to the horizon. "Your word, Elissa."

"All right. I won't say anything to her before she gets on the plane."

"And you won't call and tell her the truth."

"Agreed. But if she calls me and already knows something, I'm going to fill in the details."

"Fine."

He wasn't worried about that. Once Kayla was in Paris, there was no way she was going to find out anything. She would be too busy living her dream.

Happily ever after. That was all he'd ever wanted for her.

Chapter Sixteen

Kayla sat in front of the French café. Her small round table and single chair were near the sidewalk, allowing her a perfect view of the quaint street and passersby. Despite the fact that it was late July, the temperature was pleasant, rather than hot, the sky was clear, and the sun shone down brightly.

She fingered the brochure she'd picked up that morning on her second visit to the Louvre. Earlier that week, she'd viewed the old masters; today she'd concentrated on the sculptures. The artwork amazed her. Some of the statues were so perfect, they looked as if they'd come from a mold, instead of being hand-carved.

She sipped her coffee, then reached for the postcards she'd bought yesterday. After staring at them for a second, she let them fall back on the table. Who would have thought that after ten days in Paris, she would have nothing to say to her friends?

A family walked by the café. Three children, all chatting happily, their parents smiling at each other. Their French was too quick for her to decipher, but she didn't need to understand the conversation to know they were happy and excited about their day together. Seeing them made Kayla feel her solitary existence even more.

"Bonjour, mademoiselle."

Kayla glanced up and saw a flower vendor standing in front of her. He held up a small bouquet and raised his eyebrows questioningly.

She shook her head. *"Non."*

The vendor moved on.

She watched him pause at the next table. A couple sat there. They were young, probably still in their teens, and very much in love. They stared at each other as if the rest of the world had long since ceased to exist. The young man bought the bouquet and placed it in his girlfriend's hands. She kissed him.

Kayla turned away from them and forced herself to look at the shops across the street. Dresses and shoes were displayed provocatively behind sparkling-clean windows. Paris was a shopper's paradise, she thought to herself, then glanced down at her tailored pantsuit. An impulsive spending spree in an exclusive boutique had provided her with several sophisticated outfits, matching shoes and handbags. The afternoon had cost about as much as she'd made in the previous three months, but she refused to worry about that. She had her trust fund. Her goal had always been to enjoy life.

"Postcards," she said softly. "Someone has to write them, and you seem to be the only person volunteering."

She reached into her handbag for a pen. Her fingers closed over a thick envelope instead. The pictures from her going-away party. She'd already looked at them a hundred times, but she couldn't help pulling them out again.

Mr. Peters and Mrs. Grisham dancing together. Jo from the clinic, talking with Sarah, probably making plans. Jo had taken over the visits to Sunshine Village. The sisters laughing together. She touched the smooth paper, remembering the good time she'd had that night. So many people had come to see her off. So many people cared about her. There were no photos of the dogs, but she often thought about them, too.

"I miss you guys," she whispered, wishing her sisters were with her right now. Paris wasn't much fun for someone on her own.

She glanced around at the city and tried to convince herself it was as wonderful as she'd always imagined. But it wasn't. She didn't speak the language well, she didn't know anyone. At the end of the day, there was no one to ask what she'd done, no one to talk to, no one to hold.

Maybe it was her own fault. She had the list of Patrick's friends and Sarah's friend's granddaughter, but she'd avoided making definite plans with any of them. What was her problem? What was she waiting for?

She set the photos on the table, then found her pen and started to write. First to her sisters, then maybe Sarah.

But instead of "Dear Elissa" or "Dear Fallon," what appeared on the card was "Patrick."

Patrick—Here I am in Paris. It's beautiful and the people are much nicer than everyone told me. I've been to the Louvre twice. As I write this, I'm sitting in a little café watching the world go by.

And I miss you more than I thought I could ever miss anyone.

The last sentence went unwritten. Partly because she didn't think he would care all that much, partly because tears filled her eyes and it was difficult to see.

She slammed the pen onto the table. Her fingers hit the pile of pictures and the top one slid to one side, exposing the photo underneath. She didn't need to blink away the tears to be able to make out the subject. She'd memorized that particular shot on the plane.

She and Patrick held each other close as they danced. The background blurred, leaving only the couple in focus. They looked right together, their bodies blending with the familiarity of lovers. She closed her eyes and remembered what it had felt like to be with him. To love him, not just physically, but with her heart and her soul.

"This is crazy," she muttered, and thrust the photos back in their envelope. "Get a grip, kid, or you're never going to make it."

She scrawled an inane sentence about the weather, signed her name, then addressed the postcard and set it to one side. Next, she wrote her sisters, Sarah and Allison, and sent a group postcard to Sunshine Village and the clinic. She had just pulled out several stamps when someone placed a bouquet of flowers on the table.

She glanced up and stared into the face of the most handsome man she'd ever seen. He was tall, with dark hair pulled back in a ponytail and black eyes. A white cotton shirt emphasized the breadth of his shoulders and chest before disappearing into the waistband of his jeans. He should have looked like a dangerous pirate, but the boyish smile he gave her chased away any fears.

"*Vous permettez?*" he asked, motioning to the flowers.

Kayla's French was improving, but she had a long way to go. She thought he was asking permission to give her flowers.

"Merci, non. Je ne suis pas—" She searched her brain for the verb "to want" and found nothing. "Thank you, but I don't want the flowers."

Great, as if speaking English would help.

He frowned, but then the smile returned. "American, *non?*"

"Yes, ah, *oui.*"

He pulled a chair over from an empty table, then sat next to her. *"Bon.* I speak English," he said, his voice thick with a French accent, then laughed. *"Un peu."* He held his right thumb and forefinger about an inch apart.

She grinned. *"Je parle français un peu.* Okay, I admit I speak French less than a little, but I'm trying."

"Bon." He shook his head. "Good. I'm Jean." He held out his hand.

She shook hands with him, then pulled her fingers free. "I'm Kayla."

"Enchanté." He repeated her name several times. "Pretty, yes?"

Despite the fact that he was talking about her name, his intense gaze made her wonder if he was referring to something else. "Thank you," she murmured.

"How long have you been in Paris?"

"Ten days."

"Your *mari,* ah, your husband is with you, *non?*"

She shook her head. "I'm not married."

Jean looked at her single cup of coffee, then took her hand in his again, and squeezed her fingers. "You are alone in Paris? *Je suis désolé.* It is not permitted. We could have dinner tonight. The, ah, restaurant is public, *non?* You would be comfortable *avec moi,* ah, with me. We talk, we laugh, I explain Paris."

She didn't know if he thought he was picking up a rich American on her own or if he was genuinely a nice man.

Maybe even a prince in disguise. It didn't matter. He wasn't the one she wanted.

She looked at the flowers, then at Jean, and pulled her hand from his. "I can't," she said.

"Tomorrow?"

She shook her head. The tears returned, and when one slipped down her cheek, he frowned. "Kayla? What is wrong?"

"Nothing." She collected her postcards and photographs and shoved them into her purse. After throwing a few bills on the table, she stood up and started for the exit.

"Kayla?"

Jean sounded confused, but he didn't come after her. Thank goodness. She was crying so hard, she couldn't see where she was going.

She kept wiping her face and walking. After ten or fifteen minutes, she gained enough control to look around and try to figure out where she was. Her hotel was only a couple of blocks away.

When she sank onto her bed, she buried her face in her hands and sobbed. This wasn't what she wanted. She missed everyone back home. She missed her life. Traveling was fine, but not without someone to share it with. Not without someone to love.

"Oh, Patrick." Her voice cracked.

She reached for the phone. It didn't matter if he didn't love her in return. She just had to hear his voice and tell him what he meant to her. In time, they could be friends again. She would rather have him as a friend than not have him at all.

She spoke haltingly with the hotel operator and asked to be connected to an international phone line. It was late afternoon in Paris. The clinic would just be opening. After several misdirections and sudden hang-ups, trying her patience to the point where she wanted to scream, she heard a ring, followed by a familiar voice saying, "Walcott Animal Clinic. May I help you?"

"Cheryl?"

Silence.

"Cheryl? Can you hear me?"

"Kayla? Is that you?"

"Yes. I'm in Paris."

Cheryl laughed. "Girl, what on earth are you doing phoning here? If I was in Paris, I would be looking for a handsome Frenchman to show me why those people have a reputation for being such great lovers."

"I could give you a name," she muttered, then cleared her throat. "Is Patrick there yet?"

"Patrick?" Cheryl said the name as if she'd never heard it before.

"Your boss. Is he in?"

"No. He's not here."

"Is he still at the house?" She could probably catch him there. She had to talk to him. She had to tell him how she felt.

"I thought you knew," Cheryl said.

Kayla's chest tightened. "What are you talking about? Knew what?"

"He's in Washington, D.C., trying to get his grant money restored."

"What?" Kayla stared at the phone. What was she talking about? Grant money restored? But that was all taken care of.

Then different memories filtered into her consciousness. Patrick being late to her going-away party, and his preoccupation that night. Elissa's odd behavior before Kayla left on the plane. As if her sister were hiding something.

"Never mind," Kayla said. "I know who to call. Do you know where he's staying?"

"Yes, but he's coming home in a couple of days. If you wait, you can phone him here."

"Thanks. I'll talk to you soon, Cheryl."

Kayla hung up and quickly reconnected with the operator. The call went through faster this time. In less than two minutes, she was speaking with her sister.

"How's Paris?" Elissa asked. "Are you having a wonderful time?"

"No, but that's not important. I called the clinic and found out that Patrick's in Washington because he's having trouble with his grant. What do you know about that?"

Elissa sighed. "I wanted him to tell you before you left, but he wouldn't hear of it. I'm sorry, Kayla. He made me promise not to say anything. Of course, I didn't promise not to fill you in if you asked."

She went on to explain about the embezzlement and the delay in funding.

"So he's in Washington to see what he can do?" Kayla asked, stunned by the information.

"Right. He's working with the original foundation. They're also helping him with emergency funding through other sources."

While Elissa told her what was going on, Kayla paced beside the bed, walking as far as the phone cord would let her before turning around and heading for the nightstand. Now disbelief made her sink to the floor.

"Why didn't he want me to know?" she asked.

"He knew you'd want to help."

"Oh, and that's a bad thing?" He hadn't trusted her. Why?

"He thought you'd delay your trip and try to give him

money," Elissa said softly. "He didn't want to ruin your plans."

"You mean he didn't want me hanging around." She knew she sounded bitter, but she couldn't help herself. She'd thought—

Her throat tightened. "I love him, Elissa. I would have done anything for him."

"Did you ever tell him that?"

"No. I'd sort of hoped he would give me a hint as to how he felt. Everything has changed between us. It happened so fast that I wasn't sure what was going on. That last night, I hoped he would ask me to stay."

"Did you offer?"

"I thought about it."

"So you expected him to take all the risks?"

Kayla didn't like the sound of that. "Not really."

"Gee, that's what it sounds like to me. Maybe you can explain it."

Kayla picked at the bedspread. "I... I..."

"You were afraid."

"Yeah."

"I know that feeling. Fear is powerful. It was easier to avoid the risk, and so very simple to go away. But what did you leave behind?"

That was an easy question. "The man I love."

"And?"

"I have to tell him how I feel. But I can't. He's in Washington. He's coming home in a couple of days. Should I call him, or just come back?"

"That's your decision."

Kayla squeezed her eyes shut. She thought about Patrick, about what he meant to her, about the years they'd been together. "He's the best man I've ever known. How could I have been such a fool?"

"We all make mistakes," Elissa said, and it was obvious she wasn't just talking about Kayla's situation.

"Thank you for telling me what happened with him. And for listening. I'm going to get a flight back tomorrow. I should be in San Diego sometime the day after."

"Call and let me know what happens."

"I will."

They chatted for a couple more minutes, then hung up. Kayla got up and found her French phrase book. For the third time, she braved the hotel operator, requesting a connection with the airlines.

Patrick waited until the plane had emptied before grabbing his carry-on bag and heading for the gangway. Once in the terminal, he walked slowly toward the baggage claim and the car park beyond.

It had been a grueling five days. He'd spoken to dozens of people, met with committees, told his story over and over, until he was hoarse.

His hard work had paid off. The funding had been restored. He'd called his contractor from the Washington airport; work should start back up in the morning.

So why wasn't he excited? This was his dream come true, after all. Everything was going according to plan.

He passed a bank of phones and wished he had someone to call. His employees would be happy when he told them, but that wasn't the same as having one special person to share the moment. When he got home, he would be alone. There was no one to hold, no one to love. Maybe he should get a dog. There were plenty of strays in the clinic kennels. He could pick one out this afternoon.

But a dog would be a poor substitute for who and what he really wanted.

Without meaning to, he pictured Kayla. Her golden-blond curls, her smile, her laughter, the way she always weaseled out of doing the dishes. The scent of her skin, the feel of her body next to his, the way she gave herself completely, unselfconsciously, the way she held him as if she never wanted to let go.

The picture shifted unexpectedly, and he saw his father. Old before his years, walking through life like a spirit biding time until he could be with the woman he loved.

"Dammit, she's not dead," Patrick said out loud. Several people turned to stare at him, but he ignored them.

The realization slammed home like a gunshot. Kayla *wasn't* dead. His father hadn't had a choice. There was no way to be with his love, but Patrick was suffering simply because he'd chosen to be noble. Or maybe he'd just chosen to be stupid. After all, he'd never told Kayla how he felt. Maybe she wanted to know that he loved her. Maybe she had feelings for him, too, but was afraid to be the first one to confess them.

He understood all about being afraid, and he was sick of it. He was sick of suffering and being noble, and maybe even of being a fool. By God, he was going to tell her the truth. If she rejected him, then at least he would know. He might spend the rest of his life missing her, but he wouldn't have the added agony of wondering, "What if?"

"I don't care if she travels," he muttered. "As long as she comes home to me."

He scanned the signs overhead and saw the one pointing to the international terminal. Walking quickly, he headed that way.

"Patrick?"

He turned toward the familiar sound, scanning faces, wondering if his mind was playing tricks on him.

"Patrick, I'm right here."

He looked at a woman separating herself from the

crowd. She wore a blue suit with matching high heels. Golden curls had been trimmed to shoulder length and tamed into a sophisticated style. She wore makeup and jewelry. His heart recognized her first, and then he saw the gold and diamond bangle on her wrist and was sure.

"Kayla?"

She laughed and flew toward him. "Yes. I just got in a couple of hours ago. I called the office and Cheryl gave me your flight number. When you didn't get off the plane, I didn't know what to do."

"I got off, but I was last."

She stopped in front of him. "I should have waited longer."

They stared at each other. His heart thundered in his chest. The awful pain that had seeped down into his bones began to fade. He opened his arms, and she slammed into him.

"Why are you back?" he asked, holding her tightly against him. Her scent, her heat, the feel of her, comforted him, thrilled him. Even if it was just for today, it was perfect.

"I had to come back." She buried her face against his chest. "I missed everyone. No, that's not true. I missed you, Patrick." She looked up at him. "Why didn't you tell me about the funding?"

There were a thousand things he could have said. Half truths, almost truths. He was done with that. "Because I love you. Because I wanted you to have your dream."

"Oh, Patrick." She raised up on tiptoe and brushed his mouth with hers. "I love you, too."

It was as if the band around his chest had been unlocked. It fell away, freeing him to breathe, to feel, to love.

"I was such a fool," she said.

"No, I was."

She shook her head. "It was me. I spent so much time putting my life on hold to wait for a magical future, I never bothered to notice I already had a wonderful present. I don't need Paris, or any of that. I have lots of people who care about me. I have a job I love, and—" She paused. "Do you really love me?"

"More than anything."

"Friendship, love, or something more?"

The doubt in her eyes pained him. "I love you the way a man loves a woman, Kayla. Romantically and passionately. I want you in my life. I want us to be part of each other."

Her smiled nearly blinded him. "I want that, too. I don't deserve you, but I want to be with you always."

He desperately wanted to believe her. "What about your prince?"

She frowned. "I saw a couple of pictures of Prince Albert. He's not as good-looking as I'd thought. I think the prince thing is really overrated."

They both smiled. He touched her hair. "You look different."

"Dumb, you mean."

"I like it. Very sophisticated."

"Don't get used to it. As soon as we get home, I'm washing off this makeup and I'm going to start growing my hair back. I'm not the glamour type. I'm just the girl next door."

"The girl of my dreams."

She hugged him tight. "Always."

Later, when they'd made love and were holding each other, he asked, "Would you like to go to Paris for our honeymoon?"

She raised herself onto one elbow and smiled at him. "Is that a proposal?"

She was so beautiful. He touched her face and her neck. "I know our love isn't the tornado you've been waiting for, but it's strong enough to last both our lifetimes. I come from a long line of men who love with their whole hearts." He tucked her hair behind her ears. "Yes, it's a proposal. Kayla, will you marry me?"

Her eyes filled with tears. She wiped them away and groaned. "Do you know how many times I've cried since I left here? It's horrible. I missed you so much. Yes, I'll marry you. I'll love you forever. I'll make you proud."

His heart filled with contentment. "I already am."

She bent over and kissed him. Their lips parted. She swept inside his mouth, igniting fires that had so recently been quenched. He put his hands on her waist, then drew her on top of him. She wiggled when she felt his arousal, teasing him with the promise of their joining.

"You're wrong about something," she said, breaking the kiss and touching her index finger to his lower lip.

"What's that?"

"You said our love isn't like a tornado, but it is. Every time I'm with you, every time I think about you, every time you hold me, I get swept away."

* * * * *

Look for the next compelling book in the TRIPLE TROUBLE series, THE SECRET WIFE, coming from Special Edition in September 1997.

From the bestselling author of
THIS MATTER OF MARRIAGE

DEBBIE MACOMBER

Their dreams were different and their life-styles clashed, but their love was anything but mismatched!

Chase Brown offered Letty Ellison love and a life with him on his ranch. She chose Hollywood instead. Now, nine years later, she's come back with her young daughter—another man's child—and as the past confronts Letty and Chase, they must learn that some things are more important than pride.

DENIM AND DIAMONDS

Available August 1997
at your favorite retail outlet.

"Debbie Macomber is the queen of laughter and love."
—Elizabeth Lowell

Take 4 bestselling love stories FREE

Plus get a FREE surprise gift!

Bestselling author

JOAN JOHNSTON

continues her wildly popular miniseries with an
all-new, longer-length novel

The Virgin Groom

HAWK'S WAY

One minute, Mac Macready was a living legend in
Texas—every kid's idol, every man's envy, every
woman's fantasy. The next, his fiancée dumped him,
his career was hanging in the balance and his future
was looking mighty uncertain. Then there was the
matter of his scandalous secret, which didn't stand a
chance of staying a secret. So would he succumb to
Jewel Whitelaw's shocking proposal—or take cold
showers for the rest of the long, hot summer...?

Available August 1997
wherever Silhouette books are sold.

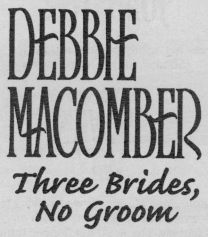